C0-DAO-037

THIS BOOK CONTAINS CRYPTIC OCEAN, SHIFTING TIDE, AND EMMY'S STORY.

THE OCEAN SERIES (BOOKS 1-3)

Contents

Cryptic Ocean

Book One

DEDICATION

To my family and friends.

ACKNOWLEDGMENTS

Special thanks to my husband! I couldn't have done this without you. (I will try to write you a spy/suspense book. Although you know me … I am a romantic at heart.)

Thank you, Meg for going through my rough drafts, circling the sentences and paragraphs that you loved, making sure they would end up in the final copy. (They are all here as I promised.)

Huge thanks to Patty, Dala and Frank for listening to my endless ideas about this book! You three, have the patience of saints!

And thank you, for taking your time to read this story... I hope you enjoy it!

Decision Time

She had watched her mother do it for nearly 20 years, so why was Victoria Garrison-Ammon struggling with this decision?

The only difference was that her mother had an affair on her father, and when he left finally she was strong, independent, and barely affected by her husband's absence. Victoria found herself standing at the crossroads of life with two options: stay or hit the road. After 16 years of marriage, her life had become nothing short of everything she despised. She was filled with disappointment and regret.

"How did I let it get to this?" She sighed, while she picked up her duffle bag and walked toward the door. Stopping short, she placed a handwritten note on the side table, along with a key, and her wedding set then shifted the strap on her shoulder and walked out the door.

She took a moment to look back at the two-story house, taking notice of the once bright yellow paint that had faded to the color of watered down lemonade. The once brilliant white shutters took on a dull shade of taupe. Paint was peeling from the eves and moss was growing along the roofline. Everything had been neglected over the past six years; everything.

Casually, and with confidence, she lifted the bag into the trunk of her car. All of her other possessions were waiting in her new apartment across town. She put the key into the ignition and, without looking back said goodbye to the life she chose so many years ago. This was her time to start over and get what she felt she deserved, without reservation or regret.

Carter had been out of town the past three days sorting out a merger. His dark chestnut brown eyes were heavy and burned as he turned onto the lane leading home. As he approached the house he noticed Tory's car was gone and the house looked eerily empty. Obviously, she had made her decision. He wasn't surprised. They had been discussing their domestic arrangement and changes in their relationship for months trying to discover those feelings of passion that once filled every room of the old farm house. The attorney had drawn up the paperwork six weeks earlier and he had signed them the day they arrived in the mail. Tory was weighing her options and he knew this decision was more difficult for her than it was for him.

She decided to return to school eight years ago to work toward a Master's Degree in writing. After the second year, Carter began putting up protective walls, knowing that the end of their relationship was looming. What would a talented, beautiful, educated woman like Victoria want with him after she realized the world was her oyster? He started withdrawing from her almost immediately, and once she realized what was going on, it was too late.

Unlocking the front door, he paused to throw his keys on the side table and noticed the items she had left for him. He grabbed the key and then noticed her wedding rings.

"Awe Tory," he sighed, "I told you to keep these." He figured she would sell them and take the money to start her new life—her new life without him. He grabbed the letter from the table and walked toward the kitchen.

Carter,

I couldn't wait any longer for you to arrive, that and I really didn't want to drag this out any more than it has been. The past few weeks have weighed heavily on my mind. We just aren't what I want us to be anymore. Thank you for your honesty about Erin.

I wish you only the best,

Tory

PS: I sent the signed papers back to the attorney today. He said the marriage would be dissolved by Friday of next week.

Sixteen years had ended with a letter. He tossed it on the kitchen island and took his cell phone out of his front pocket. He pressed two, then, waited for her to pick up.

Victoria turned into the apartment complex and pulled into space 15. With a quiet smile, she turned off the ignition and popped the trunk. The apartment was a studio, about 1,500 square feet with a modern kitchen and beautiful view of the Pacific Ocean. She had agreed to pay an addition $50.00 a month to have a balcony, and as she slid the French doors open, she stretched her arms and inhaled a long healing breath. She stood with her eyes closed feeling the salty air tickle the goose bumps on her arms. She was just beginning to drift off into another world when her cell phone started buzzing in the kitchen. Leaving the doors open she turned and made it quickly to the counter. Reaching her phone she checked to see who was calling.

"Hey Carter, did you just get back?" Her tone was friendly and warm as though she were speaking to a friend.

As soon as he heard her voice, Carter could tell she was smiling and not feeling any negative emotions from her decision. How was it that he had forgotten how simply forgiving and caring she was? He still loved her, still needed her, but he wanted her to love and need him as well.

"Hi Tory, yeah, I just got here a little bit ago. I found your note. Thanks for sending the papers back. I thought though, we agreed that you were going to keep the rings?" His voice wasn't accusatory but his tone seemed clipped, almost as if he were annoyed that she had left them there. Not that she had to keep them, but they talked about it and it stung to see them sitting on the table.

They were Tory's, and when he purchased the set he was sure they would be together forever. He had spent days going from shop to shop trying to find the perfect engagement ring to present to her. He finally decided on a quarter-carat princess cut diamond solitaire surrounded entirely by 13 deep, ocean blue, Montana Sapphires. The wedding band was plain but complemented the diamond and sapphires perfectly. He chose white gold and waited 12 weeks before picking up the finished product. To see them sitting on the table nearly made his knees buckle from shame.

"I know, but what am I supposed to do with them? Maybe Erin can use them for something." As soon as she said the words she regretted it and wished she could take them back. But it was too late and the next thing she heard was a click. The line went dead.

Her reply set his blood on fire. *Give them to Erin!* What the hell would Erin do with them and what would possess her to say something so hurtful. He couldn't speak as a lump of guilt made its way to his throat. He pressed "end" on the phone and threw the rings against the marble countertop. He slid his back down the cold stainless steel refrigerator and ran his fingers through his hair. How was he going to keep up this façade? Eventually, Tory would figure it out.

"Oh Carter, you made your bed! Don't make me feel guilty for calling you out on it," she hissed as she hung up the phone. One minute he could be the Carter that she married. The kind hearted, selfless person that had always put her needs first. The next minute he was a selfish jerk and she wondered why she ever felt any love toward him at all. Especially now, the cheating had been the clincher. They hadn't been intimate for more than seven months, and Tory now knew the reason.

She went to the kitchen to find a radio station, but instead chose her phone and selected her "Party Anthems" playlist. As soon as the music started she began singing along while unpacking. For the moment, she was carefree, nearly single, and had a bright future ahead of her. Graduation was only two days away and she had yet to prepare the speech she had been asked to give.

The past six years had been challenging both mentally and emotionally. She planned to get her Master's Degree in writing, and publish a book about the struggles of mixed families. Tory came from a dysfunctional home and married a man that refused to have any contact with his parents. There was a fine line between spouse and friend and it took Tory years to develop a relationship with his parents. Once she had, she found that the relationships were unfulfilling. She decided quickly not to spend any more time or energy attempting to fix the permanent strain.

His parents were manipulative and invasive. Always hanging on gossip and trivial things that Tory and Carter would not even consider stressors. After spending a weekend at their house, his mother had pulled Tory aside and told her that she and Carter needed marital counseling. Ha! That was nearly two years before Tory started attending school.

Perhaps they did know their son better than she had. She wondered if Carter was seeing another woman then and had perhaps confided in his Mother. It mattered little now. Both of his parents died in a car accident four years ago. His Father had been drinking and ran through a guardrail, sending the car flying down a ravine. His Father died on impact. His Mother, Leila, was sent by helicopter to the hospital, but died shortly thereafter. Neither she nor Carter attended their wakes.

Graduation Ceremony

Carter spent the afternoon picking up his dry cleaning and some fresh daisies. Tory was going to be speaking at the graduation ceremony tomorrow and he planned to attend. After all, he was very proud of her and he wanted to show his support. Sixteen years of together made three days apart, very lonely for him. The house had a constant quietness to it as he moved like a ghost through the rooms.

Tory always had music blaring from the music docking station in the kitchen which filled the whole house. It drove him mad when he was trying to watch TV. Now he wished to hear anything but silence. He imagined Tory dancing around her new apartment enjoying her freedom. He was really looking forward to seeing her tomorrow. He could only hope that she would be happy to see him as well.

Carter sat in the audience waiting for Tory to take the stage. He felt guilty and wanted to run from his seat to the parking lot. Just then he watched her stand, throw her shoulder back, and approach the audience. Her lips stretched into a smile and he could see the spark in her eye from where he was. His pupils contracted as he absorbed her poise. Tory had always stopped conversations simply by walking past a crowd of people. He never knew what it was that made others stop and notice her presence, but he missed that. He missed her presence, her poise, her ability to turn rain into sunshine. Her speech was pure Tory; exuberant, optimistic, jovial, and full of hope. If she was nervous she hid it all too well.

Applause filled the auditorium as Tory took one last glance out at the crowd of colleagues and fellow graduates. The speech had gone well and she sighed realizing that she was now ready for whatever life was going to throw her. For a moment, she was frozen in place when she realized Carter was in attendance. He was sitting in the back near the exit wearing a new gray tweed blazer, white collared shirt, and a bright blue tie. He was standing, clapping for her, and smiling wider than anyone near him. Tory tried to compose herself but her heart was pounding out of her chest.

"He came!" She smiled to the crowd and returned to her seat on the stage, all the while thinking about him. The rest of the ceremony was a blur. She sat motionless in her seat and never once took her eyes of Carter. She questioned her own surprise and near giddiness that he was in the audience.

Shouldn't Erin be with him or was that too distasteful even for him? Oh the range of emotions she felt with even the thought of him. Happy, sad, elated, angry—all because of him, and all in under two seconds.

You could have stayed with him! You could have allowed a little affair to slide by. You made a choice and now you have to stand by it. Either be civil or tell him off, but quit with the "oh I had the perfect life bit". You didn't!

Awe, the little reassuring voice in her head. Just what she needed, a little reality check.

When Carter stood to applaud, he realized that she had spotted him. Her brow crinkled, her eyes narrowed, and his greatest fear was realized. She stared at him during the remainder of the ceremony, but he couldn't read her face. The crowd started to disperse and he saw her crossing the parking lot toward him. She was smiling as he held up the bouquet of daisies to her.

"I can't believe you came!" Her voice squeaked. *Control yourself! Be kind, but don't give him the satisfaction of knowing that he tore your heart in two and given the opportunity you would crawl back to his arms because you know nothing else.*

"Really? You thought I would miss this?"

Carter handed her the flowers and gently hugged her with his other arm. *Oh, she smelled so good.*

"Um, yeah. I was kind of rude the last time we talked, by the way, I'm really sorry I said that. I really don't know what I was thinking." Although she knew the sudden rush of jealousy had prompted the outburst. Here she was, working hard to better their lives and he was sleeping around with Lord knows how many women.

He had only told her about one… Erin. Ugh, there are those feelings again. This is why she was no longer married to his two-timing ass.

"Oh, yeah, well... I kind of deserve that right? Anyway, I wasn't going to miss this. It's a big day for you. Are you upset that I came?" His words trailed off hoping she would not confirm what he was feeling between them.

"No, not at all. I was surprised to see you though. You look tired, is everything okay at home?" She laughed. *Nice Tory, tell the guy that you think he looks like crap after he hands you a bunch of your favorite flowers! No wonder he moved on.* She shook her head and said, "Never mind I asked, please don't answer that." *Shoot, as mad as I am, I can't be uncivilized.*

"No, it's okay. It has been a long couple of days. You know, adjusting to everything. How is the new apartment? Are you all unpacked?" He was trying to keep the conversation light. He could see the range of emotions stretching across her face.

"Uh, kind of... really, not at all. Truth be told, I have had a lot to do and I have been really focused on today rather than getting my life organized." The same thing he had accused her of four years ago while they stood in the hallway of their house. He was trying to tell her back then that he was unhappy and she needed to be more present for him. He hadn't wanted her to quit school, but he needed her to be with him when they were together. It wasn't an outlandish demand and looking back and if she would have listened to him then, she may not have the pending regret of a divorce looming in her near future.

"You should stop by sometime and check it out. There is a beautiful view of the ocean from the balcony, and..." her words trailed off. She lowered her eyes and shook her head, "I guess you probably wouldn't really care to come over. Sorry, I was just, I don't know, this is weird you know?" *Because you have a girlfriend you son of a...*

"Yeah, I know." Carter reached out and placed his palm under her chin raising her head up, forcing her eyes to follow. "I would like to see your new apartment though, maybe Thursday? Dinner?"

"Really? Thursday would be great and it will give me a few days to throw more boxes in the closet." She laughed and cocked her head to the side while shrugging her shoulders. *Yup, he still has the power to make me forget.*

Dang it, I need to be stronger, either that or live with his mistress. Ha! Like that would ever happen.

"Great! I will pick us up something to eat before I come. Will you send me your address so I can find it?" And at that moment, Carter realized that he had no idea where Tory lived now. It hadn't crossed his mind before, as everything just happened while he was out of town on business.

Tory pulled her phone out and promised to text him the address before she gave him another quick hug. Carter walked to his car and headed home happy to have seen the love of his life accomplish another goal. He beamed with pride and couldn't wait for Thursday.

She watched Carter's car disappear from the parking lot before turning toward her car.

"Hmm", she thought, "that car looks really familiar". She focused on the muscle car parked in the spot next to hers. *I think that's...*

"Congratulations, Victoria," he said while he climbed out of the driver's side. A goofy grin plastered to his face. He had been about ready to leave when he saw her talking to Carter. He decided to wait and make sure she was okay before going home and imagining her naked in his bed.

"Steve? What are you doing here? And thank you, is everything okay at work?"

"I had a nephew graduating today," he lied. He watched as she placed the flowers on the trunk of her car and walked toward him. Her eyes were bright green against the red graduation gown. The closer she came, the more prevalent the blush on her cheeks. Either she was embarrassed to see him, or she was feeling the same sexual tension he was. Carter was a fool, he thought as he watched her. Who in their right mind would cheat on a woman like this? *'Oh, Tory,'* he thought, *'I could give you so much more.'*

"So, your nephew graduated today? You will have to tell him congrats from me. How's everything going at the office?" Although she didn't really care, just being in his presence outside of the office was enough to make her forget Carter, forget Erin... forget everything. She could feel her heart rate increase then had to look at her shoes to catch her breath and dispel the thoughts racing through her mind.

"I am buried in post-it notes, and I cannot tell you how much I have missed you this week. I mean, I just didn't realize just how much a part of my life you have become. You know… at work." *Smooth move jackass! Just rattle out a validated sexual harassment lawsuit here in the parking lot.* Just then Tory's head jerked up and she was staring straight through him. *Say something, say something …*

"Well, it is nice to know that I am missed. Job security is a good thing now that I have to start paying back all of these student loans!" She was joking of course, trying to lighten the mood. *Was he serious? Did he really miss me?* The butterflies started and she felt a little light headed. *Steve Gage misses me… part of his life… I am really reading far too much into this I'm sure.*

"Victoria, do you want to have dinner with me? Um, maybe to go over some work before you come back on Monday? That way you won't have the hit the ground running first thing?" *Well,* he thought, *that kind of sounds innocent right?*

(Coughing)… "Um, sure." *Is he asking me out on a date? Oh mother of pearl, what has happened today? Ugh, I had no idea that he was interested in me. Wait, he said to go over work right? Is that code for… awe who knows anymore, it has been far too long since I was in the dating pool.*

"How about Friday?"

Yes, Friday was perfect, the divorce would be final and if he was interested in her in a more personal manner, well things could take their course and she could go along for the ride without fear.

Wow, ex on Thursday, sex on Friday! A chuckle escaped her lips as she clicked her seatbelt. Today had been a great day.

Stood Up

Where could he be? Tory questioned in her mind while pacing from the balcony to the kitchen which was about 20 steps. She pulled out her cell phone to see if she had missed a call, but there was nothing. She decided to call him but his voicemail picked up,

"Hey this is Carter, leave a message." Beep…

"Carter, it's Tory. Um, it's 6:30 and I was wondering if we were still on for dinner? (Sigh.) Give me a call back when you get a chance." She sat down on the wicker chair watching wave after wave crash against the rocky shore. It wasn't like Carter to forget, or not to call if he was going to be late. She waited another thirty minutes before sending him a text.

'Where r u?' *Sent 7:00*

'R U OK?' *Sent 7:25*

'Pls call me, I'm worried.' *Sent 8:01*

Her cell phone rang at 8:45. She must have fallen asleep listening to the constant hum of the ocean. She picked it up but didn't recognize the number. Instead of answering, she let the call go to voicemail. A moment passed and the phone rang again, same caller id. She again let it go to voicemail. A few minutes passed and her phone rang again. *Seriously?* She thought as she huffed over to the counter. *Same number!* As she was placing her finger on the icon, a loud knock came from her front door.

"Carter?" Of course it had to be Carter. No one else knew where she lived. She laughed to herself and sat the phone on the counter without answering.

The Accident

Nervous didn't even begin to describe how Carter was feeling. It was Thursday afternoon when he pulled into the parking lot of Risk Management Resources. He had hopes of taking Tory out to dinner rather than eating at her apartment. He really wanted to talk to her about Erin. Tell her that there had never been another woman and beg her to reconsider the divorce. He didn't want to tell her everything in her apartment because it would be too easy for her to throw him out. At least in public, she would feel obligated to listen to his entire plea before turning him down. His nerves were getting the better of him as he climbed out of his car and walked toward the large glass doors.

He walked to her office and realized her door was closed… a sure sign she was either on the phone or in a meeting. He turned to leave.

"Hey Carter, what brings you here today?" The husky voice startled him from behind.

"Gage, hey, I was uh, just going to see Tory but her door's closed. Is she going to be long?" Carter asked.

"She's not here Carter. I gave her the week off." Steve didn't elaborate. *Weren't these two "considered" divorced already? What in the hell was Carter doing stalking Tory? You had your chance Carter and you weren't man enough to keep her happy.*

"Oh, she didn't mention it at graduation the other day. We are having dinner tonight and, well, I was hoping to see her before." Carter was divulging more than he wanted to, but he could see the concern etched on Gage's face. Carter wasn't a slight man by any means, but Steve Gage towered over him by more than six inches. They weighed about the same; although Carter was less muscular and more … how would one say … padded.

"Really?" Gage raised an eyebrow to Carter. "And how does Erin feel about that Carter?" He couldn't hide the smugness from his voice. Yes, Tory had told him about Erin. She was upset in her office a month or so ago. Gage walked in and she couldn't stop the water works. She had quickly pulled herself together after apologizing profusely, but the memory of her tear-stained cheeks was a reminder to

Gage that Carter really hurt her deeply. He took a step forward toward Carter.

"Yeah, well that's what I need to talk to her about. She needs to understand some stuff before the divorce is final tomorrow." He was trying to hold his ground, but Gage was invading his personal bubble. Carter was so nervous that the words ran from his mouth like the lead horse at the races. "I've got to come clean with her. There never was an Erin. Gage, there was never anyone but Tory. I just didn't think she would want to stay with me if she really had a choice, so now I'm going to find out. Tonight." He paused, noticing that Gage's mouth was hanging wide open.

"Anyway, I have to go. Um, nice to see you, Gage." Carter had to get out of the building. God that man made him so stressed! Tory always spoke so highly of him but every time Carter was in the room with Gage, he couldn't help feeling like he was going to get his arse kicked. And Gage could definitely take him.

"Geez, when did I become such a weenie?" he said to himself. He still had an hour before he needed to pick up dinner, so Carter drove to Callihan's and ordered a beer. It helped ease the stress of seeing Gage, but only took the edge off. His mind drifted to what he was going to tell Tory. He hoped she would forgive him and take him back. All he wanted was for her to be sure that he was the one she wanted to spend the rest of forever with. *One more beer*, then I will head to Tory's.

He looked down at his phone and realized he had missed a call from Tory.

"Shit! I'm late. Hey can I get my tab over here man?" He paid his bill and raced out the door. He was a few blocks away from Tory's when his phone buzzed. He picked it up from the passenger seat 'New Text Message'. He knew it was her wondering where he was. He entered his password and looked up from the message just in time to see the red light, the blue truck… there was a loud, thundering crash and blackness.

The Scanner

He had given Tory the week off per her request. She had told him that she needed to get unpacked and prepare for her graduation speech. By Tuesday afternoon, Steve was overwhelmed by post-it notes. Tory was his right-hand and took care of more than Steve had realized. He was the Director of Risk Management Resources and most of his clients were members of Police, Sheriff and Fire Departments. His schedule was hectic before hiring Tory. He travelled to different states and spoke to large crowds about what to do when the inevitable occurred. His passion was always his central theme of keeping public safety personnel safe. Risk Management Resources was the largest company in the United States and the C.E.O. was seeking the opportunity to branch out to other countries this year. Steve had hired Tory to assist with the additional workload.

By late evening Thursday, Steve was ready for the week to end. He left the office and had planned on working from home tomorrow. He really wanted to plan something nice for his evening with Tory. He wanted to go over the top, roses, bubble bath, massage… but he needed to slow down. He wasn't all that sure she had feelings for him, other than professional. *Although, her blush at graduation was a good sign,* he thought.

He walked into the house and was greeted by silence. He was 38, never been married, no children, no pets … he had never taken the time to invest in anything but work. *Then walked in Tory and her black nail polish … I would give the world to her if only she'd allow it. Here's to finding out soon enough.*

"Shit!" She's meeting Carter tonight for dinner. He's going to bear his soul and tell her that he faked an affair. Who fakes a damned affair? Carter Ammon! *Slick little snake that he is.* Tory was smart, she wouldn't take him back… not after everything he put her through. He hoped that she would give her decision 24 hours at minimum. Maybe he should call her. NO! He had waited seven years … if this was meant to be it would work out. He needed to wait.

He walked downstairs shedding his jacket and tie. He flipped on the lights and the police scanner while looking over all of his training equipment. His basement was filled with cardio, weights, and a punching bag. It looked like an expensive gym where one would need to pay a high price for membership. Steve believed that fitness and being in top physical condition was the first step toward maintaining a healthy and balanced lifestyle. He spent three hours a day in this room with the scanner buzzing in the background.

He was beginning to unbutton his shirt when the scanner came to life.

"All units, we have a report of a possible intoxicated driver heading northbound on Crystal Lake Drive," the dispatcher announced. He recognized the female voice immediately. Janine had assisted him many times during the trainings he had at their facility. He had realized quickly that she was a model communications specialist, calm, constant, and always professional. Janine had even shown an interest in him personally and, although he thought she was adorable, he had never wanted to mixed business and pleasure *with anyone other than Tory*. It was always nice to hear her soothing voice over the scanner.

"417, enroute. I have visual on the … Stand by station 11."

Steve grabbed his workout binder and flipped through the pages. He needed something different tonight. Maybe a nice warm up with the bag to get Carter-the-Creeper out of his head. Getting Tory out of his head would take more than a strenuous workout and a cold shower. The scanner chattered voices in the background as the thought of her.

"417, that plate returns to Carter and Victoria Ammon, clear, no wants," Janine clicked the microphone. Steve shook his head trying desperately to clear his thoughts. The scanner buzzed again, this time it was a female officer.

"Station 11, this is 417. We are going to need medics for one male, unresponsive but breathing. The other male will require the on-duty medical examiner."

"Copy 417. Medics enroute and I will advise M.E."

Steve grabbed his cell phone and dialed…

"Crestville police."

"Janine, it's Gage."

"Hello Gage. May I put on hold?"

"Of course."

Janine finally picked up the line and confirmed what Steve thought he had heard. A drunk driver had collided with Carter and killed him. The medical examiner was on his way to the hospital to accept Carter's body. Janine told Steve that the sergeant was going to try and make contact with Carter's wife, Victoria.

Cruel Joke

The knock came louder and more persistent as she walked toward the door. She was going to give Carter an earful for being late. *The least he could have done was called me back,* she thought.

"Tory, it's Steve. Please open the door."

"Steve?" She opened the door and quickly realized something was terribly wrong. "What's going on? How did you get ..." her voice trailed off.

"Did the police call you yet?"

"Police? What? Why are the police calling me?" Then she recalled the past three calls on her phone.

"Victoria, Carter has been in an accident. I need to get you to the hospital. They need you to identify the ... um, they think Carter may have been killed by a drunk driver." His voice was quiet but sure.

"What? He's dead? Steve, what the hell is going on and how do you know this?" Her tone was much more of a screech than she meant it to be but seriously! This sounds like a terrible warped dream.

"I heard it over the scanner and came right over. Well, I had to call Bryce in HR to get your new address, but then I came right over. I thought someone would have notified you already."

"They did, I mean, they tried but I didn't recognize the number so ... he's dead? Oh my God," she said in more of a whisper than a sentence. That had to be who was calling her, and if Steve wouldn't have heard it over the scanner she would have ignored the calls. The hospital, Carter's dead. *Please let this be the worst nightmare that I will ever have, and for shit's sake, someone wake me the hell up!* Her head was spinning. She was feeling small. *DEAD? How can he be dead! He was coming over for ...*

She couldn't bring herself to look Steve in the eyes. Instead, she lunged toward him while her entire body shook violently with every sob. She buried her head in his jacket and she felt his arms wrap around her. Silently thankful that he had come to her with the news rather than hearing it from some stranger. She held him tighter.

She had worked under Steve's direct supervision for the past seven years. It wasn't her dream job, but he was a wonderful boss. Always giving her the most difficult assignments, challenging her ability to calculate and predict outcomes. He had been supportive when Tory decided to go back to school and patiently adjusted her schedule to accommodate her exams and labs.

She buried her face in his jacket, recalling her Psychology class. In class, they had learned that divorce was like experiencing the death of that person. Tory thought to herself that it had made sense at the time, but knowing full well that Carter was dead made it much harder to interpret the meaning. At least in divorce, she would see Carter around town or at an occasional friendly dinner. Now that she had been informed he was dead it changed the game completely.

Steve wrapped an arm around Tory's shoulder and she became more aware of the comfort he was providing her. Suddenly, her thoughts were interrupted by a constant vibration emanating from her ribcage. She felt Steve's arm slide between them while he retrieved his cell phone.

"Gage," he said into the phone and she was lost again, shaking, sobbing into his chest. She focused on his heartbeat and the sound of his voice. She refused to hear the words he was speaking and instead, listened to the controlled vibrations in his chest. The call ended quickly and she brought her eyes up to search his. His normally crystal clear blue eyes were slated gray and cold. She silently pled with him to tell her what he knew, while she wanted most to wake up from this horrible dream.

"Tory, we need to get you to the hospital. I will answer any questions you have in the car." She nodded, slowly releasing her hold from him. He kept his hand between her shoulder blades while straining to grab her purse from the table. Her keys were hanging by the door so he grabbed those as well, hooking the key ring with his index finger. He led her gently to the stairwell locking her front door.

"I'm parked street side. Can you walk that far?" His voice was calm and quiet, deep and controlled. Tory nodded again, and attempted to walk down the stairs but her knees buckled and she nearly fell. Steve grabbed her elbow to steady her, and she lowered her head.

"Tory, it's fine. Please let me help you to the car." Another nod.

She vaguely remembered Steve lowering her into the seat of his '65 Mustang fastback. He reached over her in order to buckle the seatbelt and placed his hand on her shoulder for assurance. She felt like a helpless and confused child.

She looked up at Steve and whispered, "Thank you".

He nodded and closed the door. After securing his own seatbelt he started the car. Her body responded to the low vibrations and she sank further into the seat.

"Gage," his voice startled her.

Everyone called him by his last name. Everyone at work and so far everyone that he had introduced her to referred to him as Gage. The first time he heard her refer to him as "Gage", he corrected her and asked that she please call him by his first name. She never questioned his intentions and always referred to him as "Steve".

Hearing his name come from her lips brought him immense satisfaction. Having her referred to as "Mrs. Gage" seemed closer to reality, but for now, perhaps it was for the better that she was still married.

"Yes, I've got her with me … yeah, we are on our way to the hospital … okay. We'll be arriving in about 20 minutes." He quickly turned his gaze to Tory. She looked like a scared rabbit slouched in her seat. Her eyes were red from crying and any makeup she previously had worn was now long gone. Her brows were pinched together and her hands were shaking in her lap. Instinctively, Steve placed his right hand over both of hers and gave them a firm squeeze.

"It's going to be okay, Tory. I am right here with you." She didn't respond to his grasp, instead she looked away staring at the street still hoping to awaken from the horrible nightmare.

He was doing everything in his power to keep calm, but he was concerned about Tory. He had never seen her so despondent. With exception of the day she told him about Erin and Carter. She was a firecracker at work, so passionate and skilled at thinking outside the box. He thought back to the first time he had met her.

She had walked into the conference room wearing a grey pencil skirt and a red collared shirt. Her black hair was spun into a taught bun. As she took a seat across from him,

Steve noticed her bright red peek-a-boo shoes and the black polish on her toes. Black polish, *hmmm* he had thought at the time that maybe it was a glimpse into her mischievous side. She had captured his imagination that first meeting.

During the interview, she was attentive, quick to answer, and very witty. He recalled stifling a few laughs when his colleagues tried to stump her with mundane questions. She was driven and exactly the addition he needed for his team. He had surprised everyone in the room when he asked Victoria to start the next day. She turned to him and smiled. That was nearly 7 years ago, and since then she had captured all of his attention.

He never acted on impulse and would never tempt her into ruining her marriage. He assumed she would move on after finishing school and he would try to forget her, but that was before Carter met Erin. Steve was in the game and he wasn't ready to give up without one hell of a fight. Right now, he needed to provide some level of comfort knowing full well she was about to see Carter for the last time. He put his thoughts aside and slowed the car.

Steve pulled into the hospital parking lot which was filled with a sea of flashing red and blue lights. A police officer waved at Steve to stop and walked up to his window. Steve spoke to the officer, and Tory heard bits and pieces of their conversation.

"Here to ID."

"Pull around … morgue … statement form." She closed her eyes as the tears fell quickly once again. Each salty drop raced down her cheeks only to fall from her chin. Once the car was parked she felt a gust of cool air as Steve opened her door and released her seatbelt. He lowered himself so that the weight of his body was supported by his knees on the inner doorframe. Tory looked over to meet his stare.

"I'm sorry," she said in more of a whisper than a voice.

"Don't be. Do you have any questions before we go in?" His eyes were soft, waiting for her to respond. Nothing. He took a deep breath.

"Victoria?" She nodded. "We are going to enter through that door," he said pointing to a large grey steel double door.

"It is the morgue and there are going to be some people waiting for us … for you. They are going to ask that you look at a body and tell them if you recognize the person." He paused, she nodded again and he continued.

"If at any time you feel sick, uncomfortable, or if you want to leave, let me know. I will be right by your side."

She nodded again and reached for his hand. He helped her from the car and held her elbow as they walked across the parking lot through the looming doors. The hallway was bright and smelled sterile, like bleach and moth balls. *Moth balls aren't very sterile, why would a hospital smell like a storage closet?* She shook her head at the thought … *Focus* … She thought she might be losing her mind.

There was a white door ahead of them being held open by a tall man wearing a white lab coat. He motioned for them to approach and then quietly—reverently, explained what needed to happen. He told them there was a police officer just beyond the entrance ready to take her statement. He asked her if she had any questions. She slowly shook her head from side to side feeling the tightening grip of Steve's hand on her own.

As the three of them crossed the threshold she saw a bright white light suspended over a sheet-draped table covering the outline of a person. Tory stepped forward releasing her grip from Steve's hand while the doctor made his way to the opposite side of the table. He took the corners of the sheet in either hand and began to gently, slowly, pull the white shroud from the top. As soon as the sheet revealed the face, Tory gasped and searched the room for Steve. He stepped toward her as she quickly crossed the room in his direction. Her eyes were wide open and … angry? She barreled into Steve's chest burying her face once again in his jacket and began to sob quietly.

"Is this supposed to be some kind of cruel joke?" Her voice was muffled by Steve's jacket. Her tiny hands were balled into fists and pressed between his chest and her throat.

"No Tory, this is not a cruel joke," Steve replied placing both of his arms around her. All he wanted to do at this moment was carry her out of this place and take her to his home where she would be safe.

Empty Glasses

Steve parked his car and raced up to Tory's apartment taking the stairs three at a time. When he arrived outside her door, he could hear her voice on the other side. He knocked and waited. He knocked again announcing himself this time, hoping she would open the door. When she did open the door Steve was surprised, because she thought he was Carter. She didn't know? They hadn't called her yet? *Shit.*

After quickly explaining what he knew he stood waiting for her reaction. She caught him off-guard when she slammed her head into his chest and began to cry. Her entire body was shaking. Gasping for air, she grabbed him tightly around his back.

Steve walked forward holding her shoulder and noticed a bottle of wine on the counter. There were also two wine glasses; one contained remnants of white wine. *Had she been entertaining someone?* Steve thought as he looked around the apartment. It was small enough that he could see every square inch from where he stood holding Tory, but he didn't see any signs of another person. He felt his face warm. He had remembered that Tory's divorce was final this week, but he hadn't expected her to move forward so quickly. Then he recalled that she was expecting Carter. Were they going to reconcile, or was Carter just playing with her and his mistress? What did Tory say her name was again … Erin? Suddenly, Steve recalled his conversation with Carter this afternoon. What a manipulative asshole. *Well Carter, you and karma are getting quite friendly now aren't you?* His smug thought was interrupted by his cell phone.

He leaned down to retrieve his cell phone and smelled the familiar scent of black cherry. Tory always smelled like a dessert—good enough to eat. He would have never tried advancing their strictly professional relationship because she was married after all… or *was* married. The thought that she may have already moved on and found someone new so soon, or had taken a step back and rekindled her marriage, he felt … he felt …

Back at The Morgue

"Steve, that's not Carter!" Her voice was shrill, cold and shaky. Steve leaned over Tory and stared at the face propped up on the metal table. The police officer stepped forward in their direction and addressed Tory only.

"Ma'am, can you identify this man?"

Tory looked up at Steve pulling herself away from his tense grasp. She walked toward the officer. With her body tightened and her brows furrowed together. She stopped two feet in front of him. Taking a deep breath to lessen her anger, she said in a low, assertive voice, "I've never seen this man before. Sir, this is not Carter Ammon." She quickly rubbed her cheeks with the backs of her hands to remove the tears. She glared at the officer as he was fumbling with a handful of papers. *How the hell does one mix up bodies in a hospital? Does this happen often enough or am I just that freakin' lucky?*

The officer took a step back, sat the papers down, and grabbed his notebook from his shirt pocket. He studied his notes, while avoiding contact—eyes or otherwise—with the woman glaring at him

Tory felt Steve's hand on her lower back and her body instantly relaxed with his touch. He must have sensed that she was going to blow up in the face of this latest revelation. *People,* her mind screamed... *is he dead, or is he alive. SOMEONE GIVE ME AN ANSWER!* Every part of her being wanted to scream, yet she remained silent.

"Um, ma'am ... I thought ... I was told," he stammered. "I was told you were here to identify this man. But you are correct, ma'am this man is not Carter Ammon."

"No shit." Steve bluntly stated, "Where the hell is Mr. Ammon?" He'd lost it! Lost his patience, lost his level-headedness, and lost his temper. Today was turning into one dramatic event after another. First, the absence of Tory at the office, then Carter's confession, followed by the information from the scanner. While in the midst of all of that, he was dealing with his anger thinking Carter had forced Tory to reconsider her marriage by faking an affair. *What is this guy's issue with trust and marriage?* Now adding to Steve's irritation, they both stood in the morgue looking at a corpse that is not Tory's husband ... or ex-husband ... whatever. Steve was livid and feeling the ever-present need to protect Tory from everything.

Tory looked back at Steve with a shy smile appearing on her lips. She had never, in the years that she had worked by this man's side, ever seen him lose his temper. She was thankful he was here with her and that he took the assertive tone with the officer. She would have never dared, but knowing that he was here, knowing that he was providing her strength and support...

"Mr. Ammon is in surgery I believe, on the third floor..." The officers' voice faded as Steve grabbed Tory by the arm and dragged her abruptly away from the cold, sterile room, past the white-faced doctor, who stood shocked.

When they reached the stairwell, Tory's hand slid free from Steve's and she fell painfully to her knees on the concrete. She brought her hands to her face as she lowered her head and began to cry with hysterical force. Steve turned around in time to see her fall. Her entire body was trembling. He bent down in front of her and gently wrapped his fingers around her wrists. She responded by lifting her head slowly and sliding her hands around his neck. Steve slid his hands down her arms and felt her back straighten. He rested his right hand on her lower back while slipping his left forearm behind her knees and slowly lifted her crumpled body into his arms.

He could feel her breath on his neck, erratic and strained. He took a moment and walked to the stairs where he sat down, resting her on his lap. Her legs dangled helplessly over the right side of his and he could feel her tears on his neck. Still holding the small of her back, he rested his other hand over her exposed cheek. He could feel the tears roll across his thumb as his fingers cupped around her ear. Her body was heaving against his chest. He turned and leaned his chin on her forehead while whispering comforting words that everything was going to be alright.

Tory didn't know how long she had been crying in his arms, but she felt a sudden rush of embarrassment. He was being so kind, so genuine trying to help her and she was a bawling, blubbering girl. Totally unprofessional for crying out loud! And that is exactly what she was doing, crying out loud. Yet, as she listened to his whispers, her breathing slowed and the tears began to recede. She felt his strength, his security—and the tears subsided.

She quickly became aware of his hand on her back. He was making circular motions with his finger slow, small circles on her back. His breath in her hair was hot, and his breathing was deep and slow. She could feel his pulse on her lips and it was in complete contradiction to his calm breath. His heart rate was spiked, pounding like the beat of an island drum. Her emotions were a mess and playing games with her imagination. Or maybe it was her imagination was playing games with her emotions; either way, she had to be misreading the moment.

She pulled away slightly, but remained seated on his lap. As she licked her lips, she could taste the salt from his neck on her tongue, or was it the tears that she had been crying? She was suddenly flushed, hot, and needing something more.

She looked up and was surprised to see his lips parted like he was going to say something, but no words escaped. She tried to swallow but her mouth was too dry and she could feel her own heart rate increase. His eyes were fixed on her lips, his gaze intense. Time stood still for a split second as Tory struggled to control her inappropriate thoughts. She felt his hand release her back and felt his thumb glide across her cheek removing the tear tracks. His other hand swept across her other cheek and stroked it gently. She closed her eyes and tilted her head back just enough that her lips naturally parted.

A small moan crept up from her belly as his hands fisted her hair on either side of her temples. As the vibration moved up her throat and vocalized she opened her eyes and met Steve's stoic gaze. She lunged forward, without thinking, and pressed her lips to his.

He inhaled sharply as she sucked on his lower lip and she felt his abdomen tense. She ran her hands up Steve's chiseled chest digging her fingernails into his pecks, squeezing while tugging on his lip. She could feel his hands grasp her shoulders, pushing her away, but her brain refused to comprehend the reasoning. His breathing was labored and with a firm push, her lips pulled away from his creating a loud pop from the suction. His fingers were digging into her skin painfully as she lowered her head.

Oh, God! What am I doing? Her silent question hung in her mind as she refused to open her eyes.

Never Was

"I am so sorry."

His hands were shaking, his mind was racing, but the last thing he wanted was for her to be sorry. Unless she truly regretted what she had done. There was no reason for her remorse, or that injured look on her face.

"Tory, unless you are truly sorry, please don't apologize to me."

"Steve, I don't know what I am right now. I don't know how I feel other than safe with you. I was waiting for Carter to bring dinner, then he didn't show up and I thought you were him. Then you told me that he was dead, but the morgue didn't have his body. Then I misread your emotions, your face and, well, now I'm sitting in this hospital stairwell staring up at you while you have a death grip on my arms!"

Steve instantly relaxed his hands slightly. He had no idea that he was hurting her.

"You did not misread my emotions. This is just not the time or place for you and me to, well…continue on like high school kids. We need to get to the third floor, find Carter and figure out what the hell is going on. You and I are having dinner tomorrow, and I am more than happy to postpone this conversation until then, if you so wish"

His voice was calming and he had lessened his grip on her arms, but he was still holding on. *Okay, so we can table this conversation until tomorrow. Perfect.* She ignored the embarrassment and stood up. "I wish to continue this conversation tomorrow. Thank you," Tory says.

With that, they started up the stairs as she continued the fight to calm her heart rate. When they reached the third floor, Steve brushed past her and opened the door. They looked to the left and saw the nurse's station. Steve took her arm and they walked toward the bustling center.

"Hello, can I help you?" The platinum haired nurse asks.

"Yes, my name is Victoria Garrison-Ammon and I am looking for Carter Ammon. I was told he was in surgery." Steve's face reddened as soon as she said her last name. *I need to get it changed back, but the divorce is not final until tomorrow.* Tory looked up at Steve and tried to relay a silent message of patience.

It's fine. I've waited nearly seven years already, what's a few more hours right? Steve thought and cocked his head to the side and gave her a little smirk.

"Mrs. Ammon, he is in recovery room 332. Visiting hours ended at ten, but I think we can make an exception, knowing what has kept you this evening." She was referring to the morgue.

"Thank you," Tory replied as her stomach sank to her feet with the thought of that face. The dead man staring at the ceiling.

We reached the door together just as a woman dressed in white was exiting.

"Mrs. Ammon?"

"Yes."

"Oh good evening, please accept my apologies for all of the confusion tonight. Mr. Ammon has returned from surgery, he's conscience, but medicated. We do expect he will make a full recovery. Shame that such a young man would throw his life away like that though." She nodded her head at Steve. "Please only one visitor at a time. We really need to get him on the mend for the trial, so let's keep the visit quick."

Tory turned to Steve who looked nearly as confused as she did. She shrugged her shoulders and walked through the doorway. Carter was hooked up to all sorts of loud machinery. As she looked back at Steve he motioned that he was going to wait in the waiting area. She nodded in return.

"Tory?" His voice is small.

"Hey Carter, it's me. How are you feeling?" *He really doesn't look that bad she thought to herself. He did not look nearly as bad as the guy downstairs lying on the cold table.*

"Did they tell ya?"

"Tell me what?" she replied shaking her head back and forth.

"Tory, I killed someone tonight." He looked up and saw confusion written all over her face so he continued. "I stopped at the bar after I saw Gage and had a few beers. Then I got your voicemail and realized I had been there longer than I thought. I called in our dinner and got your text. The next thing I remember was the red light and a really big truck. I think it was blue. As soon as I came out of surgery, an officer was waiting to read me my rights. They took a blood sample Tory. They took a sample and my blood alcohol level was 0.12, and that was an hour after the accident." His throat started to tighten.

"You were the drunk driver? Carter they told me you were dead! I had to go to the morgue and they showed me a dead body ... Oh my God! That was the guy you killed?" She was staring at the stiches above his eye and the bandages on his arm. He looked so fragile, so broken.

"It was going to be the perfect night Tory. I was going to come clean, beg for your forgiveness and hope that we could move forward. But now it doesn't really matter. No matter what, I am going to jail for manslaughter." He was sobbing.

"What were you coming clean about Carter? Have you had more than one affair on me? Go ahead, lay it on me!" She was yelling now. "I can handle just about that and then I am done today!" She glared at him, no sympathy at all in her stare. *Come on Carter. Give me your last best shot. Better go for the gut, because my heart is no longer yours to break.*

"Tory, there never was anyone else. I was afraid that you were going to leave me as soon as you graduated, as soon as your world opened up. So I made her up. Erin was not real. She was an excuse to let *you* decide which life *you* wanted. The one before your dreams came true, or the future where you had the opportunity to start over. I was hoping that you would be willing to consider forgiving me and..." he gasped and the alarm let out a shrill set of sounds.

Beep, beep, beeeeeeeeeeeep. Nursing staff flooded the room with loud voices, shouting out different orders. Code blue! Adrenaline! Again! Clear!

Tory felt her eyes grow huge, she was standing in the middle of the chaos and she couldn't move. Her feet felt like she was wearing cinderblock shoes. The doctor she had seen earlier raced around the corner. Time froze for Tory, while everyone else continued to move about.

"Time of Death, 23:58"

The nurse said something to her, the doctor said something, but nothing made any sense. He was just telling her that his girlfriend was imaginary, that he murdered someone with his car, and that he was driving drunk. She backed out of the room, eyes glazed, in utter shock.

"Tory. Tory. Victoria!" She turned her head in the direction of her name and saw Steve quickly making his way toward her. "I got you a coffee from the cafeteria. Shit, what's going on?" She said nothing, staring past him. Her eyes were glassy as though she were in shock. He sat her in a chair next to Carter's room and caught the attention of one of the nurses. She informed him that Carter had suffered from a sudden heart attack, and nothing had shown pre- or post-surgery that indicated he was a candidate. Tory didn't move.

Steve knelt in front of Tory, but she didn't acknowledge his presence. She was stiff, but shaking like she was freezing cold. He removed his jacket and cursed himself for forgetting to grab hers before they had left her house.

"Steve, please take me home." Her voice was a whisper and her eyes had still not moved from where they were looking. He reached down to lift her, and she responded by wrapping her arms around his neck. By the time they arrived at his car she had stopped shaking, but she was still in shock.

"Tory, I am going to take you to my place. I don't feel comfortable leaving you alone right now."

"I would rather go to my apartment please. I can't handle anymore unknowns today. Please Steve. Please just take me to my apartment."

Slowly he pulled into her apartment complex. The entire ride from the hospital was quiet; Tory didn't say a word. She sat still and stared out the passenger window with no expression on her face. Steve turned the ignition off and waited, but there was no response from her. He walked around and opened her door. As if by memory only, she slid her hand and unbuckled the seatbelt.

"Steve, this is not how I pictured today. This is not how I pictured anything."

He shook his head as he picked her up in his arms. She felt tiny, scared—almost like nothing at all. He reached for her purse and grabbed her keys from the center console. After unlocking her door, he walked her into the small, but open, apartment and sat her down on her bed. He locked the front door, secured the French doors and then knelt in front of her. She looked mortified as he removed her shoes.

"Tory, please don't worry. You are home, and you are safe." She nodded and stood for just a moment before disappearing to the bathroom. When she returned, she collapsed onto the bed, sleep wrapping around her like a cloud.

He couldn't let her fall asleep fully clothed minus the shoes he had removed from her feet earlier, but Steve was hesitant to wake her. Today had been a fire-storm for her … him as well, considering everything that had happened. This was not how he wanted to begin any relationship, but especially one with Tory.

He moved cautiously toward her bed trying to make as little noise as possible and trying to keep his thoughts appropriate. *Task at hand Gage, task at hand.* He started with her socks. Sliding his thumbs between the material and her ankle and gently removing them. He couldn't help but stare at her perfectly-pedicured feet and those infamous black polished nails. He started a pile on the corner of her bed where he placed her socks. Next were her pants. He quietly unbuckled her belt then button. With a quick pull, her zipper was down exposing a lacey dark colored fabric. *Of course they would have to be lace…*

He felt her tense under his fingers. "Shhh, Tory I just want to get your pants off and put you to bed," he said, sounding a little too excited. She let out a moan while planting her heals into the mattress and raised her hips high into the air.

Oh, God. Task at hand! Task at hand!

He pulled them off and she settled back on top the covers. He went to the opposite side of the bed and turned down the many layers of bedding.

Sheesh, is she always cold? She really needs someone to help her stay warm all night long. There was no way she would need these layers of material on top of her if I were lying next to her. Task at hand!

"Tory," he said, but she was sleeping too deeply for him to wake her. He walked back around the queen-sized bed and picked her up once more. She wrapped her arms around his neck and exhaled a deep sigh into the hollow under his ear. Her breath was so soft, but as Steve was placing her on the other side of the bed he noticed that she hadn't shaved her legs. There was definite stubble.

So, perhaps dinner with Carter was really just dinner. He chuckled to himself as he laid her head on the plum-colored satin pillow case. Before he could get her covered, she rolled away from him exposing her bottom, barely covered by tiny boy-short panties. *Argh.* He gently placed the weighty covers over her body and went to the kitchen for something to drink. He sat near her bed, staring at her for the longest time until sleep captured his body as well.

His dreams were filled with the image of Tory. In his dreams she was wearing much less than she had been when he tucked her into bed. The woman captivated him and made him question his bachelor status even in his subconscious.

Steve woke many times during the early morning to the sound of Tory moaning and talking in her sleep. Once she had even cursed Carter's name and then gone quiet again. This poor woman was struggling with her feelings even as she slept, and all he could do was listen to her internal struggle as she vocalized her thoughts. Her dreams were not as pleasant as his.

A Little Time

Mmmm, coffee. Oh that smells so good. She could feel the warmth of the sunlight on her back as she inhaled the scent of coffee brewing the kitchen. *How am I smelling coffee? I don't have a programmable ... Oh my God!* Her eyes shot open as she swiftly sat straight up, pulling the sheet to her chin. Her eyes moved from side-to-side as she looked around her apartment like a trapped animal.

"Good morning Tory, how did you sleep?" He was propped up against her counter wearing his under-shirt and boxer shorts.

"Steve? Did you stay all night? Where did you..." she looked at the opposite side of the bed which was still made.

"I slept on your couch. I didn't want to leave you after last night."

"Did we... um, did you take my pants off?" She blushed.

"No we didn't, and yes I did, with a little help from you." His mind flashed back to her heels pressed into the mattress and her hips thrust high in the air. *She is a flexible little thing.* "I hope, though that you plan on shaving your legs before our date tonight," he said trying hard to hold the laughter in his throat.

Instinctively, she reached under the comforter and felt her leg. "Holy crap! You felt my legs? I've uh, been a little busy this week."

She grabbed an extra pillow and threw it in his direction. Catching it, his smile turned into a mischievous grin. Holding the pillow he slowly stalked toward her bed. When he was only a couple of feet from the edge, he jumped and landed inches from her face. Her pupils dilated as she reached for the pillow behind her.

Ugh, he was too fast and within seconds she was pinned under him. She was laughing so hard it was shaking both of them.

"You are beautiful when you laugh." *You are beautiful when you cry too. You are the most beautiful woman I have ever met.*

His smiled faded quickly as he leaned closer to her lips.

"Steve!" She shrieked. "I have standards! I don't kiss before brushing my teeth, and I don't have sex before shaving my legs." She was still giggling. "I can't believe you would say something about that! So not-gentlemanly of you," she teased.

"You are right, but I never claimed to be a gentleman, Victoria." A wolfish grin stretched across his face.

I either need to get out of bed and brush my teeth or break my rule! She shifted her hips below him and his brows shot up like a rocket.

"Is the coffee ready?" she asked in her most innocent voice.

"I'm sure it is. Do you want a cup?"

She nodded with enthusiasm.

He wrestled himself off the bed and as soon as his back was to her, he heard her shuffle to the bathroom. He chuckled to himself at her act of innocence. "Do you take cream or sugar?"

"Cream please." *Toothpaste, toothbrush. Oh my Lord! I look like a really scary version of myself! Fluff the hair, pinch the cheeks... I don't have time to shave my legs! This is going to have to do. Ha! And he thinks I'm beautiful when I laugh! She smiled at her reflection. It feels so good to laugh again. When was the last time I laughed with Carter?*

Steve half expected to see Tory fully clothed when the bathroom door swung open. Instead, the only thing different about her was the smell of peppermint emanating from her sweet mouth. He watched as she popped herself onto the counter next to him. He placed a cup of coffee in her hand and tried not to admire her shapely legs that seemed to stretch nearly to the floor.

"I will make sure they are smooth by tonight," she giggled again.

Before she could even take a drink of her coffee, Steve took the mug from her hand and set it down next to her. He positioned his thighs at her knees and waited for her invitation. When she relaxed her legs, he pressed himself against the counter, grabbed her by the bottom and pulled her forward until the only thing that separated their desires was cotton and lace. Her tongue slid slowly out of her mouth and wet her lips. He claimed her mouth before giving her tongue a change to retreat, capturing it with his lips. He sucked hard for a quick second then released it only to enter her mouth and continue to explore. He felt her hands tighten into fists, his shirt tightening around his back as she clinched.

Her tongue swirling with his, she was panting peppermint breath into his mouth, and he was moving closer to losing control.

"Steve," she pulled away. Breathing rapidly, trying desperately to catch a natural rhythm. He buried his head into her chest trying to follow her in breathing, trying to calm himself. Moments passed and she kissed the top of his head. "I need to get showered. I feel like I have been through the wringer for the past twelve hours." His head snapped to attention. "Alone, I need some *alone* time," she emphasized as she ran her fingers across the prickly hair on her legs.

"I could um… help you…" he said running his finger along the same path.

"No, no. There will be time to test your pampering skills later. But right now, I just want to gather my thoughts, clean myself up, and come to terms with everything. You, Carter, make-believe Erin, dead morgue guy, all of it." (sigh)

Steve took a step back. The absence of his body between her legs caused an automatic response and she crossed them.

"He told you?" his eyebrows pinched together.

"Told me what?"

"Told you that he made her up?"

"Yeah, right before…" she closed her eyes and shock her head. "I just need some time to process all of this information."

"Alright Tory. What time do you want me to come back? Are we still going out tonight?" His tone was clipped. "What time is it now?" He reached for his cell phone. "10:58. Okay, how about I pick you up at 6:00 sharp." She glared at him. "I'm sorry, it's really not you. Well it is you," he said looking down. "I need some time too." He smiled and shrugged his shoulders.

"Understood and 6:00 will be perfect." She leaned forward and kissed his cheek.

Steve gathered up his watch, phone, keys, put on his pants, and threw his button down shirt over his shoulder. One last kiss on her forehead and he promised to return. Looking down at her legs he whispered, "I can't wait to inspect those later."

After securing the front door and taking a gulp of coffee from the mug, Tory went straight to the bathroom for a much-needed spa treatment. After an hour, she was satisfied with the smooth, glowing results. There was still plenty of time left for her before Steve said he would return, so she headed to the beach. As she sat on the towel and dug her feet into the warm sand. She shifted her weight to her elbows behind her and listened to the waves, one after another, slowly break against the beach and recede back into the ocean.

Tory's thoughts returned to Carter ... and the infamous discussion that lead to their divorce.

Manila Envelope

"Tory, we need to talk."

"Carter. It is the middle of my last term! I am buried in homework. Can we talk in about an hour? Just give me that long to finish this paper."

He said nothing. He threw a manila envelope on the table and stormed out the door. She grabbed the envelope and carefully slid the large stack of papers out. It took her a moment to realize what the packet was. "Oh my God." She raced to the front door.

"Stop! Carter! Stop!" She was crying and holding up the papers as Carter was backing out of the driveway. He put the car in park and waited. Tory walked over to the passenger side and he rolled the window down.

"Really Carter? You want to have this conversation in the driveway of all places? Come back into the house." It wasn't a request and through the tears, Carter couldn't tell her no.

Once they crossed the threshold and she had shut the door, she turned to Carter who was standing three feet in front of her.

"What the hell are these Carter?" She was shaking the bundle of papers in front of her.

"They are what they are, Honey."

"Honey? Honey! You place an envelope filled with divorce papers in front of me, walk away and that's it? No discussion, no …"

"Tory, you said that you were *too busy*. It's nice to see that I've found a way to get your full attention." His remark was sarcastic and his tone was patronizing.

She was fuming inside. Her blood was so hot she felt at any moment she would self-combust.

"Why are you doing this?" But she knew the answer. Numerous arguments had occurred in the past years. He was jealous of the time she spent at school, at study sessions, at the dining room table doing homework and he refused to understand.

"I am doing all of this Carter, for *us*! All of it! All of the late nights I sit studying at this table, all of the hours I have sacrificed. Damnit, Carter! I am doing this so that you and I can have a better life." Her strong voice had faded to nearly a whisper, "I am doing all of this for you and me."

"Bullshit, Tory. You're doing this to better yourself. You want more that I can obviously give you…"

How can you believe that is true? You were my first boyfriend, my first love! I gave you my virtue, my heart, my promise of forever…

"Carter," her voice was low, "graduation is only a month and-a-half away. After that, it will be just us again, no more school. Please. Let's work this out. Let's talk this out with someone, a counselor. Please." She was sobbing.

"I'm done Tory. I am just done." He knew he was breaking her heart, but he couldn't focus on that. He knew she wouldn't sign the papers, she wouldn't let this happen. He needed to do something drastic.

"There's someone else Tory. Her name is Erin."

Awakening

Opening one eye at a time, Tory tried to focus on the bright water in front of her.

Figure it out Tory! Make a list, throw stones, get mad, cry, scream and yell... but get this shit worked out. You are graduated, divorced, widowed, beautiful, smart, employed and... laid out on the beach dreaming about a conversation that already happened. Is this how you want to live today? Constantly looking back at yesterday rather than living in the right-now?

"Oh, Carter. I would have chosen you over everyth..." but she froze. Steve! Knowing now that there was such a powerful attraction between the two of them, would she have chosen Carter? Her mind raced back through the past 18 hours. Steve had arrived in her time of need and, not only did he provide her with comfort and strength, but he had given her a glimpse into a possible future.

Removing her t-shirt and shorts, Tory stood in her swimsuit, staring once again at the blue water in front of her. Walking slowly through the surf, she continued further until the water was just below her chin. Filling her lungs with fresh air, she held her breath as she dropped into the quietness. She could feel herself sinking gently until her bended knees made contact with the sandy ocean bottom.

Closing her eyes, she said a silent prayer for Carter.

Over the past six months, she had screamed, she had cried, she had been weary and insecure. There was nothing she could do to change what had happened. Tory could not change the events leading up to this moment. So she let it go. She let it all go. The hurt, the anger, the doubt, the fear, the disappointment—everything. She could feel the waves gently rocking her body, carrying away all that she was willing to release. She planted her feet firmly on the sand, exhaled her remaining air and pushed upward. She opened her eyes in time to breach the surface and took a deep, healing breath.

I don't know what tomorrow will bring, but I will not dwell on yesterday ...

I will live in the right now ...

Shifting Tide
Book Two

A. L. Elder

Prelude

"Hey Tory?" He said walking in and closing the office door behind him.

"Hey yourself!" She replied with an eyebrow raised and a crooked smile.

"Do you want to get a bite to eat before we ..."

"Sure, that sounds good. Can I meet you downstairs in about ten minutes?" Cutting him off mid-sentence.

"You got it, see you in ten," as he turned on his heel and walked out of her office.

Rejuvenated from the week, Tory sat down at her desk and looked at her calendar. She had circled today's date nearly a month ago. It had been eight months since Carter's fatal car accident. Eight months since Steve walked through her front door and rescued her from her nightmare. He was so strong and caring, even tucking her into bed that night. Oh, what a night it had been. Although, the following night…well, that was a little less-than-exhilarating, to say the least; but it was what they both had needed.

Tonight however, Tory knew that she was in for a surprise. Steve had been vague, only telling her that she needed to block out the entire weekend—make sure she had clothes for three days and two nights ... the suspense was killing her!

The First Date

At ten-minutes-to-six, Tory ran into the bathroom to check her appearance one last time.

Oh, he is going to be here any minute! I am about as nervous as a... as a... ahhh, even my subconscious is nervous!

There was a familiar knock at the door and she walked briskly toward it. She paused and took a deep breath before opening. *Breathe Tory, just breathe.*

"Good evening Sir," she said and curtsied.

"Well, good evening Miss," laughter resonating in his voice. "What's with the fancy greeting?"

"Um, I am just a little nervous. Sorry, I ..." her face turned hot. She was totally mortified!

"Well, there's no reason to be nervous Tory, you look beautiful, and tonight ... I have no expectations. Whatever happens, whatever doesn't happen, is fine."

"Really? You don't have some romantic retreat planned for us this evening? Some guarantee that we will end up ..." her voice was sarcastic but still smart.

"Tory, I didn't plan some elaborate event for our first date." His voice was firm. "I have no hidden agenda, no desire to do anything you aren't fully committed to doing. Relax. I just want to *get to know you.*" His voiced warmed up toward the end of his statement.

He was dressed in a pair of dark blue jeans, a white t-shirt and his black jacket.

"Cowboy boots? Really? I had no idea you were a cowboy Steve."

"Tory, there are a million things you don't know about me. That is why we need to start off with this date."

"Where are we going tonight?"

"That, my dear, is a surprise. Grab your things and let's go."

She gathered her purse and locked the front door as Steve gestured for her to lead the way down the stairs. When they arrived at his car, Steve opened the door and she slid into the familiar seat. She reached for the seatbelt and was suddenly catapulted to the night before. Images of Steve, the dead eyes staring at the morgue ceiling, the staircase, Carter's deathbed confession, waking up without her pants on, and the kiss the following morning. She froze, unable to move—unable to bring herself back to reality. The entire world was moving in slow motion.

Steve watched as her face fell, and her green eyes paled. She was remembering. She was reliving the nightmare.

"Tory. Tory, are you okay?" *Close your eyes, take a deep breath Tory, this will pass. Come back to me, please come back to me.*

"Yes, it all just rushed back. It took me by surprise. I'm good. I'm sorry," she replied sneaking a quick look in his direction while nodding her head.

Steve was not convinced, but put the car in gear. He had no intentions of taking her to a public place. He had a feeling that what took place in the stairwell of the hospital and in her kitchen this morning was a one-time or two-time deal. Victoria Garrison was not a woman to give herself physically to anyone unwilling to earn it first. As much as he was tempted last night to return her kiss, as badly as he wanted to touch her when he placed her into bed, it was wrong and he knew it.

He sensed her hesitation as she sat on her kitchen counter this morning, and her giggle seemed forced. But her exuberant laugh when he jumped on her bed was real. That was the Tory who had captured his attention. He wanted to help her find her strength again, even if it meant taking things painfully slow. Starting with tonight and that was what he planned to do.

"I finally listened to my voicemail this morning." Her tone was matter of fact, no emotion at all. "The Sergeant had left me a message saying that Carter had been in an accident." She stopped abruptly and her eyes darted to Steve's. Tory knew that Steve would blame himself just as he had last night. She wasn't upset with him over the miscommunication at all.

"I called Janine, the communications operator that was on duty during accident. She was the one I spoke to last night. Tory, it was my fault that you and I ended up in that morgue."

Her eyes shot up again and she stared at Steve in disbelief.

"Tory, I have spent my entire adult life, my entire career lecturing public safety officials about concentrating, recalling and retaining correct information when under duress." He paused, shaking his head. "I heard what I wanted to hear. I never stopped to think for a moment that Carter could have been the intoxicated driver when I had Janine on the line. She only had a sliver of information from the responders at the scene, and I must have filled in the details and drawn my own conclusions. My response was in complete contradiction to what I know is right in those circumstances. She told me that they took the injured man by ambulance to the hospital and the deceased man was going to be transported to the hospital morgue. I put the pieces together all on my own. I never questioned. I just reacted. I am so sorry." He lowered his hands on the steering wheel and she watched as his entire body shifted lower in the seat.

"If you are expecting me to scream and yell at you, or even try to wrap my head around being angry with you … you are sorely wrong Gage." Now she had his attention! "I can't imagine what would have happened if you weren't there. I cannot imagine standing in that bright, sterile room staring at a dead stranger without knowing that you were not within reach. I don't even remember getting home. I don't remember taking my shoes off or my pants. I can't remember crawling into bed. All I remember was feeling safe." Without a doubt she had rehashed the events of the previous evening over and over in her mind.

"You provided me with so much more than you will ever know. I don't remember everything about last night, but I remember feeling safe." She reached across the seat and placed her hand on his shoulder. "I will never be able to repay you for your attentiveness, Steve. Please don't beat yourself up over last night."

Of course she needed to talk to him about the intimate moments that had happened. She would not be comfortable talking about such things in a restaurant with potential eavesdroppers seated nearby. She had thought so much of their stairwell encounter. Feeling his strong arms wrapped around her, gently and deliberately removing the tears from her face. So tender and forceful. She rubbed her upper arm and felt the sore spots where his fingers had dug in. He said he had removed her pants, but she didn't remember him doing so. She smiled at the memory of her unshaven legs! Guh, of all the things! But then, in the kitchen this morning, kissing him. It was an amazing feeling. He felt right, but the timing felt wrong. She only knew him from work. And, although the glimpse she caught last night was pure kindness, she wasn't ready to commit to having a physical relationship. Not yet anyway.

I don't want this to be weird. I know I am nowhere near ready to jump into a relationship, let alone jump into the bed with someone. Awe, how do I tell him without sounding like a total hypocrite? I made the moves on him, I advanced, and I pounced... oh my God! I am freaking cougar! Wait, isn't a cougar older than the man she's seducing? Shoot, I'm just a prude.

Steve slowed the car and turned into the driveway. Tory had that lost look in her eyes again. He put the car in park and turned off the ignition. "Tory, we're here." He said quietly, trying not to alarm her.

She quickly turned her head in his direction, and then focused out the front windshield. Her mouth fell open as she gawked at the beautiful three-story Tudor-style home. The front door glittered in the evening light. The beautiful shade of old world red complemented the black trim and shutters. The main color resembled a white picket fence—one that even young Sawyer would have been proud of. The landscaping was equally breathtaking. Daisies grouped in the colors white, red, and orange lined the walkway leading … inviting her to the door. On the porch were two large decorative planters with the largest purple wave she had ever seen. The front yard had the look of a well-manicured golf course. Every blade bright green and plush almost looking like a carpet of grass.

"This is where we are having dinner?" She asked while taking in the scenery.

"Yes. Welcome to my home Victoria."

Oh no. Oh crap! What am I going to do? He thinks I'm going to … he thinks we are going to…

"Tory, I wanted to bring you here rather than take you to a crowded place. It has been an unforgettable 22 hours. I told you before, and I will tell you again, I have no intentions. If you want to go out, we can. If you would like to spend a quiet evening in, again, no intentions …" his voice trailed off giving her a moment to process what he was saying.

She unbuckled her seatbelt, and Steve rushed around the car to open her door. *Always the gentleman.* He held out his hand to offer his assistance. Smiling, Tory nodded her acceptance, and they walked hand-in-hand up the path.

"These are my favorite," she said as she bent down to touch a white daisy.

I know Tory. I know that you love daisies; that you prefer white tea; that you hate milk chocolate; that you cannot drink more than two cups of coffee, because it causes you unbearable heartburn. I have listened and cataloged every like and dislike you have shared with me over the past seven years.

"Did you do all of this yourself?"

"Most of it. I had some help from my sister and brothers along the way. It has been a constant work in progress for the past five years."

"It's beautiful! Absolutely beautiful! The house, the flowers, the yard … all of it, I love it."

He moved in front of her to unlock the front door and she continued to scan her surroundings. *There's so much more Tory, so much more.*

Crossing the threshold, Tory gasped. The three-story house had been remodeled into a high vaulted ceiling, two-level home. Natural wood beams laced the ceiling and latte-colored paint covered the walls. The crown molding was painted black which was something she had never seen before. She was still standing in the doorway but could see the living room, the dining room a hallway and a…Oh my God!

"Is that your kitchen?" She paused at the entrance. Then, walking quickly across the space, she approached a five-burner gas stove. As her eyes perused the culinary delight worthy of any designer magazine, her eyes traveled up the free-standing range hood. There were double ovens built into the wall and the sink was an old farmhouse style in white. There was an island with barstools resting on a sea of slate tiles. She swore the tiles were 20x20, maybe larger. The counters looked like granite, but they weren't radiating a reflection from the lights. *Oh, pendant lighting over the sink, over the island. A lot to take in for a girl with a passion to cook,* she thought to herself.

"Do you like it?" He asked watching her eyes dart around the room like a child on Christmas morning.

"This is my dream kitchen. Are you kidding me? Steve, this is gorgeous!"

"May I make you some dinner?"

"You cook too!?"

"Well, it would really be a waste to have this much stuff if I didn't. Sit there," he said pointing to one of barstools. "What's your pleasure?" He asked while pulling a glass from the cherry-wood cabinet.

"Uh-huh, um water?" She choked out. *No alcohol!*

"Water? Okay, that was my fault. How about a few choices … I have peach iced tea, lemonade, or milk."

"Oh, well then, I guess I will have a peach iced tea. Is it sweetened?"

"No, but try it first before you go adding anything to it. I think you will find the peach nectar really adds a soft sweetness to the white tea." He slid the glass in front of her and watched as her lips parted. He saw her neck flex as she swallowed.

"This is amazing! Let me guess … your own recipe?"

"Nope, my Mom's. She never really takes credit for her creations though."

"Steve, I can't have sex with you tonight." *Where the hell did that come from? Earth to Tory … the nut house is calling!*

"Um, alright. Thanks for getting that cleared up so abruptly. Not that I was asking you to go to bed with me Tory. I just wanted to offer you a beverage." His eyes were full of light and humor. There, it was out and she had said it first. No Sex!

Although it was the most awkward moment afterward, she felt so much better for getting it off her chest and out in the open. She watched for his reaction, waiting so see disappointment, but, instead, she saw that he wasn't at all surprised. Perhaps he knew her better than she thought.

"I'm not sure what happened with us last night. I mean, I remember what happened but I don't normally act like that in public." *Or even in private, Steve, I am a total prude! I have only ever slept with one man and from what I've read in my romance novels ... our relationship was extremely boring.*

He shook his head as he reached into the fridge for two chicken breasts. He also retrieved some vegetables from the crisper.

"Tory, I am just fine with taking this slow. If I thought for a minute, even a second that we were going to consummate the relationship tonight, I would have cancelled out. That's not really where I see the events leading to this evening." He carefully arranged all of the ingredients in a small glass baking dish and popped it into the top oven. "Thirty minutes and we'll have dinner. Can I show you the rest of the house?"

Taking her hand, Steve led Tory from the kitchen to the dining room. The walls were the same color of warm vanilla latte with the same black crown molding, but the table—now that was the show stopper. A beautiful walnut table with ivory cushioned chairs. The centerpiece was a huge vase filled with daisies, Tory assumed from the front yard. As he moved her to the living room, the openness took her breath away. *This is absolutely perfect. The colors he chose look so modern, but there is an old-world charm to the furnishings. There are stories inside these walls just waiting to be shared.*

"That grandfather clock was my great-grandmother's," he said pointing to the far wall. "She passed it down to my mother who then gave it to me when I bought this house. She said it felt right in this room."

Tory smiled, *It does look right in this room.*

Near the fireplace was a lounger couch. Tory imagined herself propped up on an elbow reading her research papers and soaking up the sunlight from the opposite window. Moving into the foyer, Steve pointed out a bathroom, a door that led to the garage, and a beautiful ornate wood staircase that went both up the second floor and down to the basement. The staircase was gorgeous! She had always wanted a large staircase to wrap garland and lights around for the Holidays. Oh, in this house she could see a 12 foot Christmas tree in the main room and another, smaller tree, in the foyer. *Maybe Steve will let me help him decorate for Christmas.*

"Which way first Tory? To the upper level or down to the basement?"

Oh geeze, basements! Her stomach flipped. For the past seven months she had read so many love stories, so many romance novels...most of them filled with fantasies of things Tory didn't even know existed. She had to search the internet numerous times. Secret basement rooms ...*oh yes, I have read books about what single guys keep in their basements behind closed doors. Whips and shackles, four poster beds ...*

"Let's see the upper level please." She was whispering now. Overwhelmed with the enormity of his home and the feeling of spending the Holidays wrapping gifts and decorating every square inch of this place. *Uh, it would probably take weeks to get everything done.*

"Do you decorate for the Holidays?" Although it sounded out-of-the-blue, but it was only a continuation of the mental conversation actually going on inside of her head.

Steve looked down and saw her eyes were bright, striking green and glowing with enthusiasm. "Yes, I decorate the house for Christmas, if that is the 'Holiday' you are referring to, and it takes forever! My family helps and then they all come over to open one present on Christmas Eve. It's a family tradition. Since I have the convenient kitchen and large entertaining space, my mom decided this was the place to have family gatherings. The whole house comes alive at about seven-thirty Christmas morning." He led her down a wide expansive hallway until she walked in to the first bedroom.

"This is really nice, is this one yours?" She couldn't contain her laughter.

"Um, no. This is Emmy's room. She picked out the paint herself and helped me put the glitter on the wall above the bed."

"And, will I meet Emmy?" *Who's Emmy? Steve never mentioned a daughter nor had he ever brought a little girl into the office...*

"Sure, she's my little sister. She's full of fire, glitter and butterflies. She has no idea that the world is filled with scary people. She trusts everyone and loves everything."

"Wow. How old is she?"

"She's 27." He noticed the shocked look on Tory's face. She was contemplating—he spoke, letting her off the hook. "She suffered a traumatic brain injury when she was six, Tory. She has no recollection of the accident. But, because of her injury, her mental age is developing quite a bit slower than normal. She is about 12 years old mentally, even though her body continues to mature at a normal rate. It has yet to hold her back though, she knows nothing but happiness. I told her this room was hers to do with whatever she wanted—and this is her masterpiece," he opened his arms and gestured around the room like a ring leader at a circus.

"I love it! I think it looks cool. She must think the world of you." She smiled and followed Steve out of the room, not wanting to delve further into the subject of his little sister quite yet.

There were three more bedrooms that were fully furnished with wardrobes, matching beds and dressers. Even the night stands were matching. Tory giggled thinking of the hodge-podge of furniture in her apartment. Here, all of the beds were made and pillows were propped up as if for inspection. Every room was proud and putting its best foot forward to impress Tory. It was working!

"Steve, do you have a housekeeper?" *Odd, I know, but really... who would have time to keep this place sparkling like this?*

"No, but I also don't own a television."

NO television! Holy crap. No wonder this place is immaculate. How much time did Carter and I waste sitting in front of the boob-tube causing our brains to atrophy? Ha! A lot...

"This is the master bedroom in here," he said while stopping just inside the door. Tory walked into the vast space and began to take a mental inventory.

A wall of glass caught her eye first. As she walked toward it Steve cleared his throat, causing her to turn in alarm.

"I knew that would be the first thing in this room you were drawn to! Watch this," he said while pressing a button on the wall. The windows began sliding on a hidden track, collapsing onto one another until the entire wall had nearly disappeared. Tory stepped out onto the deck, which was suspended over a twenty-foot-rock-faced cliff. The ocean waves beating against the rocks just beneath Tory, spraying the salty froth high into the sky. She walked over to the deck railing. Closing her eyes, she listened to the water smash violently against the rocks time after time...after time...after, *oh this is better than even the soft, rhythmic sounds that float in through my French doors.*

"The tide is just starting to come in. The high tide really produces the best waves." He was standing next to her, watching the calm envelope her entire body. *Tory, you are so beautiful.*

"This is amazing Steve," keeping her eyes closed. "I can only imagine sitting out here each day. It's relaxing and rejuvenating at the same time."

Waiting, Steve continued to watch the tension drain from her body. Slowly, she opened her eyes and focused again on him.

"Sorry, I have always had a fascination with the ocean. It draws me into it. I find its power is both soothing and complicated and I always feel alive when I can hear it. But this, this is almost too much! This is nothing like the view from my apartment, and the sound! Oooh, I just love it out here." She turned, reluctantly and walked back into the bedroom. Her attention was immediately captured by the painting that hung above the king-size sleigh bed.

"Oh, my God! That's the Caprietta Lighthouse isn't it?" Steve nodded. "I have been enamored by that lighthouse since I was a little girl. I've never seen it in person, but I've dreamt of seeing it one day." Lost in her thoughts, Tory continued around the room. Everything was coordinated from the dark, rich-chocolate bedding to the cherry-wood furniture. The walls were a smoky gray, and the molding was painted a glossy black. As she turned back toward the door, she noticed the oversized walk in closet.

"There's a washer and dryer in here!" She squealed.

"Uh-huh. Seemed like the most sensible place to do laundry in a three-story home."

"Smart thinking. Did you design all of this yourself?"

"For the most part, yes. But I had a lot of inspiration along the way, Tory," he was referring to her, but she did not pick up on the innuendo. Instead, she made her way over to

the seating area complete with a chase lounge and recliner.
A wall of books separated the sleeping and dressing area.

"You have quite the library. Why put it in your
bedroom where only you can enjoy it?"

"Because I like to read on the balcony. I enjoy listening
to the ocean after I unwind from the day." His eyes
wandered back to the open bank of windows.

"Hmmmm, yes, I can see that." *Seems like we have
more in common than I had thought.*

"The master bath is just beyond that door there," he said
pointing to her left.

"Whoa!" The giant claw-foot tub nearly took her breath
away … until she saw the double shower. Better than any
fancy hotel she had ever stayed in. The shower floor was
river rock, and the walls were bamboo. Two large, rain
shower heads were positioned equally off-center and
numerous shower heads jutted out from the remaining three
walls. There was a piece of seemingly invisible frosted light
blue glass that matched the paint on the walls. A double-
sink vanity rested below a large-framed mirror. On the
counter was an old-fashioned shaving brush and straight
razor with a small pewter bowl that contained what she
assumed was shaving soap. The bowl was engraved with the
initials W.H.G.

"My father … William Henry Gage," he said after
realizing she was questioning the initials.

"Do you use them, or are they just for display?"

"Tory, nothing in my home is for display. It all has a
purpose, all of it." He smiled and held out his hand. "I'm
pretty sure that if we don't go back downstairs our dinner is
going to be well-well done."

Once they entered the kitchen, Steve took her glass and
refilled it with peach tea. Placing the drink on the table, he
pulled out her chair.

"Thank you." She said, smiling up at him.

He returned to the kitchen and reappeared with plates,
flatware and napkins. Another trip and he was serving her
dinner.

"This is amazing Steve! I am impressed." *There's
rosemary, and thyme, mmm I can taste the basil.* She
glanced his way and realized he was watching her as she

enjoyed her meal a little too eagerly. "Sorry, I am eating like a moose, this is just so good."

"I am really glad you like it. I enjoy seeing you happy, Tory."

I am happy—but I am miserable in the same moment. While there is nothing remotely sensual about tonight, so far, I feel guilty. I feel like I am moving too fast, imagining myself in your home, in your life. Carter and I became roommates so long ago. Married roommates sleeping in separate quarters, saying hello in the hallway. I was happy once ... with Carter. I was happy, but then, I was sad and angry too, for so long. Lonely and heartbroken for so long. Tory was once again lost in her world of depressing thoughts.

"Tory ... talk to me. Tell me what you're thinking. Please, have I done something to upset you?"

"Nothing! You have done nothing to upset me. I was just lost in thought for a moment. I'm sorry," she said looking up at the ceiling. "I have never seen crown molding painted any other color than white. What made you decide to paint it black?"

Instinctively, Steve looked down at Tory's foot. "It just came to me one day."

"I like it," she said smiling. "It's really different and makes the entire space unique," she said, lowering her eyes to meet his.

"I agree this is a very uniquely-inspired home. Now tell me, please, what is on your mind?"

"I just can't get over how many things you have done in this house that I have always dreamed of doing in my own home. Like the kitchen ... it is perfect! You really have a knack for eclectic design.

"Maybe, it's my eclectic inspiration that created this home. I am so pleased that you like it." And with that, they finished their meal. Tory took in every detail of the room, as Steve enjoyed the glimmer in her eyes.

"Please let me clear the table. It is the least I can do after you made such a wonderful supper," she stated, gathering the soiled dishes. She placed them all in the dishwasher while Steve cleaned the counters.

"Thank you. That was one of the best meals I have eaten in such a long time."

"I'm happy to cook for you anytime, Tory. Hey, next week I have my father's Memorial Gala, and I was wondering if you would accompany me."

"Sure, like for work?"

"No, Tory, as my date." He said with a bit of annoyance in his tone.

"I would love to!" *I am going to need to unpack some more boxes ... OR go shopping!! A Gala, now this would be something Carter would have never attended. He absolutely hated wearing a tie and getting all gussied up.*

"Should we go check out the basement now?" He asked extending his hand.

... awe nuts, the basement! Am I ready for this? Oh geez, what if he is one of those kinky guys who likes ... Ugh, I need to really stop reading so much!

"Sure, let's see what you're hiding down there," her voice was a little shaky.

To her surprise, the basement was filled with cardio equipment, free weights, a punching bag and on the far wall hung a few jump ropes. *Ha! This is a far cry from what I was thinking.*

"Do you charge a membership to bring people down here?"

"No. You are the only person, outside my family, that has ever been down here, Tory. This is the room I spend most of my time in each day. Although I love the rest of the house, this is the one room that I designed around *my* wants and needs," *everything else is for you.*

"Wow, this is really something. All of this equipment looks so new and intense."

"You are more than welcome to use this room anytime you want."

Hesitantly, Tory looked at Steve. *Is he saying that I am fat and should shed a few pounds in this room? Rude!*

Steve continued, "Not that you need to lose weight or anything, I just find working out a great way of getting rid of the day's stressors. You don't have to use the room. I just want you to know that if you ever want to ... the offer stands."

"Thanks. I am more a run on-the-sand type of girl. You know, music blaring in my ears and salty air in my face.

But when it's cold, I will keep this in mind. So, where is the stereo in here?"

"Um … I listen to the scanner when I work out," his tone flattened.

"Oh! So you were working out when you heard about, um … when you heard about Carter's accident?"

He nodded his head, "I was just getting ready to begin when the information came across. Tory, again, I am so sorry that I jumped-the-gun and gave you the wrong information." He held out his hand and led her back up the stairs to the living room. She sat down on the couch she had eyed earlier, propping herself on one end with her elbow. He sat down on the floor just below her.

"You have all of this furniture and you choose the floor?" She gestured around the room filled with many pieces of suitable seating.

"I really just want to hear what is going on in your head. Tell me what you are thinking; tell me how you are feeling, please."

"Steve, I don't know how I feel and the feelings change so quickly. One minute I am awe stricken by your beautiful home and the next, I feel guilty for leading you on. I miss Carter, but not as I should and I think that may sound odd. I don't miss him as my husband because we stopped being married a long time ago. But I miss him as a friend. He was the first boy I ever fell in love with … he was my first for everything for the past 16 years," her cheeks reddened. "I thought a lot about you, and Carter, and the things he said before he died. I can't understand why he would make up an affair in order to have me sign papers. It's all just so confusing and draining, I am sorry that I can't tell you exactly how I feel." She curled her arms around her knees and brought them up to her chest.

Steve stood and walked over to the recliner. He grabbed a blanket and draped it over Victoria.

"Carter came to the office on Thursday looking for you," he said returning to the floor.

"He did? Wait, I think he told me that he spoke to you. What did he want?"

"He was hoping to catch up you before you left, and when I told him that I gave you the week off he seemed surprised and disappointed. He started rambling about how he made Erin up, that he wanted you to have a choice to love him…"

"He said the same thing in the hospital, but to make up an affair? Doesn't that seem a bit far-fetched?"

"Tory, people do crazy things for the people they love. I think he just wanted to give you the opportunity to find happiness. If that meant that your happiness was no longer with him, he would give you up. It's an odd way to look at it, but as angry as I was when he told me, I don't think the man had it in him to cause you pain. He thought he was doing what was right for you."

She pulled the blanket tighter around her shoulders and gazed at the ceiling. "I think I should get back home. Either that, or I'm going to end up sleeping on your couch.

Rose Garrison

Tory closed the front door to her apartment and took her cell phone from her purse. She noticed that she had missed two calls and had voicemail. She pressed the message icon and hit the speaker button.

"You have two new messages. To play your new…

Beep. Message received today at 8:29 am."

"Hey Tory! It's Melanie. I just got back and saw the newspaper. I am so sorry sweetie. Please give me a call. I will have my phone all day. If you're not busy, let's plan lunch tomorrow. Love you."

"Next message received today at 2:18 pm."

"Victoria, this is Annette at Century Cove Care Facility. Would you please call me regarding your mother? Our number is 503- …"

"End of new messages."

(Sigh)

"Hello, this is Victoria Garrison. May I please speak to Annette?"

"Sure, one moment Miss Garrison."

There was a long pause and she could hear the scuttle on the other end. Apparently, Mr. Trahan had refused his medication and was racing down the main hall with nothing but a bed sheet tied into a cape around his neck. Poor Mr. Trahan … he always sat next to her mother at mealtime and even afterward, watching her while she stared blankly toward the television. Her mother's Alzheimer's had progressed so rapidly in the past year-and-a-half, that Tory doubted she even recognized Mr. Trahan sitting in the same room.

"Hello, this is Annette."

"Hello Annette, this is Victoria Am-um Tory Garrison. I was returning your call … something about my Mother?"

"Oh, yes dear, hold on just a minute while I get her file."

She could hear a woman yelling at Mr. Trahan to get down from the table and she couldn't help but giggle. "Interesting evening over there?"

"Oh, honey, every evening is interesting. Okay, here

it is. Yes, I am sorry dear, but your Mother took a little stumble getting into the shower this morning."

"Is she, is everything okay?" Tory could feel the rush of blood heat her cheeks.

"Yes, we had the doctor take a look and he said that we need to keep an eye on the bump, but she should be fine. He's coming back in the morning to check on her. Tory, do you want me to have him call you when he is done?"

"No, no. I will be there tomorrow morning. I will see you then, and thank you for calling Annette. Best of luck with Mr. Trahan," she giggled.

"Thank you, and we will see you tomorrow."

The last time she had visited her Mother, she was caught off guard by the memory deterioration.

"Who's Tory? I don't know any Victoria's. Are you Rhonda's daughter?" Her Mother had prodded.

It was exhausting and emotionally draining. (*Sheesh. There's a constant theme in my life over the past year.*) It had been one of the most difficult decisions she had made in the past year. Brad, husband number … um, four? He had called and told Tory he was unable to handle the constant care that her mother required. Understandable, especially considering that Brad was 20 years younger than her mother. Carter had dropped the "divorce ball" in her lap and there was no way Tory would move her mother into his house only to move her again so quickly. She knew that Century Cove had been in business forever; her grandfather, an aunt, and a cousin all lived out their last days there. Playing Bingo and taking creative arts classes.

She debated driving over immediately, but it was late. She was tired, and there was nothing she could do until she spoke to the doctor in the morning. Instead of worrying over a little bump, she picked up her phone.

"Hey! This is Melanie … you know what to do, wait for the beep …"

"Hi Mel, it's Tory. Sorry, I missed your call. God, I am so glad you are back! Lunch would be great! I have to go and see mom, she had a fall… I will give you a call when I get into town and we can do lunch. Love you."

Tory turned off her phone and placed it on the charger. She opened the French doors and felt the immediate comfort of the ocean breeze. She walked into the bathroom and turned to fill the bathtub. Sprinkling lavender bath salts into the base she grabbed the white tea bubble bath and squirted some into the cascading, steamy water.

She sat on the edge of the tub and slowly removed her shoes, socks, jeans, shirt, and undies. Slowly, she descended into the scorching hot water and laid her head back on the cool slant of the porcelain. She turned off the water and listened as the waves rolled along the beach.

Spending the evening with Steve had been wonderful and relaxing. His home was so beautiful and absolutely perfect. She thought of the giant claw-foot tub and imagined herself sinking lower and lower into it as the white tea and lavender filled her lungs.

Steve had been nothing but a complete gentleman, even lightening the mood after Tory mentioned abruptly that copulation was off the menu. *Just a day ago, I was willing to give myself to this man ... now the thought just scares me to death! I was taught that intimacy was between two people that loved one another enough to promise forever.* The emotions were still present; the desire to kiss him still lingering from the night before. The way he held her. The way he wiped her tears, and kissed her so intensely this morning. *God, I am so glad nothing more happened. I know I would have regretted it.*

As she soaked in the hot, steamy comfort she thought of Carter again.

I wish you were still alive! She said in her thoughts. *You were my best friend long before you were anything else, and I miss you. I could really use your insight right now. (sigh) Not that it wouldn't be strange to have the conversation with you. I just want to move on. I want to let you go, but the way things ended between us ... Oh, Carter! If I could go back, I would haves spent less time at the dining room table. I would have assured you that I loved you. I would have tried harder to convince you that you were the only thing in my life more important than myself. I would have forgiven you even if you wouldn't forgive me. I would have still chosen to work things out. But now... now that you aren't here, I can't keep holding back. I am going to eventually move forward. I hope.*

(Shiver)

With her toe, Tory pressed the knob and the tepid water began to recede from the tub. She stood and grabbed her bathrobe, wrapping it around her body. She pulled her hair into a ponytail, grabbed a bottle of water from the fridge and walked out onto the balcony. After what felt like an eternity of listening to the muffled waves, she closed the screens and put on her pajamas. Crawling under the dense covers, Tory drifted off to sleep still thinking about Carter and Steve.

Catching Up

The sunlight was bright as Tory opened her eyes. "Uh," she exhaled as she stretched her arms above her head. "I need some coffee." She quickly prepared the coffee maker and pressed "Start". She turned on her phone to see if Melanie had left her a message, but there was nothing. Returning the phone to the charging station, she prepared her coffee cup and waited for the brewing process to complete. Her phone began vibrating on the counter.

"Hello?"

"Hello, may I speak to Victoria Garrison please?"

"This is she."

"Hi Tory, It's Frank Watts. How is everything going?"

"Hi Frank. Good, I think, other than getting a call from my husband's divorce attorney on a Saturday morning is a bit alarming. Is everything alright?"

"I hope so, I tried to call you yesterday, but I got too busy. I just wanted to let you know that I got the divorce papers filed in court on Thursday instead of Friday. There was a cancellation on the docket, and I was there for another case. Anyway, I just wanted to tell you that the divorce was final on Thursday afternoon. I tried to call Carter, but his voicemail is full. Did he take a vacation or is he out on business again?"

"I—uh, Carter was involved in an accident on Thursday and he—he passed away in the hospital."

"Tory! Oh, my goodness. Honey I am sorry. Is there anything I can do? Can Martha and I do anything?"

Explaining the situation, Tory reiterated too many times that she was okay, and that she didn't need anything. "Frank, I will be okay, it's just a lot to take in right now you know?"

"I can only imagine, Victoria! Please don't hesitate to call us if you need anything at all, and I am sure Martha will be in touch. She never takes my word on things such as this."

Tory hung up the call and shook her head. The benefit of living in a small town was that everyone knew who you were, where you were, and they became an extension of family in a way.

At 9:30, Tory parked her car in the "Visitor's Only" area of the parking lot. As she entered Century Cove she saw Annette.

"Tory! Hi, how are you this morning? It is so nice to see you again."

"Good, thanks, how's Mom?"

"Sweetie, Dr. Baker is in with her now. Go ahead Dear, I told him that you were coming this morning."

As she was approaching her Mother's room, she saw Mr. Trahan sitting in the hallway. He didn't notice as she walked up nearly touching his shoes with her own. She bent down and his eyes shot up.

"Oh, hello Miss. Are you here to check on Rose? They won't let me in her room. I think she may have died, but I don't know. Could you check for me?"

"Hello Mr. Trahan. How long have you been out here?"

"I don't know … a bit, I think my ass fell asleep!" He started to shift his weight and Tory helped him stand. "Yip, all tingly back there," he said as he rubbed his backside.

"If you wait a minute, I will see how she is and let you know." Tory had to stifle a giggle at the old man as she cautiously walked into her mother's room.

"Good morning Dr. Ba… Oh my God! MOM!" Her face darted from her mother to the doctor. She moved quickly to the bedside and reached her hand toward her mother's eye. There was goose-egg the size of a ping pong ball surrounded by blue and purple bruising. Her mother instinctively pulled away, wincing in pain as Tory brushed her fingertips across the area.

Dr. Baker gently took Tory's hand withdrawing it from her mother's face. "It looks much worse than it is Victoria. You know how quickly your mother bruises and the bump has gone down quite a bit since yesterday." His voice was calm and his eyes were soft as he tried to reassure Tory.

"I'm sorry, I just wasn't expecting … expecting to see her like this. Is she going to be okay?"

"Who is this rude woman that thinks touching other people is okay?" Rose spoke to the doctor, never making eye contact with her daughter.

"Mom, it's me. Tory."

A blank expression crossed over Rose's face and she stared at Tory for a moment trying to place the strange face. "Tory who?"

"Tory, I am your daughter."

"Rose, do you remember you have a daughter? Victoria?"

"Victoria? Who's Victoria? I never had a daughter. I was a gold medal figure skater! Having a baby would have ruined my career. I won 30 gold medals you know …" Rose faded away into her thoughts.

"This is not a good memory day, Tory. Sorry." Dr. Baker finished his exam and led Tory out of the room.

"So? Is my Rose dead?"

"No, Mr. Trahan, she is not dead. Lord knows that woman if far too stubborn to let a little slip in the shower end her life," Tory said.

"Oh sweetie, thank you. That is the best news I have heard since Ford took office last year," Mr. Trahan said. Then he kissed the top of Tory's hand and walked down the hallway.

Shaking her head, she exchanged information with Dr. Baker and he promised to call her if anything changed with her mom. Walking back to her car, she called Melanie.

"Tory?"

"Yeah, Mel, hey I am in town. Do you want to meet at Jackie's Place for some breakfast?"

"Sure, give me 20 minutes to throw some makeup on and I will see you there."

Melanie walked through the door and saw Tory waiting in a booth holding a menu.

"You look amazing," she said wrapping her arms around her best friend.

"Mel, oh, it is so nice to see you! Look at you! Sheesh, Maui was good to you! You are glowing!"

"Thanks, it was so nice to just get away. Thank you so much for all of the recommendations! I loved the banyan tree … oh and the sushi! You weren't kidding about getting fresh seafood anywhere. Oh, here," she said reaching into her bag. "I stopped at that little stand and got you some banana bread before I flew out yesterday."

"You are the best! I love this stuff," Tory replied placing the heavy loaf up to her nose trying to inhale through the plastic wrap.

"How is your mom?"

"She had a fall and earned a goose egg above her eye. The doctor says she will be fine. She had no idea, again, of my existence," Tory replied setting the bread loaf on the table.

Melanie shook her head, "Sorry Sweetie, I can't even imagine how frustrating that must be."

"It's okay, I think she is happy in her little world."

"So, tell me what has happened. I mean, I saw the paper and ..."

"Well, I signed the papers last week and sent them off. Graduation was a blur. And then Steve showed up at my door and told me that Carter was killed in a car accident by a drunk driver." She took a deep breath as her friend interrupted.

"But, I thought, I mean, the paper said that Carter was charged with DUII and manslaughter ..." Melanie scrunched her face in confusion.

"Yeah, I know. So, after Steve picked me up, we went to the hospital morgue and, uh it smelled like mothballs believe it or not! And there was this person, on the table, and a white sheet. The doctor or mortician, no the Medical Examiner, pulled the sheet down and it wasn't Carter! Steve totally lost it and yelled at the police officer. Poor kid, he had to have been new on the force. Anyway, I kissed Steve in the stairwell and then we went to the third floor because Carter was in surgery."

"Whoa, wait... you kissed Steve? Your boss Steve?"

"Yeah, in the stairwell of the hospital. I don't know, I—he was being so nice and I was feeling so safe. And I looked up at him and I got lost in the moment. I wasn't thinking of Carter, or Erin, or anything but kissing him." She rubbed her arm.

"Anyway, he pushed me away and said that we couldn't continue to sit on the stairs carrying on like high school kids. Mel, I was so mortified!" She shook her head and looked down again at the menu. The waitress came and took their order.

"Okay, so then what happened? The paper said that Carter died!"

"So, we got to the third floor and Carter was already out of surgery. I went into his room and he starts rambling about killing someone and blood tests. Then he tells me that there never was an Erin." She stopped and stared across the table waiting for Mel's reaction.

"WHAT? Wait, so what do you mean? Erin was the reason he wanted a divorce, right?"

"I thought so, but he told me that he made her up so that I could have a choice whether I wanted to stay with him or start over."

"Tory, this is unbelievable. So, what did you tell him?"

"Nothing, the machines started beeping and then the doctor said something about time of death. The next thing I remember is Steve standing in my kitchen making coffee the next morning."

"You slept with Steve? Oh my God Tory! I leave for a three week sabbatical and you turn into a hooker?"

Tory broke out in laughter. A rolling laughter that rumbled from her empty stomach. "I—I didn't sleep with him! Geez! He brought me back to my apartment and put me to bed. He slept on the couch! Nothing happened. He didn't try anything. I think I would remember if something would have happened. But we did kiss again before he left."

"I didn't even know you were interested in him. Why didn't you ever say anything to me? For crying out loud Tory, I tell you everything!"

"Seriously? I wasn't interested Mel. I was married and it didn't matter if it was a happy marriage or otherwise, I wasn't going to allow myself any feelings for anyone but Carter. I was just as surprised when he asked me to dinner after graduation."

"Who asked you to dinner? Carter or Steve?"

"Well, yeah, Carter was supposed to come over Thursday night for dinner. He wanted to see the new apartment. But then, Steve asked if I wanted to go to dinner on Friday. He said the there was a lot of work to go over …

ugh, I don't know. So much has happened in the past two days!"

"Holy crap! So..."

"Mel you are the worst! Yes, I went to dinner with Steve last night. He took me to his house and we HAD DINNER. Nothing else." Tory emphasized the dinner part because Melanie's eyebrows started wiggling in interest.

"So, now what?" Mel asked shrugging her shoulders.

"Who knows? I go back to work on Monday. I guess we will keep taking things slow and see of anything comes of it. I am in no hurry to get back in the saddle."

Mel threw her head back and laughed so loud, the waitress nearly dropped the plates in her hand. "No pun intended, right Tory?" She threw her napkin at Mel, still shaking her head and blushing in embarrassment.

"He invited me to his father's memorial party next week."

"So, you want to do a little closet shopping?"

Giggling, "Yes, if you think any of your stuff will fit me." Tory had always borrowed clothes from Mel, but found Mel's style a bit more provocative than her own.

"Tory, I have the perfect dress for you! It's a black tie event right?" Tory nodded. "I have just the dress ... a bit of sexy and a whole lot of sophistication. I haven't even worn it yet! I purchased it when I was dating James ... what an arse!" They both giggled.

Unexpected Guest

Monday morning arrived far too abruptly, as Tory reached over to turn off her alarm. Steve had called yesterday asking her how her weekend was going. They talked for a few minutes about the memorial until his family arrived. She heard a high-pitched squeal in the background and he explained that Emmy had just walked through the door. Her exuberance radiated through the phone. *I can't wait to meet her,* she thought to herself. Steve had extended an invitation for her to have dinner with him and his family, but she declined. There was too much to unpack and far too much to do before tomorrow she had told him. But really, it was just too soon to meet his family; she would feel awkward. It would be uncomfortable enough to be introduced at the memorial.

Her desk phone rang and she answered the call.

"Victoria?"

"Yes, hello Colleen."

"Sorry to bother you right off the bat this morning, but there is a gentleman in the lobby by the name of Eric Tomlinson requesting to see you."

"Oh, well, I don't have any meetings scheduled today. I would be happy to see him. Did he say why he wants to see me?"

"No, I didn't ask. He's sitting in the lobby with a briefcase. Looks pretty professional, I don't think he's a reporter."

Steve had called an early-morning meeting, knowing that the press would be waiting to speak to Tory. This was the biggest thing to have happened in their little town since his father was shot and killed in the line of duty. Steve was concerned that Risk Management Resources would be a topic of gossip as well, since their company worked extremely close with law enforcement personnel. He gave explicit instructions to his staff that no one was to speak to the press on-or off-the-record. The company would release a statement this afternoon. Any visitors would be closely scrutinized before being allowed access to any employee, but especially Tory.

"Thanks Colleen. I will double check with Gage, and then I will be up there." Clicking the receiver, she called Steve's extension.

"Morning Tory."

"Good morning Steve," she said with a smile in her voice. "Hey, do you know an Eric Tomlinson?"

"Um, the name doesn't sound familiar ... why?"

"Oh, I don't know, I don't think it's anything but he's in the lobby and Colleen ..."

Cutting her off, Steve said quickly, "I'll come with you," abruptly hanging up the line.

Before she could hang up the phone, Steve was standing inside her office wearing his serious expression. Her blood warmed and she could feel her cheeks flush. Smiling, she stood and together they walked into the lobby.

"Mr. Tomlinson?" Tory asked the gentleman.

"Yes. Are you Victoria Ammon?"

"Yes sir, how may I help you this morning?"

The man reached into his briefcase and, before she realized what was happening, Steve was partially blocking her body with his own. As soon as Steve saw what the man was reaching for, he moved and took his place behind Tory. It had happened so quickly, Tory didn't know if the man noticed at all. But she had.

As the man shifted his weight to stand, he was holding a manila envelope in his hand. Tory began to feel unsteady on her feet. She felt Steve's hand on her lower back and could sense his tension as it radiated through her body.

"Nothing good EVER comes packaged in a manila envelope," she thought as she remembered the divorce papers.

"Mrs. Ammon, I represent Dana Melson. If you don't already have one," he said handing her the packet, "I recommend you hire an attorney."

Tory watched as the man picked up his briefcase and exited through the glass door. She looked down at the envelope then up at Steve.

"I hate manila envelopes," she said walking toward Colleen.

"I am so sorry, Mr. Gage. He didn't look like a reporter. I should have questioned him. I should have asked what he needed from Miss. Garrison." She turned her head toward Tory and whispered, "It will not happen again."

"Colleen, you did nothing wrong," Tory replied while looking over at Steve's expression. *Oh, he looks angry!* "If he were a potential client, he most likely would have chosen another company after an inquisition from the first face he saw." She smiled at Colleen and turned to walk to her office. Steve was right behind her, closing the door as he entered.

She sat in her chair and tossed the offending envelope on her desk.

THUNK

"Are you going to open it?"

"No, not at work. I'm going to call Todd and see if he can get me in this afternoon."

"Who's Todd?" Steve asked as his expression changed and he shifted in the chair across from Tory.

"We went to high school together. Todd went to college and became an attorney. He set up a little firm on the other side of town about 12 years ago …"

"Todd Reynolds?"

"One-in-the-same. Why do you know him?"

"Not personally, but I have heard good things about him."

"Well, knowing that the name of the man Carter, um … anyway, Dana must be his wife, or widow now. So, the only thing I can think of is to take that wonderful packet to Todd and beg him for his help."

Tory called Todd only after finishing the daily report for Steve. Todd said that he could see her at 12:30 that afternoon. Tory adjusted her lunch hour and raced over to Todd's office with the heavy manila envelope.

"Victoria Garrison!"

"Hey Todd! Thanks for squeezing me in so quickly."

"Awe, that's what friends are for. Hey, I talked to Mel this weekend and she filled me in. You good?"

"Yeah, as good as can be expected, right?" She held up the mighty manila envelope. "So, this morning, this attorney named Eric Tomlinson delivered this to me. Said I should get an attorney …"

"Wow! Eric Tomlinson, huh? He's a pretty heavy-hitter in the playground, Tory. Let me take a look at what you've got there."

She handed him the envelope and plopped down in the chair nearest her. She watched Todd's eyes scan page after page.

"Holy shit, Tory!" He had read nearly half of the stack, "She's suing you for one million dollars!"

"Suing me? For what?" She could feel the blood drain from her face. She was going to pass out. "Where the hell am I going to come up with that kind of money? Todd, I don't own anything but a bunch of 'assembly required' furniture and a nine-year-old Honda. Carter got the house and that was the only thing that was really valuable ..." *One million dollars?*

"Tory, who was your divorce attorney?"

"Um, Frank Watts. Why?"

"Nothing really, I am just going to need a copy of the decree and Carter's death cert..." He stopped mid-sentence.

"It's fine Todd. You didn't spill the beans," she whispered leaning forward, "I know he's dead." *One million dollars? One million dollars!*

"Guh, Tory. I'm trying to be delicate here, I'm sorry. This is just really a really shitty thing to be happening to someone like you."

Shaking her head she inhaled, "I have a copy of the decree in my car. Frank filed the papers early, but I can't remember what time he told me. Do you want me to get the copy?"

"No, I will need certified copies. So what time did Carter..."

"Seriously Todd, I promise I won't fall to the floor and curl up in the fetal position if you say the word DEAD!" *I am not made of glass!* "Carter died at almost midnight, I think. It was still Thursday night, but it was really late."

"And you said Frank filed the papers early. Do remember when?"

"Well, he was going to file them on Friday, but he said there was an opening or something when he was in court on Thursday. It was sometime in the afternoon on Thursday. Why?"

"Tory, if all of what you just said checks out, this lawsuit will be thrown out faster than the first pitch of the World Series." He saw the confusion wash across her face. "Tory, you were already divorced before the crash, before Carter passed away. You are not responsible for any of the money she is suing you for. She can go after his assets, the house, everything that was his. But she can't have anything that is yours."

"Oh."

"So, was Carter under arrest at the hospital?"

"When I spoke to him, in his room, he said that an officer had read him Miranda something and told him that his blood alcohol level was 0.1, um there was another number with that but I don't remember. He told me that he was going to prison for manslaughter."

"Alright, well if he was awarded to the state, then it wouldn't matter if you were married or not at the time um … when he passed away."

"So, because my ex-husband was in the custody of the state, he owes no restitution to the Melson family?" Tory was getting lost. The logic just seemed wrong.

"Maybe. All of his assets are in limbo until the District Attorney's Office either files the paperwork or completes a disposition stating otherwise. Right now, I need to get some copies and make some calls. It's probably going to take me a few weeks, Tory. When I have some answers, do you want me to call the office or you cell?"

"Better make it my cell … I may not get to talk to you if you call the office … Steve has the place locked down like Fort Knox," she said feeling defiant.

"Mel mentioned something about him …" he wiggled his eyebrows.

"Seriously! You too? Ugh!" She grabbed her purse and turned to leave.

"Love you, Tory."

"I know, love you too, Todd." She was smiling, feeling a little better about the morning. She headed out the door to her car and grabbed an iced tea on her way back to the office.

A million dollars seems like a lot of money especially when I don't have anywhere near that amount at my fingertips. If Todd is right, then Dana would have to wait until the papers are filed with the DA's Office. That could take forever. Poor thing, she loses her husband and now she's planning a funeral. Shit! Who's taking care of Carter's funeral? Her thoughts continue to race as she parked her car in the familiar space.

With her purse in one hand and a beverage in the other, she headed across the parking lot. "I need to call Frank and see what Carter wrote in his will about a funeral. Pretty sure we agreed that we would go the cremation route ..." she said aloud, but to herself.

"Victoria Ammon?" A small voice whispered behind her.

"Yes," she said turning around and feeling the goose bumps on her neck. She had a sudden eerie feeling.

"I'm really sorry for bothering you here. Um—I. Is there any way I could talk to you for a few minutes?"

"I'm sorry, do I know you?"

"No... not really, um ... I'm Erin."

Tory was squeezed her iced tea so tightly that the lip popped off and some of the beverage spilled out.

"You're Erin?" She asked.

"Yes, I just need a couple of minutes and then I promise I won't bother you again. Please?"

"Not in the parking lot. Follow me." Tory secured her lid and walked into Risk Management Resources. Stopping at the elevator she pressed the call button. Too quickly it opened and she entered followed by *her.*

Perky little bimbo. What the heck was I thinking getting into an elevator with this woman or girl, ugh, she looks like a kid? I could strangle her right here, and no one would ask any questions. Wrap my hands around her pretty little neck. Argh, how freaking old is she? By the look of her, I would guess about 25. Carter you lying sack of ... what am I going to do? What does she want from me? "Oh, hi, my name's Erin and I just wanted to introduce myself so you would have a visual when you think about your husband and I ... he probably told you that I don't exist, but SURPRISE, here I am!"

The elevator opened and Tory stepped out. She walked all-too-quickly by Colleen without making eye contact. Then, as she passed Steve's office, she looked over and saw him peek up from his work. He smiled and then quickly looked confused.

"In here," Tory said firmly. "Sit there." She pointed to the chair directly across from hers. She was far too irate to sit so she paced back and forth behind her desk.

"Erin, how old *are* you?"

"Um, I am 24," she said looking down at the floor.

Just as she was contemplating her next question, Steve came busting through her office door. He gave her a *what's going on* look.

"Oh, Gage. Please let me introduce my guest," she said as she outstretched her arm toward the *bimbo*. Erin stood and faced Steve, while Tory came around from her desk.

Before Tory had a chance to introduce them, the freak-of-nature extended her hand.

"Mr. Gage, it is so nice to meet you. My name is Erin Sherman."

"Tory, may I see you outside for a minute?"

Tory followed Steve to his office. Closing the door he ran his hands over his temples.

"Erin?" He asked.

"Uh-huh. She was waiting for me in the parking lot when I got back from the attorney's office."

"Erin? Like the imaginary Erin? Tory, I don't like this. I—geez. What are you going to do?"

Pull her hair out by the roots, pin a 'kick me' sign to her back. Hell-if-I-know!

"I have no idea, but I didn't want to do anything to make a scene in the parking lot." Flustered she sat on the corner of Steve's desk.

"Why do you think she's here?"

"Who knows, the past, what four or five days, have been such a cluster. Maybe she wants me to set her conscience clean. My God … she's just a kid!"

"I'm going to go in there with you. I won't interrupt, but I want to make sure you're okay."

Stopping outside her office door, Tory took a deep breath and looked up at Steve. *Showtime.*

Erin jumped as the door opened. On her feet now, she walked toward Steve and Tory.

"Mrs. Ammon, I just wanted to thank you for seeing me, I ..."

"Okay, let's just cut to the nuts-and-bolts okay? What do you want?"

"Uhhh, okay then, let me get my notes," she said as she rummaged through her satchel. Tory and Steve watched and she clumsily fumbled, pulling out numerous items.

An ID badge fell onto the floor and Steve bent down to pick it up. He turned to face Tory.

"You're a reporter?" He asked as he handed Erin the press pass.

"Yes," she replied. "I cannot thank you enough for allowing me this opportunity of the first interview. My editor said I was wasting my time," she paused. "But I told him that it was my time to waste, right?" She asked, looking at Steve first, then at Tory.

"So," Tory started, "you never knew my late husband?"

"No," Erin replied shaking her head back-and-forth. A bewildered look on her face confirmed that she had no idea who Carter was.

Tory made her way to the chair behind her desk. She took a deep breath and tried to dispel her feeling of suspicion.

PRESS PASS

Registered Post

Erin Sherman
Intern

Big Night

"Steve?"

"Hey Tory, come in. Have a seat." He gestured as he stood to close the door.

"I have all of the assorted notes from last week organized and the meeting is set for Timberland Police Department. They will be coming here for the initial training and then we can send a consultant to them. I thought perhaps Duston would be a great fit for their people," she said while placing four folders in front of him.

"Have I told you how much I missed you last week?" He was grinning as he flipped through the pages. "You really do have quite the knack for this, Tory."

She flushed at his words. He was honestly just what she needed today. His reassurances made her smile and cock her head to the side.

"So, I was wondering. Since the memorial is this evening, and I have yet to meet your family ... well, would it be okay if I left a few hours early? I want to make sure I pass inspections!" She instantly caught Steve's look.

"Inspections? So you're telling me that you need to shave your legs?" He said holding in a laugh.

"Gage!"

"Of course you can leave early. If I were to pick you up at 6:00 ... would that give you enough time to..." he was laughing out loud now. Watching as the blush tone flooded her face.

"Yes. That will be plenty of time. Thank you. I will see you at 6:00, Mr. Gage."

"I look forward to our evening, Miss Garrison."

She wished she could say the same, but truth be told Tory was as nervous as a church mouse. She hadn't met someone's family since Carter and that had been easy since they went to the same school. His parents were always around for events and of course, graduation

The 21st Annual W.H. Gage Memorial Gala

Steve left the office shortly after Tory. He had some errands to run before he was to pick her up. At 5:55, Steve pulled up in front of her apartment.

After knocking on the door, he heard her call out, "Be right there." A few moments passed and when the door opened, Steve exhaled all of the oxygen from his lungs.

She was wearing heels, at least five inches, maybe more. They were sandal-type, showing off her black polished nails. Her dress nearly covered them, but as she shifted in front of him, Steve got a glimpse of the black satin ribbon tied in a bow near her achilles. The dress itself was deep black cherry with a slit up the back that ended just above the back of her knees. Steve's eyes continued up the back of the dress as Tory retrieved her clutch. Her entire back was exposed! Her shoulders were bare, and as she turned to face him, he noticed the dress came together with a choker around her neck. The choker was attached to the dress, but opened in the front, exposing the tops of her breasts. Her hair was down, curled in big ringlets. Her makeup was dark, even her lipstick was the color of merlot. She looked stunning. He had never realized just how curvy she was. This dress left nothing to his imagination.

"Are the gloves too much?" She asked holding up her arm.

"No, no they look, you look great!" *I didn't even notice the black satin gloves that wrapped each arm from her fingertips to just above her elbows.* He fidgeted with his tux.

"You look very nice as well. Should we go before we are fashionably late?" She said, tucking her arm in his.

The Memorial Gala was held on the second floor of the City Hall building. Photographers lined the walkway, snapping photos of each guest as they arrived. Tory felt like she was walking into a red carpet event when they finally reached the front door. Two men dressed in white tuxedos held the heavy doors as Steve and Tory walked through. Another man, dressed the same, was waiting at the elevator.

"Good evening. This way please. Enjoy your night," he said gesturing toward the elevator. Inside was yet another man in white. He pressed the button labeled "2", and they waited as the elevator hummed to life.

"Have a nice evening Mr. Gage and Miss Garrison."

"Thank you," Steve replied as they exited.

"How did he know my name?" Tory whispered into Steve's ear.

"You are my date. Your name is listed next to mine on the list," he said leaning into her hair. *Oh, you smell like black cherries again! Focus Gage!*

"Oh," she replied quietly as the rounded the corner to the main ballroom.

Tory stopped in her tracks as soon as she saw the room. The back wall was filled with photos of Steve, his brothers, sister, his mother and a large photo of his father in his class A dress police uniform. There were white twinkling lights everywhere, with hundreds of white butterflies suspended from the ceiling. People were seated at tables, visiting and telling stories about the infamous Will Gage. Her thoughts were interrupted by a high-pitched squeal. *Emmy!* She thought to herself remembering that sound when she was talking to Steve on the phone. Tory scanned the room trying to hone in on the source. Walking quickly across the makeshift dance floor, a beautiful woman approached. She was wearing a bright yellow dress that had a black and white polka-dot flare skirt underneath. She was shorter than Tory wearing a pair of black ballerina-style shoes. Her hair was a beautiful shade of golden blond and by the time she put her arms around Steve, Tory was awestruck.

"Emmy! I want you to meet someone," he said returning her hug.

"Okay."

"Emmy, I would like you to meet Victoria," he said while gesturing toward Tory.

"Hello, Emmy. It is a pleasure to meet you. You can call me Tory."

"It's nice to meet you, Tory. You are very pretty!"

Tory smiled, "Thank you. I was just thinking the same thing about you."

Emmy smiled a huge grin, displaying beautiful white teeth, and then turned her attention back to her older brother. "Mommy wants you to come over to our table, follow me. I will show you where it is." And with that, she turned and quickly took the lead through the crowd of police, fire, military personnel and City Officials.

"Gage! How are you? Oh, it is so very nice to see you."

"Jenny … good … things are good. Victoria, this is Jenny. Jenny this is my date, Victoria Garrison."

Jenny extends her hand and Tory accepts. "Nice to meet you Miss Garrison."

"Very nice to meet you Jenny, please call me Tory."

"Jenny, I would stay longer, but if we don't catch up, Emmy will come looking for us," he said as they turned to the table. Steve stopped for a moment and turned back to Jenny, "I like the butterflies," he said and gave Jenny a wink.

"She is so easy to please, Gage. Enjoy your evening, both of you." He nodded as they reached the table where his family was in conversation, Emmy included.

"… so pretty mommy and she has …"

"Good evening everyone," Gage interrupted, knowing that his sister would not stop otherwise.

"Oh Steven! You always look so nice in a tuxedo. So grown up." All eyes were on Tory and she was feeling somewhat anxious … two brothers, his sister and his mother all sizing her up.

"Mom, this is Victoria. Victoria, this is my mother, Edna."

"It is so nice to finally meet you. My son says the nicest things about you."

"Thank you, it is nice to meet you as well. Please, call me Tory."

"Tory, these are my brothers. This is Corbin, and this is Tylar, and you have already met my little sister, Emmy," he gestured in their direction.

"It's very nice to meet all of you," she said, smiling.

Steve noticed who wouldn't? As soon as Tory entered the room, every person, gasped. They stared in complete silence, and she was too busy looking around to notice. If she had the presence to captivate a room filled with decorated firemen, police officers, spouses and government officials, what would she do to a crowd of complete strangers? His mind was quickly processing the information. He would have to get her in front of a crowd of total strangers to test his theory.

Dinner conversation was light. No one at the event asked her about her divorce, Carter's accident, his death, or even work. The night was filled with memories of Will. Everyone was sharing the joy of having had him in their life.

"… like the time Will forgot to tell Dispatch where we were headed. So what's he do? Radios in our location! Thank God our 'friends' didn't have a scanner so they didn't know company was coming …" Everyone laughed.

"Remember the night he was on duty and Edna called saying she was going into labor? I swear he wanted the whole fire department to take her in the ambulance. And then … THEN after all that fuss, it turned out to be a false alarm! But that was okay. Hose jockeys are used to false alarms right?" More laughter and even more stories.

Somewhere between the main course and dessert, Tory felt Steve's hand brush against her knee. At first, she thought it was just an accident, but then it happened again. Her breath caught in her throat as she tried to stay still, smiling and laughing with the others at the table. She moved her knee slightly closer to his without actually making contact. She waited and finally felt Steve's hand resting on both of their knees. It was such an innocent moment. She was thankful for his touch and refused to move, or read further into the action for the rest of the evening.

They pulled into Steve's driveway and he helped Tory out of the car.

"How are your feet doing?" He asked looking down, catching a glimpse of her black polished toes, her ankle and that little satin bow.

"Really not bad. Not nearly as bad as I thought they would be." She smiled and walked with him to the front door.

"Although, had I known we were coming back to your house I would have grabbed a change of clothes."

"Not a problem, I am sure I have a pair of sweats and a tee shirt you can borrow."

After the Gala

"I left some sweats on my bed. Feel free to wear whatever you want. Um, there are tee shirts and sweatshirts in the closet."

Tory was sitting on the couch as Steve approached.

"Let me," he said kneeling on the floor in front of her. "I really like these shoes!" Slowly, he pulled the loose end of the ribbon. Watching as the loop got smaller and smaller then releasing completely. He gently caressed her foot with brief massaging movements. He reached over and took her other foot and placed it in his lap. He ran his finger around her ankle, gently up her calf, and the back of her knee. He watched as her expression changed. Her pupils dilated, and her breath hitched.

He felt her tense, "You passed inspection," he said smiling. She shook her head side-to-side and smiled back at him. Taking both free ends of the ribbon between his index finger and thumbs, he slowly pulled them in opposite directions. Once her shoe was removed, he began rubbing her other foot. *Oh, that feels so good ... I should give him 20 minutes of this before ...*

"I should go change," she said blushing.

"Of course, I will get you some tea and meet you out on the deck."

A few minutes later, Tory appeared dressed in sweats.

"Hey! Nice outfit slick!"

"You like?" She asked as she pivoted.

Even in sweatpants and an oversized football sweatshirt, the girl was striking.

"I really like that fact that you wear all that makeup when you work out, yet your skin is so clear!"

"Ha, nice one! I have no plans to work out, but if I were, I would wash all of this makeup off," she said as she slid up next to him on the lounger. A cool breeze was drifted off the water carrying with it a little spray. "Must be high tide huh?"

"Yeah, are you too cold? Do you want to go inside?" He felt her snuggle into his side.

"No, I'm warm enough for now."

They sat quietly together, listening to the crash, then the roar, only to repeat over and over again.

"You are too quiet Tory. What's on your mind?"

"I was just thinking about that poor little intern. Sheesh, I felt like total crap when you showed me her press badge."

"You? I swear Tory all of my common sense goes right out the window when I am with you! I shouldn't have assumed that she was anything but a total stranger," he said shaking his head.

"You have to admit though she'll probably get a raise because of it. So far, she is the only person I have allowed to interview me." She laughed and rolled her eyes.

"I doubt she's an intern for very much longer," Steve said joining her in laughter.

After their laughter subsided, Tory looked up through heavily mascara layered lashes asking, "What do you think your family thought of me tonight?"

"Are you kidding? They loved you! Didn't you notice the whole room took a deep breath when you walked in?"

"Whatever," she said rolling her eyes. "They were most likely looking at you. Your mom was right, you do look very nice all dressed up." She paused. "Did your mom say anything about me? Do you think she approves of me … of us?"

"She must have! She said she hopes you'll come to Sunday dinner," he replied. "We have one every week, here. Everyone comes and has a nice family meal together."

"I would love to!"

"So, you tell me what you thought about my family," Steve said. "I will tell you whether or not you have them figured out." It was really more of a test to see if she had the ability to read people.

"Well, let's see …" she said. "Corbin, your oldest brother, is super protective of your mom and Emmy. He didn't let anyone he didn't know even near your table. He's quiet—didn't say too much—more of a listener. He was polite though … to everyone. I think he tries to fill your Fathers' shoes, but he struggles because he doesn't feel like he is able to take care of everyone the way your Father would have."

Steve nodded his head for her to continue. "And Tylar?"

"Hmmm, Tylar is a fire ant! I get the impression that he is the wild child in your family. He's loud but respectful. He's the daredevil of family—dirt bikes, bungee jumping—I would imagine he has a few tattoos that match his defiant personality."

"Okay, now Emmy?"

"Emmy is the innocent one in your family. She has three older brothers who have kept her sheltered from the evils of this world. She has a secret way about her though, like she's holding something back."

"And my mom?"

"Ah, Edna. Your mother absolutely adores each of you. She seeks strength from Corbin, assurance from you, challenge from Tylar, and love from Emmy. She does not have a selfish bone in her body. She was a little suspicious of me and still wants to know what my intentions are with her son," she said and looked over to see his reaction.

"Huh, you're pretty spot on. I'm impressed! I think you read each person correctly, except for Emmy. I doubt she could keep anything to herself for very long before spilling the beans."

"Steve, tell me about your father."

"You already know a lot about my father. We just got back from a Gala filled with nothing but information about him."

"I know he was shot and killed in the line of duty, but what happened?"

"Tory, I promise to tell you the story, but please not tonight okay? And please don't bring it up in front of Emmy. She doesn't remember what happened."

She nodded *yes* then laid her head again his arm. "Okay," she whispered.

Steve could hear her breathing become shallow and knew she had fallen asleep. Rather than disturb her, he laid his head against the back of the lounge chair and quietly contemplated the evening.

"Steve, I really should get home," Tory said pulling herself up.

"I'll grab your shoes," he said rubbing his eyes.

They reached the door to Tory's apartment and both stood staring at the door feeling the awkwardness.

"I would invite you in, but..." Tory said with hesitation.

Steve bent down and kissed her forehead. "No expectations Tory. No intentions. I will see you tomorrow. Thank you for going with me tonight, I had a wonderful evening."

"Me too," she said unlocking the door. "See you tomorrow then." And she watched as Steve made his was back down the stairs. Opening the doors to the balcony, she leaned against the railing as she watched the taillights on his car slowly diminish in the darkness.

Mrs. Melson

Tory began the day by making a to-do list. Steve was out of town until noon. He was taking Duston through the ropes at Timberland Police Department.

___Call Todd regarding Dana Melson

___Call Melanie… lots to catch up on

___Call Annette/Mom

___Dress to the drycleaners

___Call Drake at Windom City Hall

___Check with Colleen (Status of report)

___

___

Knowing there would be more before lunch, she left the last two spaces available on her notepad. Steve hadn't left her much to do this week, but she assumed it would get busier once he returned this afternoon.

Tory tapped the green icon on her cell phone. "Hello?"

"Good morning, Tory, it's Colleen. There is a gentleman in the lobby named Todd Reynolds who says he is your attorney? Um, he has a woman with him too."

"He is, Colleen, thank you. I will be there in just a moment." She moved her paperwork to one side of her desk and walked to the lobby. Todd was sitting on the lobby couch. Beside him sat a woman nervously cracking her knuckles.

"Hello, Mr. Reynolds, it's a pleasure to see you." She was going to keep the meeting formal for now. Perhaps that would change once she found out who the woman was accompanying her high school friend.

"Hello, Miss Garrison. Sorry to stop by unannounced, but I … we have had an interesting morning already," he said looking at the stranger.

"Would you like to meet in my office?"

"That would be great. I hope we are not interrupting anything."

"Not at all. I am happy for the distraction. Please, follow me," and she led the way to her office. After offering them both chairs, she closed the door and seated herself.

"So?" Tory said looking at Todd and then at the woman seated next to him.

"Tory, this is Dana Melson."

WHAT! The Dana Melson? The woman who is suing me for a million dollars?"

"It's nice to meet you, Miss Garrison. I am sorry to intrude on your day like this, but I—I ..." her voice trailed off as she looked over at Todd.

"Tory," he took a deep breath. "Mrs. Melson came to my office this morning to discuss her lawsuit against you," he looked over at Dana. "She doesn't want to pursue it any longer."

"What?" Tory gasped.

"I, well ... when everything happened, I was on my way to the hospital morgue and I saw you. I saw you leaving the morgue and you looked more upset than I ever seen anyone look. I thought for a moment that maybe it was Rick that had killed someone. Anyway, after I went into the building and saw Rick on the table, I was actually relieved. When the officer told me that you were there too, I mean ... he said you were told that your husband, I mean ... ex-husband was dead. I don't know what kind of person he was but I can tell you that I have shed very few tears for Rick since the accident."

"I'm sorry, I don't understand. You saw me at the hospital?"

"Yes, when I was walking in I saw you. You were crying, but I didn't know who you were at the time. It wasn't until ... well, I asked the officer and he told me."

Tory thought back to that moment, but she didn't recall seeing anyone other than Steve as he rushed them both out of the room.

"Anyway, after all that happened, I thought it was over. Then I got a call from a lawyer," she continued.

"Eric Tomlinson," Todd interrupted.

"Yeah, Mr. Tomlinson called and said he saw the accident in the paper and wanted to help me. He said that you had a lot of money it was only right that I get some of it. He said that I deserved it because of what your husband ... I mean ex-husband did to Rick. At first, I thought it was a good thing, you know? I figured if you had a lot of money that you wouldn't really miss a million of it," she sighed and lowered her head. "But, then I saw that article in the paper last night, and I felt horrible. So I came to see your lawyer to let him know that I don't want to sue you anymore. It just doesn't seem right, ya know, and I'm sorry."

"Todd?"

"Tory, I have already called Tomlinson's office. The lawsuit has been dropped."

"But," Tory looked at Dana. "Dana, would you mind if I spoke to my attorney *privately* for a moment?"

Tory led Todd to the conference room.

"What is going on?" she asked with a pitched voice.

"She came in this morning, out of the blue. I had no idea who she was, and then she dumped all of this on me. She dropped the suit, and she doesn't want anything from you. I guess Rick and her have had this on-again off-again relationship … if you can call it that … for years. She said she had a restraining order against him when the accident happened, because he beat the living … Anyway, I thought this news would make your day."

"It's news, that's for sure! So, she wants nothing at all?"

"Nope, she just wants to move forward and get through this chapter in her life."

I can relate … I am trying to do the same thing, she thought as they made their way back to her office.

"Miss Garrison, again I am so sorry for putting you through all this. I hope everything turns out good for you," Dana said while extending her hand to Tory.

"Mrs. Melson, it has been a surprisingly interesting morning I must say! It has been a pleasure to meet you, although I do wish it were under different circumstances." She shook hands with both Todd and Dana and walked with them to the lobby.

"Is everything okay Tory?" Her secretary asked.

"I think so Colleen. Every minute changes my outlook on life though," she smiled and walked back to her office.

I am getting very little work done this morning. I will work late and make it up. The last thing I need is for my life to get in the way of my career.

Tory made a quick detour to the kitchen, where she brewed a cup of Chamomile tea to counteract the adrenaline rush she had just experienced. Now seated at her desk, she noticed her right hand tapping her pen nervously on her desk. *Deep breaths ... in with the good air ... out with the bad air.* Her left hand quickly flattened against her right hand to stop the tapping. *I need to know what the article says.*

Curiosity got the better of her as she went to the online version of the newspaper and found the story Dana had mentioned. After a few minutes she sat back in her chair reading what Erin had written.

The Register Guard
Column: Interview with Victoria Garrison-Ammon
Tagged: Fatal Car Accident, DUII, Carter Ammon, Rick Melson, Victoria Garrison

I waited in the parking lot at Risk Management Resources, Inc. for three hours before I finally saw her. Victoria "Tory" Garrison-Ammon was exiting her car when I took a chance and approached her. She graciously led me to the second floor where her office was located.

Before writing this column, I believed—like most people—that Tory must be a horrible person. To know that her husband killed another and then died at the hospital. I found out last week that the widow had filed a lawsuit in civil court for one million dollars.

I reckon everyone wants to know how much of a villain Tory is, but I am going to disappoint every expectation. I didn't ask much about the accident after Tory informed me that she and Carter Ammon had filed for divorce six week prior to the incident. Instead, this is what I found out about the now in-famous Tory Garrison ...

She graduated college last week with high honors, earning a Master's Degree in Writing. She married her high school sweetheart, which ended in divorce 16 years later. She has a personality that lights up a room. The fact that she agreed to speak to me—even after seeing my credentials, was probably the most impressive thing about her.

Tory is nothing but a victim of circumstance. She was bright, kind, energetic and honest during my time with her. I wanted a juicy story and instead I met an everyday woman struggling to put her life back together after experiencing a traumatic event.

Erin Sawyer, Columnist

"Columnist, well good for you Erin," she said with a smile.

"Hey!" Gage burst through her door.

She jumped, "Hey, you scared the bejesus out of me!"

"Ha, sorry. Thought I'd go get lunch, want to go?"

Tory told Steve about Todd and Dana during lunch. After his initial response of anger, he shook his head and told her about Duston's training. She had a good gut feeling and everything was back to running at normal speed. After lunch she called Annette and was told that her mother was doing fine and that Mr. Trahan hadn't left the hallway until she was allowed to accompany him to dinner.

She called Melanie and regurgitated several weeks' worth of information and apologized for not returning her dress and shoes right away. She promised to bring them to her within the week. The press lost interest in the story and eventually, things returned to normal around the office, as well as at home. She had returned to a regular routine of running along the beach after work, eating better *thanks to Steve*, enjoying life and the challenges at work.

"Are you ready for this, Baby?" Steve asked as she unbuckled her seatbelt.

"You have no idea how much I have thought about this! Oh, the things I have imagined! I am more excited than I ever can remember being in my entire life!"

The front door opened with a mighty whoosh as Emmy came running toward them.

"Mommy has all the boxes ready. Did you find a tree?" She squeaked, hugging Tory tightly around the neck.

"We found three! And purchased them all!" Tory replied, just as the large delivery truck rounded the corner. Unloading the trees and setting them in the bases took only a few minutes. Christmas music filled Steve's house as everyone rummaged through box after box revealing one decoration after another.

"Emmy," Tory called from the stairs. "I need your help."

"I'm on my way," she replied taking the stairs two-at-a-time. "Where are you Tory?"

"In here—I am in your room."

As Emmy rounded the corner, Tory watched her face light up. A huge toothy smile appeared on her lips.

"I get a tree of my own?"

"Yep, and those bags are for you. I hope you like them," Tory said sitting on the corner of Emmy's bed.

She watched, delighted as Emmy pulled each of the items from the bag and inspected them one by one. The bags were filled with white butterflies of all sizes. Some with glitter wings, some were made with opaque material, others were made of lace and several were crafted with beautiful paper. The purple twinkle lights were a huge hit. Tory had shopped for an eternity online finding every white butterfly known to man. In October, she had found the purple twinkle lights, on a Halloween website. Another bag contained tinsel—silver and white. Ornament balls—clear, white, and purple—would also adorn Emmy's personal Christmas tree.

As she watched, she saw tears forming in Emmy's eyes.

"This is the best Christmas gift you could give me. Will you help me decorate it?"

The next hour was spent decorating, changing, and standing on tip-toes to reach even the tallest of branches. When the tree was sparkling, Tory turned to Emmy and said,

"In your wardrobe is a special gift I found that I thought you might enjoy."

Emmy raced to the wardrobe and gently grabbed a beautiful two-foot by three-foot butterfly made of white tulle, white lace, and clear glitter. Her eyes met Tory's.

"It's my very own angel," she whispered. "You are my very own white angel."

Tory thought perhaps Emmy was talking about the butterfly, but the way she stared through Tory made her question the meaning behind the statement.

"Can you reach the top?" Tory asked.

Emmy pulled the chair close to the tree and placed the butterfly perfectly. She wrapped her arms around Tory one more time then asked, "Can I show everyone?"

"Of course Sweetie, it's your tree," she said with tears running down her face. But Emmy didn't notice. She was halfway down the flight of stairs yelling for her family to hurry. Hurry and see what she and Tory created.

Emmy was the first up the stairs, followed closely by Tylar. Corbin, Edna and Steve walked in just as Emmy was presenting her tree with pride and joy none of them had ever seen her exhibit before. Tory was sitting on a chair watching the expressions wash over their faces. First awe, then smiles. Then all of them looked at her.

Edna crossed the room first.

"Emmy, this is the most beautiful tree I have ever seen. Did you tell Tory, thank you?"

She nodded her head. "She is my white angel Mommy."

"That she is my dear," Edna said and turned to look at Tory. "That she is."

"Can I stay here tonight? PLEASE?"

"That's not up to me Honey, you need to ask your brother."

Before Emmy could open her mouth to speak, Steve told her she could and she began jumping on her bed.

"Emmy, it is getting late. You need to put your pajamas on, brush your teeth, and get ready for bed," Edna said as she was pulling pajama pants out of the dresser.

"Can I leave my Christmas tree on all night, Tory?"

"Um," she looked over at Steve. He shook his head. "Of course you may. Now go brush those teeth and get those PJ's on you silly girl."

After the rest of the family had left and Emmy was sound asleep, Tory snuggled up to Steve on the lounger.

"I'm sorry you didn't get to do a lot of the decorating," he said inhaling into her hair.

"That's alright, there's always next year. You will have to save the banister for me."

"Where did you find all those decorations?"

Tory giggled and said, "I have been collecting for over two months! After I saw how much she liked the butterflies at the Gala. I—I just had a vision."

He kissed the top of her head, "You are one of the most thoughtful, and giving women I have ever met Tory Garrison."

"And you, Mr. Gage, are one of the most patient men I have ever met."

"My family was completely shocked you know? I was shocked. I mean, I knew we were getting the tree for her room and all. But what you did ... you have no idea how much that meant to me ... to all of us. Thank you."

Tory laid her head against his chest and whispered, "I love you."

He leaned down and kissed her forehead, "I love you more."

Next Level

Steve had asked Tory to consider staging for the conferences which meant, in short, she would become the voice and face of the company at PR events. Introducing the programs and sharing success stories; but most of all, getting the audience motivated to invest in the product. It was a great opportunity, and Tory agreed to give it a shot.

She even began collecting research material on her book. She and Emmy had spent the past five Saturday afternoons building sandcastles on "Tory's Beach" because the other beach had too many rocks. She absolutely adored Emmy and enjoyed the time the three of them spent together.

Things were smoothing out and tonight, she was ready to take the bull by the horns. What is life if you are too afraid to live it? Christmas had been magical and spending time with the family on a regular basis had Tory wanting for more. It gave Tory insight into being a mother and imagining Steve as a father. She wanted a life with this man and his wonderful family. It had been so long since she felt loved and felt free to share her love with others. She had thought about it, made a list, mole-hilled her agenda, and simply decided to surprise him. She was ready to take this relationship to the next level.

I'm ready to let what will happen just happen. I am a grown woman with a strong sense of self, I'm independent, and I'm ready for this! I want to love him forever.

"Hello?" Steve said as he answered his cell phone.

"Hi, may I come over?"

"Sure, I thought you had things to do today. I was doing some work out in the yard. You alright, Tory?"

"I am. So, is 20 minutes good?"

"Uh—yeah. See you then," Steve said as he hung up the phone. *That was a little cryptic*, he thought to himself as he pushed the mower into the garage. He left the front door unlocked and rushed up the stairs to take a shower.

Tory opened the front door and listened for Steve. She heard nothing and decided to walk upstairs. Perhaps he was in the study.

Alright. It's either now or never.

Reaching the top of the stairs, Tory walked down the hallway and then into his room. The bathroom door was closed and she could hear the shower running. She slipped off her flip-flops clicked off the main lights, turned on the far reading lamp, and lifted herself onto his bed. She pulled her up her legs and crossed them, resting her elbows on her thighs. The comforter felt cool against her exposed skin as she sat, waiting. She heard him turn the water off and waited.

A plume of steam rolled out as he opened the door ... and then he stepped into the bedroom. He stopped as soon as he noticed her sitting on the bed. His mouth opened, but nothing ... nothing came out. Tory held her breath. Holding the red towel around his waist he walked toward her. She could see little droplets of water escaping from his hair, dripping down his shoulders and traveling down his chest. She watched as his muscles tensed. She shifted toward the edge of the bed, still looking at the beads of water race down his body. He stopped moving. She could hear his breathing was fast and labored.

Tentatively, she reached up and slowly ran her fingernail from his naval, following the natural crevasse of his stomach to his chest. She flattened her palm over his heart and slowly raised her eyes. His brows were drawn together. She reached up with her other hand and wrapped it around his neck, feeling the wet hair in her hands, as she gently pulled him toward her. Making her intention clear, she whispered to him, before softly kissing his lips. She felt his arms around her and heard the towel slide onto the floor.

"Tory," he whispered lying on his back. Her head was on his shoulder, her hand pressed flat in the center of his chest.

"Hmm?" She replied, pulling the sheet up to cover herself.

"You are quiet."

"Nothing is wrong. I'm just enjoying this moment. I have thought so much about you ... about this. I just want to lie here and know there is nothing I need to do. Nowhere I need to be. There is nothing right now but you and me." She sighed, content, sated, and happy. Steve reached across her to open the windows. The sounds of the ocean filled the room as Tory fell further and further into her subconscious.

Tory awakened to the sound of the waves crashing outside Steve's bedroom. She rolled over and ran her hand along the mattress, but he was already out of bed. She sat up and stretched her hands above her head. At the edge of the bed was a pair of sweats and a tee shirt. She scooped them up as she went quietly and quickly into the bathroom to dress and brush her teeth.

"Good morning," she whispered into Steve's ear then kissed his neck.

"Good morning, how did you sleep?"

"Well, thank you. I slept so well." She felt her face flush as she turned to get herself a cup of coffee.

"Remember when you asked me about my dad?"

"Yeah," she replied as she sat next to him.

"Do you still want to know what happened?"

She slowly nodded her head while taking a sip of coffee. She put the mug down and turned toward him. His face was solemn as he took a drink.

"We really don't talk about … my family I mean. And we *never* talk about in front of Emmy." He looked at her, and then lowered his eyes.

"It was June 8th and it was Emmy's last day of first grade. She'd spent that whole morning whining and begging my Mom to let her walk home from the bus stop by herself. My Mom has always been protective of Emmy," he said looking up at her again.

"Anyway, Mom caved and said that she could walk home. It was only a block and mom was pretty sure it would be fine. Dad was on duty when the call came in that a suspicious person was seen near the corner of Elm and Fifth Streets, which was only a block or so from Emmy's bus stop. So, Dad, thinking that my Mom would be waiting for Emmy, took the call and headed over to see what was going on. He had no idea that Mom agreed to let her walk home by herself." He took a deep breath and continued.

"The rest of the details are pretty sketchy, at best. We know the suspicious person shot my Dad and when he instinctively returned fire, he got Emmy. My Dad radioed for back-up but by the time the other officers arrived he had already bled out. Mom heard the shots from the front porch and she arrived to the scene before the medics. Emmy was rushed to the hospital but they were re-routed to Pacific

Regional, because the bullet was lodged in her brain." Steve took another deep breath.

"So, after Emmy survived a nine-hour surgery, things were touch-and-go for about three days. After she was stable, we buried my dad. My brothers and I tried hard to protect Emmy from everything. We all grew up pretty fast after that."

"But they caught the guy right?"

"Yeah, they caught up with him a few blocks away from the scene. He was covered in Emmy's blood. It came out in the papers that he was under the influence of a controlled substance. He died though, two weeks after the trial began."

"Oh my gosh, that's awful. So your family never got closure."

"Well, if you mean an-eye-for-an-eye kind of closure, no we didn't. But his daughter donated all of the assets from his estate to a memorial fund for my Father. The Gala is because of her."

Her? Tory thought back to the Gala and the many faces she was introduced to.

"Jenny?"

"Uh-huh, she's organized and been in attendance every year for the past 21 years. She told my Mother years ago that even though her Father wasn't able to pay penance to our family, she could and she would.

"Wow, that's actually quite admirable of her. When you introduced me, I thought she was just a close friend of your family."

"It was a little awkward at first, you know, when my mom told us about her. But once we all met her and spoke to her, it was really difficult to hold any ill feeling toward her."

"So, everyone knows who she is then?"

"What do you mean?" Steve asked turning his head to her.

"Your brother's. Your sister, they all know who Jenny is and her relation to … well, your family now … I suppose?"

"If you are asking me if we told Emmy that it was Jenny's Dad that shot our Father and that Emmy was accidentally shot by our Father that day … no! She doesn't remember anything about that day. At first, after the surgery, she was so fragile and we didn't want to add anymore trauma to her healing process. Then, after the weeks turned into years, we all just made a pact that we would never tell her. Really Tory, what good could come from it? She doesn't remember anything."

Ashes to Ashes

The state finally released the report on Carter and declined prosecution. With probate complete, Victoria was named in Carter's Last Will and Testament as beneficiary of his estate. She knew exactly what she wanted to do with the money…

"Hey Todd, it's Tory. Give me a call when you get a chance. I need a *really* big favor. I need you to send the assets from the settlement of the estate to Dana. Don't ask—just do, please? Love ya!"

Carter's ashes had been delivered to Tory's house yesterday, and she spent the following morning on the beach with the wooden box. Carter had asked her to send him off in the ocean.

"May you find the happiness that you are searching for Carter. May you always know that I loved you with every beat of my heart. If we ever meet again, I will embrace you as a friend and thank you for helping to make me the woman I am today."

Walking past the surf, Tory placed the wooden box on the water. With tears in her eyes, she stood watching as the gentle waves carried him further and further out toward the horizon. When she could see him no longer, she turned slowly back to her apartment. The sun was just setting into the black water as she climbed into bed.

Back to the Beginning

"That was 18 minutes Tory!"

"Ha ha. What's a couple of minutes?" She was still laughing as Steve put her luggage in the car.

"Do you think you have enough luggage for a weekend trip?" He asked putting the third bag in the backseat.

"Well, you didn't tell me where we're going. I didn't know whether to pack for warm or cool conditions … so I packed everything." She replied cocking her head to the side.

"Awe, it would be easier to be annoyed with you, if you weren't so beautiful." He opened Tory's door and walked around.

"Ready?"

"Are you going to tell me where we are going?"

"Nope. You will find out soon enough," he smiled and put the car in Drive.

"Tory. Honey. We are here."

"Did I fall asleep? Uh, I am the worst co-pilot ever. So, where are…" *Tell me I am not dreaming, but if I am please let me stay asleep.*

"Really? We are staying here all weekend."

Steve shook his head and walked around to open her door.

She immediately walked to the front door and read the brass plaque aloud.

The Caprietta Lighthouse
    In 1912, an Italian settler landed on the beach below the eighty foot cliff after his ship sank in the Pacific Ocean. His beautiful bride had escaped the shipwreck as well, but had not arrived safely on the same shore as her beloved. Refusing to accept that his love had drowned, he erected the lighthouse in hope that it would light her path back to his arms.

    It took three years for Meikel to complete the structure. Night after night for seventy years he lit the fire and signaled into the darkness waiting for her return. On the seventh night of the seventieth year, he heard a light tap on the front door. Meikel eighty six years old, hobbled down the stairs and opened the door. He squinted to see the frail, gray-haired woman walking away on the path.

    "Caprietta?" he whispered.

    "Caprietta!" he yelled running after her.

    "Meikel?" the woman turned and saw outstretched arms welcoming her back to where she had been trying so long to return.

    The Caprietta Lighthouse is dedicated to Meikel and Caprietta, *the eternal couple.*

    "I can't believe we are staying here this weekend, this is such a dream come ..." her voice failed her as she turned to see Steve bended on one knee. He reached up and took her shaking left hand in his.

    "Victoria Garrison. I fell in love with you the moment you walked into the conference room over seven years ago. I don't want to wait until I am too old to take care of you, and I already know my life would be mediocre at best without you. You don't have to answer tonight, you can ..."

    "Yes! Yes Steve! I will. Of course I will!" Tears were streaming down her face as she looked down at the ring he was sliding onto her finger.

    Later that evening, after crawling into bed, Tory laid her head on Steve's shoulder and whispered, "I love you," into his ear.

    Steve turned his head, kissed her cheek and whispered, "I love you more."

The Beginning… Emmy's Story

Tory checked her phone, one missed call and a new voicemail.

"Hi Tory, it's Emmy. I was wondering if I could come over and make castles with you? Are you there?"

She heard Steve's voice in the background, "Honey, tell her to call you back."

"Steve says to call me back. Bye."

She pressed seven and deleted the message. Steve had brought Emmy by one Sunday when he was picking Tory up for family dinner. Emmy was impressed by "Tory's Beach" as she referred to it. She had spent hours with Tory and Steve building sand castles. Steve always took her home before the tide came in. Every time she returned to the beach, she would squeal and ask where her castle went. Steve had told her once that the sand fairies take them to live in. She giggled and told him there were no such things.

"Hello?"

"Hey! I just got Emmy's message. I'm home now if you guys want to come over."

"Emmy," Steve yelled. "Tory's home, do you still want to go over there?"

She heard Emmy in the background telling Steve that she was getting her 'stuff'. "Um, I guess I will see you two soon then," she said, smiling into the phone.

A few minutes later Emmy came bursting through the front door. "Tory? Are you ready to go?"

"Yup, let me just get a couple of towels and I will be right there."

"Do you want me to get everything out of the car Emmy and carry it down to the beach?" Steve asked while Tory grabbed three beach towels.

"Okay," Emmy replied grabbing Tory by the hand, pulling her out the door.

They were half way through the second castle when Emmy told Steve she needed some sea shells for the moat. As soon as Steve had walked far enough that she thought he couldn't hear her, she turned to Tory.

"I remember everything you know."

"What?" Tory turned her entire body so that she was facing Emmy.

"I remember everything that happened that day."

Oh my God!

"Sweetie, why haven't you told anyone?" Her voice was quiet and etched with concern.

"I'm telling you," Emmy replied matter-of-factly. "If I tell you, you have to promise not to tell anyone ..."

Author Note:
Emmy's Story is written in first-person. A little change from
the previous books. When I was writing Emmy's Story it just
felt right to tell it from her own perspective.

A.   L. Elder

Emmy's Story

Book Three

A. L. Elder

DEDICATION

Dedicated to my Mother. The strongest and most supportive woman in my life.

ACKNOWLEDGMENTS

Thanks…

To Dala, Patty, Valerie, Bernie, Corinna, David, Jill, Amy, Scott, John, Jeremy, Frank, Lisa, Sue, Lou, Chelle, Jon, Hayden, Jamie, Reva, Mary Lou, Shelly, Dennis, Jeannie … I know I am going to miss someone.

Thank you to my Mother for her inspiration, and supporting my passion of writing!

Thank you to Miss Megan for the inspiration on the cover of Emmy's Story.

And finally, thank you to the *Ladybug*. Your insight and comments in the margins made it easy for me to improve the entire storyline.

All my love,

A. L. Elder

Chapter None

Really, all I know for sure is the brain, the human brain, is one of the most adaptable organs in our body. The changes and re-wiring mine went through was for my own survival. Still, I can't be sure that some of what I experienced wasn't just the vivid imagination of a young girl.

I was born on January 12, 1983, to William and Edna Gage. I was the fourth of four children and the only girl.

I was six when the incident happened. It was my last day of first grade.

Everyone told me it was *normal* that I didn't remember what happened that day. I never told them for fear they would think I was not *normal*. I lived for 21 years in a world where everyone else decided what was right, wrong, or indifferent. Then, I told my story and my life changed dramatically.

My most recent psychiatrist, Dr. Lesley Weston, challenged me to write down my story. She said it may help me put the pieces together. So, before I get too far ahead of myself, let me first apologize for the first portion of this book. I needed to get into my old mind in order to write everything down the way it happened. It was extremely frustrating for me to put all of this in writing, knowing my memories were of a six-to-twelve year old mentality. But, again it was imperative to my personal healing process.

Confession…

January … 21 years after the accident

Mommy and I are over here, at Steve's house. I call Tory but she doesn't answer. Steve is telling Mommy that Tory said yes to his question.

I ask Steve what question and he tells me he asked Tory to be his wife. He tells me Tory will be like my big sister. I have never had a sister and the thought of having Tory in my life as family makes me really happy.

Mommy is really happy too, she tells Steve, Tory is a wonderful choice for a wife.

I wonder if I will ever find someone to marry and be happy with.

Tory is home now. Steve and I are going over to build sandcastles on her beach. She builds really good sandcastles. Her beach is only sand and seashells but Steve's beach is just rocks. It is really hard to build sandcastles on his beach.

I see her bright light when she opens the door. She is so pretty. I really missed her. Tory grabs some towels and Steve gets the stuff from his car. I have a lot of stuff to make sandcastles with. I have shovels, buckets, rakes, little bowls, big bowls, straws, buttons, crystals, and lots of pretty seashells too.

We sit on the beach and I pull out all of my stuff. I give Tory some too because she likes to get water for me. I give Tory the big purple bucket for water because we always need a lot of water. We start building a really tall castle with a river around it and I tell Steve we need seashells for the river and for the outside of our castle. Steve always finds the best seashells and he takes the yellow bucket to fill. I watch his color until I can't see him very well. He is far away.

I turn to Tory and tell her I remember. I tell her I need to tell her but I need her to promise not to tell anyone.

Tory is crying. She asks me if I am okay. She asks me why I never told anyone.

She tells me I have to tell my family. I tell her I will tell them at my birthday. She promises not to tell anyone and she makes me promise I will tell them at my birthday.

I promise Tory.

January 12th

It is my 27th birthday and everyone is here, at Mommy's house. I am helping Tory clean up the dishes. She tells me she thinks it is a good time to tell them my memories. I say okay. Tory asks everyone to come into the living room. Tory is holding my hand as we walk behind them.

I smile at Tory. Her light is even brighter than it was in the kitchen. I look at my Mommy and she looks scared. Corbin has his arms crossed over his chest, and Steve is sitting by Tylar because Tory is sitting by me. They are all looking at me.

I look down and stare at Tory's hand. I tell them I remember everything. I remember Daddy and the old man, and Daddy's gun. I tell them I am getting off of the bus and there is a really old man standing the sidewalk. I tell them his clothes are really dirty and he looks so scared. His hands are shaking, and he is talking to someone I can't see. I keep looking at Tory's hands because I can hear my Mommy crying and I don't want to look at her. I have to tell them all of my memory.

I tell them I hear squealing sounds of a car stopping and I cover my ears. It is a police car! The pretty lights are flashing red and blue.

Daddy gets out of the car. I'm so happy to see Daddy because I think he is going to take me for a ride. But, then I am mad at Daddy because Mommy says I can walk home like a big girl.

I yell to Daddy. Then I feel a scratchy hand on my arm. I am being tugged by the old man. Daddy is yelling at the old man.

The old man has a gun, just like Daddy does.

Daddy is yelling at me now. He is telling to run. He keeps yelling for me to run.

The old man points the gun at my Daddy. I am trying to run. I am almost wriggled free from him when there's a really loud boom. I try to cover my ears as I watch Daddy. He is falling to the ground. He yells at me again to run, but the scratchy hand pulls on my arm harder than before.

I see fire come out of my Daddy's gun. It goes to nighttime. The scratchy hand is still holding me. I feel his arm behind me. I can't see anything, it is just dark. He is laying me down on the sidewalk. I can feel water coming out of my head. The old man says a really bad word and then I hear his footprints. He is running away.

I can hear Mommy now. She is screaming at me and Daddy. She is telling someone to call 911. Mommy is yelling at me to hold on. Mommy is crying and telling Daddy she loves him. She tells him he can't leave her like this. My head starts to hurt really badly. I fall asleep and …

I lift my head and look up at Tory. She has tears running down both of her cheeks. I am so upset I have made the white angel cry. All I can think of is to give her a hug.

Mommy is wiping her eyes. She is sniffling. Mommy asks me why I never told anyone before.

I tell her the doctors said I wouldn't be normal if I remembered. She asks me how long I have remembered. I tell her since I woke up from the Nighttime.

I tell Mommy, Daddy can't go to Heaven until I tell the white angel. Mommy, Corbin, Steve, and Tylar all look at Tory. Then they look at me again. Steve is starting to cry now.

Mommy asks if I have seen Daddy. I tell her I have. I talked to Daddy on my birthday. I tell her Daddy told me I needed to tell *her,* pointing to Tory, and then he can go to Heaven.

I tell Mommy not to be mad at Daddy. He says it was an accident. He says he was trying to shoot the old man. I tell Mommy that Daddy says he loves me.

Mommy is shaking her head no. She says she is not mad at Daddy. She says she knows it was an accident. Corbin and Tylar are crying.

Steve asks me what the white angel is? I tell Steve I have never stopped seeing lights around people. I tell him I can still see his light, and Corbin's light, and Tylar's light. I can even still see Mommy's light.

I tell Steve that Daddy told me to tell the white angel. I tell Steve that Tory's light is white. Her light is really bright. I tell Steve that Tory is my white angel.

Mommy tells me she doesn't know what to say. Mommy says she is so sorry. I tell Mommy it is okay now.

I am not mad at Daddy anymore. I tell her Daddy can go to Heaven now.

Dr. Lesley Weston

Mommy says we are going to meet a new doctor today. It has been a couple of weeks since I told my family about Daddy and my memory. Mommy says this new doctor does not want to take pictures of my brain. Nobody has taken pictures of my brain for a really long time.

My new doctor has a pink light, just like Jenny. My doctor is Lesley Weston. She talks to me for a really long time. She asks me what I want. Nobody has ever asked me what I want. I think about it for a minute and then tell her I want to get my Driver's License, like Katie. I tell her I want a house of my own. I tell her I would like to have a piano at my new house. I tell her that her light is pink. She smiles when I tell her this. I ask her if she wants me to tell her what happened with my Daddy. She tells me she wants me to write everything down instead of telling her.

She hands me a book with a lot of blank paper in it. The book has a white cover on it and my name in silver letters at the top. It is cursive writing and it looks really fancy. The pages are white and when the book is closed, all of the pages are silver around the edges. I really like my new book. I think it is pretty. Mommy says she will help me fill up my new book. We leave Dr. Weston's office and go home. Mommy makes me macaroni and cheese for lunch.

We start writing in my new book.

June 8th
My journal begins…

  This is my favorite dress. It is purple, my very best favorite color. There are ruffles around my neck and ruffles around the bottom. I am wearing my shiny black shoes and white socks. I tell Mommy it is hard to play kick ball because these shoes are so slickery. She says I look pretty. She tells me little girls shouldn't play kick ball anyway. I try to tell Mommy that I like playing kick ball, but not in my slickery shoes. Mommy shakes her head and says kick ball is for little boys to play—not little girls wearing dresses.

  I stand in front of the mirror while Mommy is taking out my pink spongy curlers. Sometime, they hurt my head while I am sleeping. Mommy pulls my hair tight and puts a purple ribbon in my hair. The ribbon matches my dress. I ask Mommy if I can walk home from the bus stop by myself today. Mommy tells me no. I tell her that I am a big girl. I am six, but she tells me no again.

  I tell Mommy that I promise to come right home. I tell her that this is the last day of school and I am a big girl! Mommy is really quiet and then she says okay. I am really happy Mommy is going to let me walk home from school today.

  Mommy walks with me to the bus stop. She tells me to walk straight down this sidewalk when I get off the bus. Mommy is pointing at the ground. I can almost still see my house. I tell Mommy okay. I promise her that I will walk on the sidewalk and walk straight home. She gives me a kiss on the cheek. The yellow bus stops in front of Mommy and me. I can see Katie sitting by the window. Katie is waving at me to hurry. I tell Mommy goodbye and climb up the stairs on the bus. I sit right next to Katie. She is my bestest friend in the whole wide world.

  We don't play kick ball at recess today, so I am not mad about my slickery shoes anymore. The final bell rings and Katie and I race to the busses. She always sits by the window, but she says since it is the last day of school she will let me sit by the window.
Katie and I sit on the bus and I am excited my stop is next. I am walking home all by myself, because I am a big girl now.

  The school bus driver just stopped at my corner. I tell Katie that I will see her next year because that is what we have been saying to everyone today. There is a really old man standing by the street. I wave at Katie as she scoots closer to the window, and I watch as the school bus drives away.

There is a really loud squealing sound that makes me put my hands over my ears.

It's my Daddy and his flashing lights are going. My Daddy is a Policeman and I think he is here to take me for a ride in his police car because, sometimes he does that. I am sort of mad though, because Mommy said I could walk home all by myself like a big girl.

Daddy is getting out of his car and I yell for him. I feel a really hard, scratchy hand on my arm. It hurts. I look up and see the old man is pulling on my arm. His eyes are red, like he has been crying and he is talking to someone. I don't think he is talking to me, but I cannot see anyone else.

He has a gun like my Daddy. He is pointing his gun at my Daddy and my Daddy is yelling at me to run.

I pull on my arm. I am trying Daddy. I am trying. Daddy, he won't let go, he is hurting me Daddy. I keep pulling but the old man is really strong. My Daddy is still yelling at me to run. Daddy! He's hurting me Daddy, I can't get away. Every time I try to pull away, his hand squeezes tighter. I scream back at Daddy the old man won't let me run. I tell Daddy to help me, that the old man is hurting my arm.

I hear a really loud boom and watch as my Daddy is falling down. I scream for my Daddy but he is falling and he doesn't look at me. I see blood coming from Daddy's neck. He is trying to yell but I can only see more blood.

There is another loud boom and I see fire come out of Daddy's gun.

I can't hear anything and the sun is gone. It is nighttime.

Many days have passed in darkness…

I can hear beeps. It is still nighttime and my head hurts really badly. I hear Mommy's voice and the voice of a man. The man is telling Mommy that I won't remember.

There are more beeps and my head doesn't hurt anymore. It is still nighttime and I miss the sunshine. I can hear Mommy crying then I feel something on my arm. I think it is my Mommy's hand.

Mommy is telling me to wake up. She is squeezing my hand telling me to squeeze her hand back. I am trying Mommy, but I can't make my eyes open, and I think my hands are broken because I can't make them move. I can hear Corbin talking to Mommy about Daddy. Corbin is crying really loud. He is asking Mommy why Daddy had to go and when can we see him again? I cannot listen to Corbin cry anymore. It hurts my heart too much.

It's daytime! I am so excited the sun is out and thankful that my eyes let me open them. Mommy's in the hallway telling everyone I am awake. I try to tell Mommy that I wasn't asleep but she is crying again.

Mommy brings a lady wearing a white dress over to me. The lady is flashing a really bright light into my eyes. She hands me a red ball and tells me to squeeze it as hard as I can. I squeeze it really hard with both hands because my hands are working again.

I look at Mommy and she is still crying. Corbin and Steve come into my new room and they hug Mommy. Tylar is sitting in a chair over in the corner and he is crying too. My family is so sad, and I feel bad for feeling happy. I think they are sad because Daddy hurt me.

I ask Mommy where Daddy is and she sits down on my new bed. Mommy starts crying even harder. I don't know why she is so sad.

Mommy tells me Daddy is in Heaven now.

My head hurts really badly again. The sun goes away and it is night again.

July

It is daytime again, and I am in my own bedroom. There are a lot of teddy bears on my bed I have never seen before.

Mommy is sleeping next to me so I try to be really quiet. She wakes up anyway and smiles. She asks me how I feel and I tell her my head hurts just a little bit. She brings me a plastic cup with some pink medicine in it and tells me to drink it. It tastes gross, but Mommy says it will make my head feel better. I stay in my room for a really long time. Mommy wants me to wait until my head doesn't hurt any more.

Mommy brings me a box of letters and pictures from a lot of people. I find four of them from Katie which make me smile. One is a picture of us that she drew on a piece of purple paper. Another one she colored me a kitten. One said that I should wake up because she wants to play with me. And the last one, all it says is she loves me with a really big sparkly heart.

Mommy says lots of people were praying for me to get better. She says I am a miracle and she is so happy I am awake. She tells me I need to rest and takes the box away. She lets me keep the sparkle heart from Katie, and I put it by my nightlight.

August

> *My brothers are eating waffles and Mommy brings me one too. I watch as Corbin cuts it up and puts extra syrup on it. He knows I like maple syrup.*
>
> *Today, Mommy says we are going to meet a really nice lady named Evalynn. Her name is really hard to say. Evalynn asks me lots of questions about my favorite color and my favorite part of school. I tell her my favorite color is purple and recess is my favorite part of school. I tell her I don't like kick ball days when Mommy makes me wear my slickery shoes. Evalynn is wearing tall slickery shoes. She is really nice. Evalynn doesn't ask me if I remember what happened. I don't tell Evalynn what happened.*
>
> *I hear Mommy talking to Evalynn in the hallway. She tells Mommy that I won't remember what happened and she tells Mommy that it is normal. She says I will heal faster because I don't remember. She tells Mommy the body has a normal reaction to reject the memories of something so traumatic.*
>
> *I don't tell Evalynn I remember. I don't tell anyone I remember, but nobody asks me anyway.*

September

I ask Mommy when I get to go back to school and she tells me my new teacher will come over to our house.

I am really excited! I ask her if Katie has the same teacher too. She says Katie has a different teacher and that makes me sad. I miss Katie.

My new teacher is a girl. She smells really pretty and she colors with me. She asks me if I remember coloring in school. I tell her I do. She asks me if I remember my alphabet. I tell her I do and say all of my ABC's to her. She smiles a lot. She asks me if I can count to 10. I tell her I can count to 50 and she tells me to count to 50. She asks me if I remember a lot of things, but she doesn't ask me if I remember the accident. I tell her that I remember lots of things, but I don't tell her about the accident. She doesn't ask me about that day. She only asks me about school.

October

Mommy says we can all dress up today for trick or treating. Corbin, Steve, and Tylar are going as Power Rangers and I am going as a princess. I even have a crown! We walk on the sidewalk and Mommy holds my hand. We knock on doors and when the people open them we say "trick-or-treat" and then they give us all candy. We have plastic pumpkins with handles on them to carry all of our candy in. We bring home all of our treats and Mommy makes sure there isn't anything bad in our candy. She says we always have to have an adult check our candy before we eat any. She says sometimes people put bad things, like poison, in the candy. Mommy doesn't find any candy with poison in it. We get to choose our favorite one to eat before bedtime. I want to eat the taffy one because it is purple. It tastes like grapes.

November

Mommy made a turkey for dinner tonight. I got to help make the smashed potatoes.

Corbin is saying the blessing and he says he misses Daddy. Mommy is crying and says she misses Daddy too, but she says that he is happy in Heaven.

I ask Mommy where Heaven is and she tells me it is where the angels live. I ask how long Daddy is going to be there—in Heaven. She says that he will be there for a long time. She says we will see Daddy again.

I don't want to see Daddy again. Daddy hurt me. I don't tell Mommy why I am crying because Mommy doesn't know that I remember. Mommy tells me everything is going to be okay. I don't need to cry because Daddy is in Heaven. She says Heaven is a really nice place and Daddy is happy there. She says he can see us. He is watching over us to make sure we are safe.

December

  Today is Christmas and Mommy hands me a present from under the tree. It is wrapped in all white papers, with a white bow on it. Corbin, Steve, and Tylar have one that looks the same as mine. Mommy says these presents are special because they are from Heaven. She says our Daddy had them delivered. My bothers' open their all white present. I tell Mommy that I don't want mine.

  Mommy starts crying. She asks me why I don't want to open my present. I tell her that I just don't want any presents from Daddy. I ask Mommy why Daddy is in Heaven. She says because Daddy was a good person, and good people like Daddy always go to Heaven where they live with angels.

  I ask Mommy where bad people go. She says bad people don't go to Heaven. She says bad people go to a bad place.

  I want to tell Mommy that Daddy went to the bad place, but I can't. If I tell Mommy, she will know I remember. Then, she will be sad again. I don't think Mommy knows that Daddy was the one that hurt me, and took away my daytimes for a really long time.

January

Mommy says Katie is coming over today to have cake and ice cream. I am really excited because it is my birthday. I am seven today. Katie has a really pretty white dress on and she says her Mommy is going to be mad because she dropped some chocolate ice cream on it. My Mommy says it will be okay and tries to wash it out. Katie and I play for a little bit in the living room and then her Daddy comes to pick her up.

She starts crying and says she wants to stay longer. I start crying because I want her to stay longer too. Mommy says we can play together again soon. She says it is almost time for dinner and Katie has to go home to her house. I ask Katie's Daddy if I can come to his house and he tells me that I can. I ask my Mommy when I can go to Katie's house and she tells me on another day.

I never remember going to Katie's house.

July

Today is fireworks day. Mommy says I have to stay home with her and I am really mad. All of my brothers get to go to the river and watch them. I like the glittery one the best. Corbin tells Mommy he will take me with them and he promises I will be safe. Mommy says she doesn't want to worry all night and tells Corbin no.

I start crying and Steve tells Mommy they will all watch me and we will come home right after. I tell Mommy I will be good and hold Corbin's hand the whole entire time. Tylar tells Mommy, please, please, please, but Mommy still says no. She says maybe I can go with them next year. Mommy tells my brothers they can go, but I have to stay home.

Mommy and I watch some on T.V. but it is not the same. Mommy can be really mean sometimes.

Spectator

Dr. Weston asks me how I am doing with my memory. I tell her the journals are coming together slowly and I find that a lot of my memory has specific events attached. I remember holidays, my birthdays, and events in my life that either made me really happy or just the opposite. I tell her I am having a hard time remembering anything from the time I was 7 through 16. Dr. Weston explains during the time period of nine years, I may have been experiencing everything as a spectator rather than a participant. She said it's like watching a movie. You only remember the parts you really like or the parts you really hate. She tells me those memories may or may not come back as I continue to write in my journal. She said either way, what I had written so far was encouraging.

We talk about my education since I don't mention it a lot in my journals. I tell her I remember learning math, reading, writing, history and science but I am not sure where those memories fit into the timeline. She wants to give me a placement test next week to see where I am as far as education level. She gives me a GED book to study and our session is over.

I return home and continue with my journal.

January (year eleven)

Katie is here and she is showing me her new car. Her new car is a Cooper and it is blue and white. Katie has her Driver's License and I am really happy for her. She takes me for a ride around the block. I want to go further, but Mommy says she is scared something will happen. Mommy is always scared something is going to happen to me.

I ask Mommy if I can go and get my Driver's License. Mommy starts crying and tells me maybe someday I can. I know I can't get one because my Daddy shot me in my brain. There are a lot of things I can't do because Daddy shot me in the brain. I hate my Daddy.

June

 Mommy tells me it is time to get ready. We are going to go to the Gala. Mommy says it is a party for Daddy and all of his friends. Daddy can't come to his party. I think it's because he is in the place where bad people go. I don't think bad people can go to good parties. Mommy says Jenny will be there and I am excited. I like Jenny, she is really nice. Jenny glows pink.

 People always dress up to go to this party so Mommy is dressed up too. Corbin is bringing a girlfriend. Tylar and Steve have to wear a monkey suit because Mommy says so. But Tylar and Steve don't wear a monkey suit. They wear a black and white suit. I think Mommy likes their suits.

 Jenny is waiting for us when we get to the party. She gives me a hug and tells me I look pretty. The tables are all decorated in flags and there is a big picture of my Daddy wearing his police outfit on the wall. There are a lot of people here and they tell funny stories about Daddy. They don't know what Daddy did to me, and I don't tell them either. Jenny asks me how I am and I want to tell her she shouldn't make a party for my Daddy. Jenny likes doing this party she says. She says it is a way to re-pay my family for what happened. I don't know what Jenny is talking about, but she starts crying and walks away from me. I don't know why Jenny is so sad.

 We are home now, and I tell Mommy that I like Jenny. I tell Mommy that Jenny has a pretty light around her, Jenny's light is pink.

 Mommy doesn't understand. I tell Mommy that her light is yellow. Corbin has a green light, Steve has a blue light, and Tylar has a red light around him. I tell her everyone has light around them except for me. I cannot see any light on me. Mommy is scared and she says she is worried about me seeing lights around people. I tell Mommy that it doesn't hurt me and I started seeing lights after I woke up from the nighttime.

 Mommy calls a new doctor. The new doctor tells Mommy it is not normal that I see lights.

 The doctor makes me come and lay on his cold table. He wants to take more pictures of my brain. He tells Mommy that I am okay but the lights that I see are not normal. He says he cannot see anything wrong in my pictures and tells Mommy that maybe I have a vivid imagination. Mommy doesn't believe it is my imagination and she asks the doctor if Mommy should take me to a different kind of doctor.

He tells Mommy she should wait and see if I still see lights in a month, then go and find another doctor.

I don't want to see any more doctors so I stop telling Mommy about the lights.

January 12 (year twelve)

Today I am 18 and Mommy asks me if I still see lights around her.

I tell Mommy no. She starts crying and gives me a hug. She tells me that I am strong and she is very proud of me.

I am afraid to tell Mommy that I still see the lights. I don't want to see a new doctor, and I don't want her to be sad anymore.

Mommy says Katie is coming over for my birthday today. Mommy says we are going to go sledding in the mountains. I am really excited we get to go somewhere. We never get to go anywhere because Mommy worries I will get hurt. I go to my room and start getting my boots on. It doesn't snow here very often and Mommy says I can wear my snow boots today and my big heavy coat. She says there will be lots of snow. Katie has to bring her Daddy because Mommy's car doesn't have four wheels to drive in the snow. I try to tell Mommy her car has four wheels but she says they don't work at the same time and we could get stuck if we took her car. I grab my itchy hat that Jenny made for me and my gloves which don't have fingers in them.

Mommy is in the kitchen and she is talking on the phone. Mommy looks really mad, but I don't know who she is talking to. Mommy hangs the phone up and tells me we can't go sledding for my birthday this year. I start crying and Mommy says Katie is sick so her Daddy can't take us. I tell her that she can take us. I tell her again her car has four wheels and they can get us to the snow.

Mommy tells me to take my boots, my heavy coat, and the scratchy hat Jenny made me, and put them back in my closet. I start crying really hard and tell Mommy that she is mean. I tell her that I never get to do anything fun. I always have to stay home when my brothers get to live away from us. I tell her that I think she hates me, and just does things to make me sad. I tell Mommy I hate her.

May

Mommy is taking me to meet a new doctor today. We walk into his office and his light is really dark brown. He is not very nice to me. He tells Mommy I am done healing from the accident. Mommy cries because I think she is happy. He tells her that he cannot do anything to help me. He says it is normal.

Mommy believes him because Mommy doesn't know. I can't tell Mommy I feel different. I can't tell her because she doesn't know. I don't want my Mommy to think I am not normal.

September

I am watching T.V. with my Mommy. An airplane hit a building in a place far from where we live. We live in Oregon. Mommy says the T.V. show is in New York. I have never been to New York. As we are watching, another airplane hits another big building. Mommy is crying.

October

    I ask Mommy why I never go trick or treating with the other kids. Mommy tells me it is because all of the kids my age don't go anymore. She says they go and do other things. She tells me that I have an important job of handing out candy to all of the little kids who come to the door.

November

   This year it is just Mommy and me for Thanksgiving because my brothers are too busy. Mommy decides we are going to go to a restaurant instead of messing up the kitchen. I don't like the smashed potatoes or the corn at the restaurant. Mommy makes better turkey too. Mommy gives me a really long hug and tells me she loves me very much. I love Mommy too, and I want to tell her about my rememberies, but I can't.

December

 I hate Christmas! Mommy makes me put the ornaments Daddy sent from Heaven on the tree. All of Mommy's decorations are from Heaven. Corbin is not here anymore. He lives with Julie. Julie is nice; she has a red light around her like Tylar. Steve isn't here anymore. He lives by the water by himself. Tylar isn't here anymore either because he is going to school.

 I ask Mommy when I don't have to live in here anymore. I ask her when I can get a house. Mommy says that I do have a house. But, I don't have a house. I have a bedroom in her house.

 Mommy says we are going to Steve's house to help him put up decorations. Steve doesn't decorate with his presents from Heaven. Mommy says all of our presents from Heaven are only for her tree.

 Someday, I am going to have a tree that isn't full of Heaven.

 Steve's house is really big and it takes us a long time to decorate. I want to live here, with Steve, but Mommy says I can't. I hate living in my house. I miss Katie. I miss going to school on the school bus.

 I hate my Daddy.

May (year thirteen)

 Mommy says a doctor is here to help me. Mommy says I am always mad. Mommy doesn't know I want to go to the bad place and tell Daddy to stop sending presents from Heaven. I am staring at the new doctor. He asks me why I am so mad. I cross my arms over my chest. I don't talk to the doctor. His light is brown like the other doctor. I don't like brown.

 I hear the new doctor tell Mommy that my anger is normal. He gives her some yellow pills and tells her to give them to me. He tells her the pills will make me feel better.

 Mommy gives me the yellow pills. They make me tired. I am not mad anymore.

(year fourteen)

 Steve is moving into a new house and we are painting my new bedroom there. He said I could paint the room any color I want. He is painting it purple. I still love purple. It's my turn to help. I get to put sparklies on my wall.

 Steve always says I am pretty. I ask Steve if I am normal. He tells me no. He tells me I am unique. He says I am a white butterfly.

 Steve is the only one tells me I am not normal.

 I am a white butterfly.

 I ask Mommy if she will get me a white butterfly. She tells me butterflies don't like to live inside. I ask her if she can help me find one outside. We look for a really long time. We see big butterflies, little butterflies, but we can't find any white butterflies.

 Mommy lets me call Steve at his house, and I ask him if he has any white butterflies. He tells me that white butterflies are really rare. He says he has only ever seen one in his entire life.

He says I am a white butterfly, because I am rare.

Placement Test

While Dr. Weston is reading my journals, I am taking a placement test. The book she gave me to study was, for the most part, review. Although, I don't remember when all of the education took place, it is all coming back as I quickly flip through the pages. Even the memory of using number two pencils is returning as I sit here.

I hand the packet back to Dr. Weston and she asks how I did on it. I tell her I am pretty confident I did well. She tells me that she will have my placement results for our next session.

She asks why my journal entries are getting less and less. I tell her there are not a lot of memories I can write about.

I tell her I am afraid the memories between the years of 17 and 27 are non-existent. I remember Corbin getting married, but not the ceremony. I remember that Tylar graduated, but I can't remember specifics. I tell her I remember being fitted for a bra. (I remember being so excited that I was finally an adult.) I tell her I am frustrated that my memory is lacking.

Dr. Weston says I need to keep journaling. If the memories return, I can write them down. But, she says, getting upset will only push my vivid memories further back into my mind.

A Visit from Daddy

February (year twenty)

It's nighttime. I get really sad when the sun goes away. I am almost asleep when I realize my Daddy is in my bedroom. He is sitting next to my bed on the floor. He is crying. I can see Daddy's light. It is white.

Daddy tells me he is sorry. It was an accident and he was trying to help me get away from the old man. Daddy tells me he would never want to hurt me. Daddy tells me he loves me and he is so sorry. Daddy is crying.

I ask Daddy if he is in Heaven. Daddy tells me he cannot go to Heaven until I am not mad at him anymore. He says that I have to tell the white angel what I remember, and then he can go to Heaven.

I tell Daddy I don't have a white angel. Daddy tells me the white angel will come to me.

I tell Daddy that I am not mad at him anymore. I tell Daddy that I love him. I tell Dad I miss him so much. I am crying. I tell my Daddy that I want him to go to Heaven. I tell him I don't want him to go to the bad place. I tell Daddy that I don't think he is a bad person. I think my Daddy is a good person. Daddy makes me promise him that I will tell the white angel what happened. I promise Daddy that I will. Daddy says he has to go. Daddy says he loves me very much and he is proud of me. Daddy says he will always be with me. Daddy says he will keep me safe.

Mommy comes into my bedroom and sees me crying. She says she heard me talking and says I had a bad dream. I am still crying. Mommy asks me why I am crying so hard. I hug Mommy. I hug Mommy really hard but I don't tell Mommy about Daddy.

April (year twenty)
I wait for a really long time. I don't know if my Daddy forgot to send me my white angel from Heaven.
Mommy doesn't give me anymore yellow pills. She says I am not mad anymore.

May (year twenty)

Mommy and Corbin are in the kitchen talking about Daddy. They get really quiet when I walk in. I ask if they are telling a secret. Corbin says they are and asks if I want to know what the secret is. I tell him yes. Corbin says the secret is he loves me. I cross my arms and tell Corbin, THAT is not a secret.

Corbin asks me if I have a secret to tell him. Corbin is not my white angel. I cannot tell Corbin my secret.

June

   I can hear Jenny! I run into the living room and see her pink light. She gives me a hug.

   Jenny is planning Daddy's Gala again. She plans it every year. Jenny says she needs my help in decorating. I tell her she should decorate with white butterflies. Mommy smiles and says she likes the idea too!

   Jenny says she will make sure there are white butterflies at Daddy's party. I like Jenny, she is pink. I can't tell Jenny though, because she is not my white angel.

   I think my Daddy forgot to send me a white angel. I cry. Mommy thinks I am crying because Jenny is gone. Mommy doesn't know that I talked to Daddy.

   Mommy is brushing my hair for the Gala. My dress is yellow. It has dots. I have black shoes on, but they are not slickery shoes. We don't ever play kick ball at Daddy's party. People tell funny stories about my Daddy.

   I miss my Daddy.

   When we get to the party, Jenny is waiting for me. She yells my name and pulls me into the room. Jenny is really excited. I walk into the room with Jenny, she points to the ceiling. There are white butterflies everywhere. I am crying and Jenny gives me a hug. She asks if I don't like them. I shake my head no, and tell her I like them. I like them very much. She gives me another hug.

   Mommy is walking over to our table. We sit in the same place every year. Corbin and Tylar are already here. Mommy asks them when Steve is coming. I look over toward the door and I see Steve. He is standing in the doorway looking at all of the people. I tell Mommy that I am going to get Steve and bring him to our table.

   I walk really fast, but I don't run. Mommy says we can't run around at Daddy's party. I give Steve a big hug and he tells me he wants to introduce me to someone name Victoria. I let go of him and stare at the woman standing by him. She has really long black hair and she is really pretty. Her light is really bright! I think she is my Daddy's white angel! I know it's her. I am so excited to meet her. She says that I look pretty. She tells me to call her Tory. They stop to talk to Jenny. I tell Mommy that Tory is really pretty. I almost tell Mommy she is my white angel, but Mommy is meeting her so I am quiet. My Mommy doesn't know that Daddy sent her to me.

We are home and Mommy asks me if I had a nice time. I tell her that I really liked the butterflies, and I really like Tory. Mommy says she likes Tory very much. Mommy says Tory is really nice.

August

Mommy says the music teacher is coming over today. Mommy wants me to learn to play her piano. Mommy use to play her piano all of the time before Daddy went to Heaven.

My music teacher is really nice. Her name is Lisa and her light is red, just like Tylar's. She tells me I have to practice every day.

I practice on the piano every day, just like Lisa says. Lisa tells me I am doing a really good job. I hear Lisa tell Mommy I am really good.

October

 Mommy tells the doctor I am playing the piano. She tells him I am learning really fast. I hear the doctor tell Mommy it is normal and, I should keep playing. He says music may be my gift.

 I start practicing two times every day.

December

Mommy brings down the boxes filled with Heaven and we decorate the tree. Mommy is crying. She says she misses Daddy.

I miss Daddy too.

Mommy tells me we are going to Steve's to decorate his house. We get there and Corbin says Steve is not home. He and Tory are getting a tree. He says they will be back soon.

Tylar brings the boxes inside, and start putting up all of the decorations. Mommy hands me an angel and tells me to put her on the mantle. We are hanging stockings on Steve's fireplace when I hear his car in the driveway. I run out the front door and yell his name. I give him a hug. He is with the white angel. She says they found three trees instead of just one. Her light is so bright.

Steve's house is really busy. There are three people that I don't know putting trees in bases. I look for Tory, but I can't see her light. A few minutes later I hear her.

She yells for me from the top of the stairs. She says she needs my help. I am excited she needs my help. I run up the stairs as fast as I can. Tory says she is in my bedroom.

There is a Christmas tree in my room at Steve's house. The white angel is sitting on my bed. There are shopping bags on the floor. Tory tells me the Christmas tree is mine. She tells me to open the bags.

I sit down on the floor and cross my legs. I am so excited I have my very own tree. I open the first bag. It is filled with purple lights. I pull them out and put them in a pile right beside Tory's feet. She is smiling down at me.

I open up the second bag and pull out a piece of white tissue paper. Inside the soft paper is a white butterfly made of feathers. There are three of them in this bag. I place all three, very carefully, in another pile on the floor.

I open the next bag and find three more white butterflies made of really pretty lace.

The next bag holds more white butterflies! They have sparkles on them! There are six of the sparkle ones. I put them in another pile.

The last bag has round ornaments. There are white ones, purple ones, and sparkle ones.

They don't look like my Mommy's decorations from Heaven.

I am crying because I am happy. I give Tory a hug and she helps me put the purple lights on my very own tree. Tory sits on the floor, in front of my piles of butterflies. I tell her which one I want, and she hands it to me. I ask her if she wants to put a butterfly on the tree too. She says no, she likes helping me this way. She says I am doing a really good job and my tree is beautiful.

I tell her she is my white angel. She smiles and her light gets so bright it is hurting my eyes. All of my butterflies and ornaments are on the tree. Tory tells me there is a special surprise in the wardrobe. I walk over and open the wooden doors.

I reach up and carefully retrieve a big white butterfly. It is bigger than my head! The butterfly wings are almost invisible. There are white feathers and sparkles just like the other butterflies.

Tory says this is for the top of my tree. I am so happy. Mommy and Steve only have angels for the top of their tree, but I have a white butterfly. I pull the chair over to my tree. I can't reach the top even on my tip toes. Tory says it's perfect where I place it. I ask Tory if I can show Mommy, Corbin, Steve, and Tylar my tree. She says yes and plugs in the lights. I run downstairs and tell everyone to come see.

They walk too slowly. They only walk up one stair at a time. I am waiting by my tree. Tory's light is really bright. Brighter and prettier than my tree! I am worries that her light is so bright my family won't be able to see my tree. Then, I remember that I am the only one that can see her light.

Mommy is crying. She says my tree is beautiful. Corbin is crying too. Steve is hugging me really hard and he is looking at the white angel. Tylar wipes his cheek and kisses the top of my head.

Everyone is crying, but I think they are all happy. I think they are crying because my tree is so pretty. Everyone touches the butterflies on my new tree.

I ask Mommy if I can stay here tonight. Steve says it is okay. Mommy says it is late, so I get ready for bed. Mommy, Corbin, and Tylar went to their homes. Steve and

Tory are downstairs. I stare at my tree as it is glowing purple. My tree is not from Heaven… but my white angel is.

We woke up early and now Steve is helping me build a sandcastle. His beach is really rocky. I ask him if we can go to Tory's beach instead. Steve says she is not home today. She had a meeting with a lawyer.

Tory's beach is perfect. There aren't any rocks, just sand. Tory says she likes making sandcastles with me. I know I have to tell her. I want to tell her because I want my Daddy to go to Heaven. I have to wait. Mommy tells me Steve is going to ask Tory to marry him.

January (year twenty-one)
I can't see her today. Mommy says Steve took her away. I want him to bring my white angel back.

Lisa tells Mommy I should play my piano at a recital. Mommy says we can have a recital at our house. I don't know what a recital is, but Mommy is really happy.

Mommy watches me practice the piano and says someday I can play in front of lots of people. I tell Mommy I don't want to play the piano in front of a lot of people.

Mommy tells Lisa we can't do a recital at our house. Lisa looks sad.

Prisoner of Mind

Dr. Weston asks me how I am doing writing everything down. I tell her it is extremely frustrating because I feel trapped inside my old mind the whole time. She tells me writing as though I am living it again may help me put together what is missing.

She asks if I want to know how I did on the placement test. *Of course I want to know how I did. But I wonder what will happen if I did badly. Shoot, I wonder what will happen if I didn't do badly.* Everything has been snapping together so easily, other than my journal.

I tell her I do want to know how I scored. She says I placed at college level reading and writing, and my mathematics score was of a senior in high school. So, I ask her if it is normal, if my scores are normal. She is laughing and asking me if anything about my experience so far in life has been normal. She's right! I am anything but normal and I need to get out of trying to fit into a box that doesn't exist.

When I see Mother in the lobby of Dr. Weston's office, I tell her my placement results. She says she is not at all surprised. She says she has all of my school work at home in dozens of boxes. She tells me all of my teachers were always very impressed with my ability to learn and retain new things.

I wonder, to myself, *why don't I remember this?* It would seem it was positive reinforcement and something I would have perceived as normal. Again, I find myself frustrated I cannot remember things.

Mother says we need to go to the bank and set up my account. She says it is very important I learn how to budget money and balance a bank account. It's funny really, my entire life has passed and I have never had a single thought about money!

February (year twenty-two)
Mom and I complete the journal and I was surprised by the amount of memory I have lost. The days and nights began to fade into one month after another. I have been suffering from headaches again. So much that Dr. Weston has had to come to Mother's house for my sessions.

March

   I am noticing the light around my Mother is beginning to fade. I tell her but she shows very little concern. She says it is most likely my brain creating new pathways and reorganizing old ones. I assume she is probably right and let it go.

   The only way I can describe the light I see is to compare it to something everyone can relate to. For example, Tory's light is white. It brightens sometimes, depending on her mood. It never dims beyond the original glow, as I have noticed occurring with Mother. I would compare Tory's light to headlights on a car. Her normal light reflection is like driving lights, but her vivid light could be compared to the bright setting of the headlights.

   Tylar and Julie both have red light around them. Tylar's light is as red as a fire engine, while Julie's is deeper like inky maroon. Corbin has a green glow around him. I would compare his light to pea soup. Steve's light is a bright—clean blue. His color is like to sky on a clear summer day. Jenny's light is a soft pink, and it reminds me of a baby blanket.

   Mother tells me that I shouldn't worry about her light fading. She tells me it might just be the re-wiring of my brain that is causing the glitch. I am worried that my Mother may be dying.

March 20th
Today I met with Dr. Weston and discussed my
continuing treatment. She is amazed, as am I, at the
progress my mind and body has made in such a short time. I
tell her I am keeping a journal. Writing things down as they
seem important and she agrees this is a good idea. We
decide to continue our sessions. We agree to meet once per
month rather than once per week.

Katie is waiting outside Dr. Weston's office to take me
to lunch. I watch as she waves from the driver's side
window. As I sit in her car, I watch her put it into gear and
apply the gas. I become jealous of Katie. We are the same
age and, yet her life is so different from mine. She was
sitting right next to me on the bus so many years ago. We
were both young and, she continued to blossom while I was
held under the confines of one roof. Katie looks so
absolutely normal ... beautiful, in fact. I can't help but
wonder if I would have turned out similar. She has a
husband, and she is a third grade teacher. I am feeling angry
her life is perfect—she has everything I could ever hope to
have.

"Have you been here lately?" Katie asks,
interrupting my thoughts.

"Not recently, mom and I ate here a few years ago."

"Oh! They have the best finger steaks I have ever
tasted," Katie says while pulling into a parking stall. I reach
for my purse and step out of the car.

"So, how is everything? I mean, what does
everyone think about your, well, the new you?" Katie asks
after the waitress takes our order.

"I think everyone is still in shock, to be honest with
you."

"So, what happened? Did you just wake up one
morning and, boom, everything was different?"

"I don't know, really. Dr. Weston thinks, because I
tried to repress my memories of the accident for so many
years my brain just reacted, making it possible for me to
survive in the world everyone else created for me." I had
asked this question a hundred times in my mind and there
really wasn't a firm answer. I don't know. Maybe it was the
confession to my family that created the opportunity for me
to move forward and begin to realize my potential. I don't

have an answer other than I know I want reclaim the life that was taken away when I was only six year old.

"What is it like? Do you feel differently?" Katie asks after taking a drink of her iced tea.

I shrug my shoulders, "It's hard to explain. Dr. Weston had me write down all of my memories to this point in my life. It was so frustrating, because there are so many holes in what I remember. Sometimes, I remember things so clearly it was like it happened just yesterday. There are other times, the only things I can remember were the horrible headaches which seemed to stretch for weeks. I can't help but wonder if there are other people out there like me. You know? Living in their own falsely created world. Too afraid to deter from what they are being told is normal."

"So, do you blame the doctors?"

"No, I don't blame the doctors, I can't blame anyone. I was the one that was too afraid to speak up. Katie, there is just so much even the doctors don't know about our brain. I was a science project from the time I was six until—well, I suppose I still am huh?"

Katie smiles as the waitress delivers our food. I reach down and grab a weird looking piece of fried meat. It is oddly shaped and could resemble a finger, that is, if the finger belonged to a really old person with arthritis.

"These are really good," Katie says. "You need to dip them in the ranch dressing it puts the flavor over the top!" Katie exclaims as she pops one into her mouth.

I follow suit and she is right, the ranch adds just a zip of zing to the crunchy little morsels.

"So, what are your plans now," Katie asks. "What do you want to do? Where do you see yourself going?"

"Hmmmm, well, I would really like to get my Driver's License," I smile. "It's really an inconvenience to depend on everyone else for transportation. I would eventually like to move out of my Mother's house. Get my own place, so I can have a little privacy and enjoy just being alone once in a while."

"You know I don't mind driving you to lunch. In fact, you can call me anytime. I will pick you up and take you anywhere you want to go, especially during the summer. What else am I going to do? Lesson Plans for fall?" She smiles and cocks her head to the side. "Besides, what are best friends for, right? How does your mom feel about all of this? It has to be a huge shock for her. I mean, you've been her little girl for so long."

"Yeh, she says she's excited to see me moving forward, but I think there is still a part of her that feels guilty. We have talked a lot about it and she thinks it was her who held me back all of these years. I've told her so many times I wasn't unhappy with my life," I look up to see Katie's expression. She is staring at me with a blank look on her face, so I continue. "I really wasn't. I was doing what the doctors all said I should be doing. Up until I told Tory and my family what had really happened, what I really remembered. Well, up until that time I just didn't know any better."

"So, what did happen that afternoon? If you don't want to talk about it here, or with me, that's fine. I guess I am just curious. I read all of the papers and my mom filled me in as I got older ..."

"Nah, I don't mind talking about it. I imagine I will be telling this story many more times to many more people."

I tell Katie what I remember about that day starting with the very memory of pink spongy curlers. Our waitress even interrupted a couple of times to ask questions about the accident. She wanted to know if I really saw the fire from the gun, and if I knew at the time my father had been shot. She also asked why I thought the old man helped me lay down on the sidewalk. I hadn't thought about it before, so I couldn't give her an answer about the old man. Perhaps, he was a nice man who made some bad choices, or maybe he was also in the wrong place at the wrong time. It is very difficult to decipher too much information about that afternoon. When I finally finished with my story, it quickly became obvious that everyone in the restaurant that afternoon knew me, knew my father, or had heard about the incident one way or another. There are nearly thirty people in the diner, all of them watching and listening to me as I share the story. A room filled with strangers to me, but I am not a stranger to them. They have all been touched in one way or another by the same events which changed the course of my life so many years ago. It feels so good to talk about what happened without fearing I am going to be told I am not normal.

I look around to room and see a woman holding her husband's hand; another woman is wiping her cheek with her napkin. In the far right corner, in a booth, there is a man with an orange glow around him and he's about my age. He is staring right through me. He looks oddly familiar but I can't place where I know him from. He has dark brown hair and brilliant blue eyes like the tropical oceans. His jawline is covered with stubble and his lips are full, almost pouty. He catches my stare and smiles. I smile back and lower my gaze to the empty plate in front of me.

Katie looks behind her to see what I am staring at, and then back at me, "Do you recognize him?"

"I am not sure, he looks really familiar, but I can't tell you if I have ever met him before."

"Oh, you've met him," she sneers. "It will come back to you—I am sure of it! Are you ready to go?" Katie's voice was low as she stood and grabbed our check. "My treat today, I am so glad to have you back!"

April

 I tell Dr. Weston I am still journaling although, the frequency is less and less. We talk about my lunch with Katie, the diner, the curious folks, and my feeling of jealousy toward Katie.

 "Lesley, do you think it will ever be possible for me to get a Driver's License?" I ask Dr. Weston. She is staring at her notepad, writing faster than I have ever seen her write before.

 "Is that what you want?" She asks, still writing.

 "Yes. Actually, I want a lot of things, but I don't know what is possible and what is impossible. I mean, what are my limits? Is there some kind of guide I can read to let me know what I should and shouldn't do now that I am, well … whatever it is I am now." I sigh.

 "Emmelia, how many times do I need to tell you there is not a set limit to what you can accomplish? Sure, there will be things you will find more difficult to do, but would you rather live out the rest of your life wondering if you could have done something? Or would you rather try then accept the outcome?"

 "I know, I know. But I have always had limits. Things other people say I can't do … shouldn't do, because 'it's just not normal in your condition'. So, I am just asking if I am expecting far too much."

 "I don't think it is a lot to ask for. Getting a license to drive is liberating, although frustrating as well. There's a lot that goes into learning how to operate a motor vehicle. Emmelia, what else do you want to accomplish?"

 I sit in silence thinking through my thoughts as Dr. Weston places her legal pad in her lap. *I want to live on my own. I want to shop for my own food. I want to meet people that share my interests. I want to ride a horse. I want to purchase clothes. I want to play the piano in a concert hall. I want to go out on a date. I want to be kissed by a boy. I want to skinny dip in a lake. I want to purchase Christmas gifts for my family. I want a family of my own. I want to reach out to others like me and reassure them there is nothing normal about life.*

 "For now, I just want to focus on getting a Driver's License," I say, not wanting to freak Lesley out with all of my irrational demands.

"Perhaps you should make a list of things you would like to accomplish in the next year. We can discuss them at our next session. As far as obtaining your Driver's License, I can help you get into a class that will help prepare you if that is really what you want."

"Yes, please." I answer quickly and Lesley makes a call. My first class is next week! I leave the office and search the parking lot for my Mother's car. Instead, I see Tory waiting in a stall. She is standing near the trunk of Steve's car talking on her cell phone. As I walk closer, I can hear she is speaking to my brother. She notices me approaching and she ends her conversation.

"Hey! How did it go with Dr. Weston?" Tory asks.

"Good. Is there something wrong with mom?" I ask, standing in front of Tory. She shakes her head no.

"No, no. She had an appointment which worked out great because I was on my way to pick up Melanie. I thought I would see if you want to come too."

"Where are you going?"

"Janessa's Bridal Boutique. I have to find my bridesmaid dresses and everyone I have spoken to says Janessa's has the best gowns. Anyway, I thought you might want a say in what you will be wearing *in* the wedding," she said emphasizing the *in*.

"Really? You want me to be a part of your wedding? Of course!" I squeal. *What a wonderful surprise!*

"Of course silly, it will be you and Melanie in my wedding party. Your brother has two in his as well. I am so glad you want to do this," she says wrapping her arms around my waist.

On our way to Melanie's, Tory tells me they have been best friends since high school. They were inseparable up until Tory married her first husband, Carter. "Marriage does something to your single friends, they don't really want to hang out with you and compete with a husband for your attention." Tory says matter-of-factly as I nod my head up and down from the back seat. "You know, you don't have to always sit in the back."

"I know," I laugh, embarrassed, "I guess old habits are hard to break. So, do you think Melanie will be okay with you marrying my brother? I mean, will that cause a problem with your friendship with her?"

"Probably not, it will just be something we adjust to. It's not like I've been single very long. Anyway, the most important thing right now is to make sure we can find a dress Melanie can fit into."

Before I have a chance to ask Tory what she means, we had stopped in front of a large apartment complex. There are huge Iris plants and a stone sidewalk leading to the glass front doors. I see a very tall, slender woman emerge from the doors into the sunlight. *That has to be Melanie.* I squint to see her more clearly. Her hair is bright red, and her eyes look black. She's wearing a pair of jeans and a purple shirt that is so low-cut, not only can I see the top half of her boobs, but I can see her bra as well! Her bra is purple too, and very lacey.

All of the bras I have are white and they have a stupid blue flower in the center near the clasp. I actually touch the center of my shirt to feel the appliqued flower. *Ugh, I need to go shopping for under-garments.*

Melanie is wearing a lot of make-up but she looks so pretty and I am trying very hard not to stare as she climbs into the front seat. She turns while clicking her seatbelt in place and extends her hand to me.

"I'm Melanie, and you must be Emmelia. Tory has told me so much about you. It is nice to finally meet you!"

I smile and shake her hand, "it's really nice to meet you too. Tory has told me a lot about you as well."

Melanie scrunches her face and leans closer to me. "Don't believe everything she says Emmelia," and then she laughs really hard.

Tory and Melanie talk the entire drive to Janessa's. Melanie has a new boyfriend so most of their conversation is about him. She says his name is Brock, he's 29 and he's amazing in bed. Tory curbs the conversation quickly when Melanie starts talking about her sex life with Brock. I'm not sure if Tory is embarrassed because I am in the car, or if she is just embarrassed to hear anything else about Melanie's love life. I for one am a little disappointed Tory asked her to stop. It's not like I have my own experience to fall back on. Cripes, I haven't even kissed a boy! I wish Tory would have let Melanie finish talking about her activities with Brock, although I am sure I wouldn't have understood.

We pull into the parking lot and there are numerous cars, it's not full by any means, but this looks like a popular destination. In the front window I can see some of the most elegant dresses shimmering in the afternoon sunlight. There is one in particular that is a deep chocolate brown with amazing bead work on the bodice. The mannequin is simply not doing this dress justice. I wonder where I could wear a dress like this and suddenly remember my dad's annual Gala. This would be the perfect dress to wear this year.

We walk through the front door and we are greeted by a tall, slender man wearing a pin-striped suit and slicked back, gray hair. He welcomes Tory with a hug like they have known one another for years. He tells her it is nice to finally meet her in person and he has pulled some dresses per her specifications and asks we follow him to a private area. He invites Melanie and me to sit on a large white leather sectional and begins to rummage through a rack of gowns. Most of them are white, full of lace, and beautiful.

"Johnathan, I specifically said I would not be wearing white on my wedding day," Tory stated with her hands firmly on her hips.

"I know, I know. But I thought these would also make beautiful dresses for your bridesmaids," he replied gesturing toward Melanie and I.

Melanie stood up and walked toward Tory and Johnathan. "This would probably be the only wedding I will ever be in where white would be worn by me! Lord knows I won't be wearing white at my own wedding, huh Tory?" Melanie laughed and slugged Tory on the shoulder.

"I am not going to have my wedding party dressed like a bride. Johnathan, please tell me there are more options than the ones in front of me." Tory exhaled loudly.

Johnathan races out of the room leaving the rack behind. Tory and Melanie start flipping through the dresses like pages in a magazine.

"Emmelia, what do you think about this one?" Melanie asks holding up a gorgeous mermaid style dress.

"I think it's lovely, although, I am afraid that I must agree with Tory. I don't want to look like a bride on *her* wedding day."

"Thank you Emmelia," Tory says walking over to me. She sits down on the sofa and shakes her head in disapproval. "I really hope he returns with something closer to what I have already asked for," she said tossing her head back.

Johnathan returns with another rack of dresses. Tory seems delighted as she jumps off the couch and races towards them. She is pulling some off the rack and setting the on them back of a nearby chair. Melanie and I watch her smile and oogle over her choices.

"Alright ladies, these are the gowns I want to see you try on please," Tory says to both of us. We each grab our respective pile and head toward the fitting room. It is one very large room and we each choose a side to hang our dresses on. I have three dresses and Melanie has two. They are the same color but completely different styles. The first one I try on has spaghetti straps and it is floor length. It's blush-colored and flowing. It has a darker colored, satin slip with a lighter, airier material sewn over it in a cascading water-like effect. Melanie zips me up.

Her first dress is sleeveless and pretty low-cut. I don't know … it seems to be a little too revealing in that area for a wedding, but Tory might be okay with it. It is the same color as mine but it's all satin, floor length, and it's really form fitting. There is a slit up the back which I notice while I am zipping her up.

"Tory, we are ready, do you want to see?" Melanie shouts, but I already know the answer. We walk out of the fitting room and we are instantly attacked by hands. Tory is touching and waving at the layers on my dress while Johnathan is tugging at the bodice on Melanie's dress.

"Okay, so Melanie's dress will need some adjustments if this is the one you choose for her. How does that dress fit you young lady?"

Johnathan is addressing me, but thankfully Tory steps in. "I think we will need to adjust this one as well. The length is right, but the waist needs to be brought in here. See how it just hangs?" she says pinching the excess material.

"Do you want to see the others?" Melanie is getting impatient.

Tory nods her head and we change quickly into choice number two. I glance at my third choice and really hope that Tory likes this dress. I really like this dress better than either of the others. We zip, we giggle and we walk out into the waiting hands.

Tory stops Johnathan before he reaches Melanie. "No, no," she says holding his arm. "These are perfect! These are the dresses! Oh my god, they both look absolutely stunning!" Tory wraps her arms around Johnathan thanking him five more times before letting him go.

"Should we complete the picture Miss Tory?" Johnathan asks in a mischievous voice.

Tory looks at both Melanie and I and tells Johnathan it's a great idea. "Do you both want to see my dress?"

We look at each other and both shake our heads. "Duh," Melanie replies. "I didn't know you had already picked one out. When did you go shopping for it?"

"I did it online and just emailed Johnathan my measurements last week," she said as she walked in the fitting room. "It won't take but a minute, that is, if I haven't gained any weight since last week," she laughed.

May

I tell Dr. Weston that the month of May has been filled with one trial after another. I don't want to complain really, but how does a normal person cope with all of the daily crap that happens to them? I am wondering if I was happier living in my protected little world where no one ever dared say anything to upset my bubble. Mother is being nearly impossible with every decision I try to make to move toward independence. She even tried to interfere with my driving lessons in order to get me to fail the class. Tory and Steve have been so busy planning the wedding and what-not, they haven't been around to help "explain" my point to Mother. Of course, Katie and her drama aren't really helping matters either. We go to lunch, or shopping and she carries on about how horrible her marriage is. She tells me she wants a divorce, but she's afraid her family will disapprove. I swear, it's like everyone forgot I AM the one who suffered a horrible tragedy and I AM the one trying to move forward.

Katie and her husband, ugh! This is so entirely ridiculous to me and I have to vent. So, Katie tells me her husband has decided he wants to start a family. Oh, I could only be so lucky to find a man who wants to marry me then start a family. But noooo, Katie says he is just trying to keep her under his control. Like that makes any sense whatsoever. Katie says they talked about having kids, years ago, when they first got engaged. They both agreed there were far too many things they wanted to do and having kids would only slow them down. So, now Katie says, her husband has had a change of heart and he wants to have at least two children. Needless to say, a huge argument ensued between us and I haven't spoken to Katie for a week now. I have tried to call her but she refuses to answer. I just don't understand how she can be so selfish.

The List:

Dr. Weston asks me to make a list of things I want to accomplish. I update as I work through, although I am not planning on doing them in any order.

1. *Driver's License*
2. *Buy new underwear and bras (anything but blue flowers)*
3. *Find an apartment*
4. *Find my own style (Tory to help)*
5. *Meet new friends (try going to a bar?)*
6. *Get a job!*
7. *Kiss a boy*
8. *Skinny Dip (but not with said boy above, or any boy!)*
9.
10.

I tell Lesley I have left nine and ten blank as I am sure there will be more added to the list later. She laughs with me as she reads through the list and assures me everything on my list is attainable. She says I can really do anything I set my mind to. I am not sure I believe what she is selling, but hope is something the month has been short on already.

Dedication

As a child, I was shot by my father who was a law enforcement officer. I know it should sound like a horror story, but it was an accident. He was responding to a suspicious person call and I was just getting off the school bus. Talk about wrong place, wrong time. Needless to say, my father was shot and killed that day, the suspect died before the District Attorney's Office had a chance to file paperwork, and I spent the following 21 years in a bubble. I survived a bullet lodged in my brain.

The doctors told my Mother my progressions were normal. I listened to them tell her what would happen next in my recovery process and I did as they assumed. When the doctors would tell my Mother something wasn't normal, I would stop the behavior altogether. It's funny what the brain is capable of when someone else is controlling your ideal of normal.

At 20-seven, I met a woman whom changed my life. I refer to her as my white angel. After living so long in a state where nothing felt right, nothing felt complete; it was a liberating moment when I told her my secret. As part of my treatment plan, I was asked by my Psychiatrist to write my story, my memories down which I did. The book is called "Emmy's Story" and it is as personal as it gets. After I finished book, I was pressured (in a good way) by the millions of people that spoke to me after reading my journals. They wanted to know more. They wanted to know how I changed my outlook after so many years. So, to all of my new friends and family… I dedicate this book to you in hopes you too realize you are a white butterfly and spread your wings.

Never settle for another person's perception of normal.
With love,
Emmelia E. Gage

Emmelia Elizabeth Gage

The Bank

"What kind of account are we opening today ladies?" The lady sitting behind the desk asks.

"Checking and savings please," my Mother replies like she has done this a million times.

"Alright, and who is going to be primary on the account?"

"I am," my Mother replies. "Emmelia will be a signer. That will give her full access to the account correct?" Mother hands her a piece of paper. I realize it is my certificate of birth.

"Of course Mrs. Gage, we can set it up so the account is yours primarily, but will allow Emmelia the same access to the funds, deposits, and withdrawals you have."

Mother produces a sheet of paper is yellowed and torn at every fold mark. She hands the clerk the paper and asks that $500.00 be transferred from that account into the new account. The lady nods her head and after completing Mother's request, hands the flimsy, yellow piece of paper back. Mother respectfully folds the paper and places it back into her wallet.

"I need both of you to sign and remember this is what we will compare should there be any problem with your account. While you are doing this, I am going to make your cards. Now, how many debit cards would you like for this account Mrs. Gage?" The lady asks.

"Two please, one for me and one for Emmelia." The lady walks toward the back of the bank.

"Okay Emmy, you need to sign here, your full name," Mother says handing me the pen.

It has been so long since I have had to sign anything, let alone with my full name. I remember writing E. E. Gage on all of my schoolwork instead of writing out all of the characters. The teachers never minded, I mean, I was a class of one. How confusing could it have been for them when grading my assignments right?

I take the pen from Mother and sign my full name, Emmelia Elizabeth Gage. I sign it loopy and full of wisps. I have one of those names that go on and on and the double

E's are fun to write in cursive. I have always loved writing capital E's.

A few minutes later, the lady returns with two nearly identical debit cards and a box of checks. She hands Mother the cards, the checks, and an envelope filled with the papers we just signed. She even gives Mother a pen with the bank logo on it.

On the way home, Mother explains that we will go over budgeting and reconciliation after dinner. Which we do, and it seems pretty straight forward to me. This is what I have, subtract what I spend, don't go below zero, and double check the statements. Debit purchases on my card are instant deductions, charges take a day or so, and checks are best saved for a later time as I don't have any bills for the time being.

The following morning, I ask Mother about the schoolwork she said she saved. She tells me there are boxes of all of my schoolwork in Steve's old bedroom closet. We walk into the room and she starts pulling large banker boxes from the space. There are three in total and we carry them to my room and sit them in the corner. I tell her I would like to go through them to see if I remember anything more for my journal. She kisses the top of my head and tells me she has some errands to run anyway. She tells me she will be home in a few hours.

I sit, cross-legged on my floor and remove the lid from the closest box. On the outside one may think the boxes are quite organized, however one would be wrong. As I rummage through the stacks of misshapen papers I begin to see a pattern of my early works. There are drawings of houses and flowers, people and animals all strewn between handwriting assignments and math homework. This must have been my first couple years of school before the accident. There is a list of supplies someone has checked off with a purple crayon. Although I don't remember doing so, I assume it was me who checked off each item as Mother put them in my backpack. I stare at the list and then read: box of tissue, box of 16 crayons, safety scissors, ruler, glue stick, white glue, Popsicle sticks, writing notebook, and a box of number two pencils. I dig further into the box and find a piece of paper that has a practice writing assignment. I must have struggled with lower case q's because half of one side is one after another. There a piece of paper that catches my eye. I pull it out of the box and giggle to myself. It is written in crayon and it says the same thing over and over again. 'I heart TH' although the word heart is not written, it is an actual heart shape in between the *I* and *TH*. I have no idea who TH is, but I must have had some crush on him. I set the sheet aside and continue to the next box.

The box is filled with more handwriting assignments and I can see where my penmanship is improving. This box has to be more recent as I have written my name as E. E. Gage rather than spelling everything out. I really did get lazy with my name during the homeschool days. More math, spelling, and a few book reports on books I don't remember reading but I did a pretty good job summarizing them.

The third box is filled with pictures and albums my Mother must have made. There is one album in particular that catches me interest. On the front cover is reads: 'The Darkness'. I open to the first page expecting to see photos of me in the hospital. Instead, I find a letter to my father from my Mother in her own handwriting. I begin to read it to myself:

Dearest William,

I cannot even begin to tell you how badly my heart aches for you. How difficult it must have been for you to watch our daughter fall to the pavement knowing the gun you held in your hand inflicted the wound that may not heal. How did this happen? How did we go from having the perfect family, your successful career, my book club, and four exuberant children, to this?

I am sitting next to her and listening to the machines breathing oxygen for her. I have been here so long I have forgotten what day it is. I cannot sleep Will, and I cannot bring myself to eat. I have lost you and now I don't know if Emmy is going to die as well.

The doctors are telling me she may never wake up and I may have to make the decision to take her off of the life support. How and I supposed to make a decision like this? How can I make the choice to end her life? The only thing that gives me resolution is the fact that if I must let her go, I know you will be there waiting to take her. I know you will never answer me but I find peace in writing you my darling. I miss

you, I love you, and I hope you know these things wherever
you are right now.
Always & Forever,
Edna

I stare at the page that has yellowed over the years. I can see where there were stains on the paper and I can only assume it was my own Mother's tears as she wrote the letter to my dead father. There are more letters, many more, as I flip through the pages of the book. Another faded yellow page catches my eye and I read:

Dearest William,

I have never seen our boys so sad than I did today when you were laid to rest. Tears streamed down their little faces. This is not how I pictured their childhood, their lives. I am angry. I am sad. There were over three hundred Officers and Firemen in uniform there today. I wonder if you know just how many lives you touched.

I sit with Emmelia, listen to the machines waiting and willing her to awaken, but nothing. She gives me nothing in response, William. Please tell them, whoever they are, if they are going to take her they had better do it soon. I cannot and will not end her life William. I will die before I unplug her from those machines.

Edna

I look in the box and find three more albums. Each one contains letters from my Mother to my father and all have been written after his death. I flip the pages in the second book and find a letter written after I had awoke from the darkness.

Will,

The attorneys called this morning and have closed the case. The young lady I wrote earlier about is overcome with grief and I cannot help but want to Mother her. It was not her fault these horrible events happened, and like me, she is left with so many questions. The doctors continue to work with Emmy and are doing so pro bono due to the scientific and medical discoveries they are making with each test they perform on her fragile brain. She is such a strong willed child and I know she gets that quality from you. You would be proud of her if you could see her now. I hope you can. I hope you are watching over all of us. I hope you know I plan on sending the children gifts from you every Christmas. I want them to know you are thinking of them but more importantly, I don't want them to forget you.

I transferred part of your pension to the children's college accounts and receive the social security benefits beginning

*next month. We are going to be okay financially because
you were lost in the line of duty. All of those policies you
insisted we take out will ensure I can stay home and take
care of our family.*

*I love you, and I miss you so badly my heart aches
constantly. If it wasn't for our children, I would chose to
join you again much sooner than I should. Please know
wherever you are, I will be there with you again. You are
my William, my husband, my love, my best friend.*

Forever and Always yours,

Edna

I feel uncomfortable reading anymore them so I gently put
them all back into the box and replace the lid. One by one, I
carry them back to Steve's old closet and close the door. I
can't believe my Mother was put in a position to end or save
my life and I cannot imagine how difficult that decision must
have been for her. I am quietly thankful she hadn't decided
to take me off of the machines. I remember her telling me to
wake up, to open my eyes, to squeeze her hand. I remember
trying to wake up, trying to force my eyes to open. My body
was unwilling to respond to the commands I was making but
she continued to have faith I would eventually awaken from
my own darkness. The thought of my Mother living without
him all of these years and writing to him regularly is
overwhelming. Truly, that is love.

I hear Mother pulling into the garage so I grab the paper I
had set aside earlier and meet her in the kitchen. I hope she
cannot tell I have been crying although, if she asks, I can tell
her it was just the overwhelming memories in the boxes. If
she asks, I will tell her I could only make it through one of
the boxes and it was just too much too soon. She would
understand and not question any further.

"How did your appointment go," I ask as she places her
purse on the counter?

"Well. How did your discoveries go?"

"Uh, pretty good. I really didn't remember any more
than before but it was interesting to see everything. Hey,
was there a time I had a crush on a boy at school?"

Mother smiles and says, "You mean TH?"

No Secret

"Emmelia? Emmy are you here?"

"In here Mother," I yell from the dining room table. I have 15 job applications spread out across the table with only three filled out.

"Land sakes young lady, what is this mess?" Mother looks across the table and the scattered papers. I have my Social Security Card and Birth Certificate to my left and an application from Readers Cove flipped to page three directly in front of me.

"Sorry mom, I am trying to fill these out before we go to town this afternoon. I promise to get it cleaned up. So how was your appointment this morning?"

"It was fine. Why are you applying for a job?"

"Mother, in order to move on with my life, I need to know I can support myself financially," I smile and look over at her. She is pulls the chair out across from me and sits. She has her hands folded and her elbows are resting on the table. "Mother, there was a dress I saw at the bridal store the other day. It is absolutely beautiful! Unfortunately, it costs $189.00, plus I would like to get myself some … um … new under clothes as well. I can't do all of that on $500.00."

Mother stares at me with a blank, unreadable expression on her face.

"I just want to have a little more independence Mother. I want to know I can take care of myself," I continue not knowing what she is thinking.

"So, this dress, you really want it then," she asks? I nod my head. "Okay, well while we are running errands this afternoon, we will go and take a look at it. We can also stop by and see if we can't find you some different under-garments as well. I just, well I am afraid you are trying to do so much so quickly and I don't want your headaches to return," she says with concern etched across her face.

"I know Mother. I worry about the same thing. But I don't want to slow down, or stop my progress for fear I will slip backward. I am more afraid of holding back and not accomplishing everything I am capable of. The only way I am going to know, is to push forward and try new things."

"Alright, if this is what you want to do. I just don't want to see you get hurt, or frustrated, or angry again. I have tried so hard to keep you safe from everything ..." Mother's voice trails off.

I grab Mother's hand, "I know, and I cannot tell you how sorry I am for not telling you sooner what I remembered. You have spent all of your time protecting me, making me your entire life. What would have been different for you had I not listened to the doctors?"

"Nothing Emmy. Nothing would have changed. You have to understand I want what is best for you. I want to see you succeed in whatever capacity that will be. But I don't want to sit idly by and watch as your dreams are squished. It would be too much for me right now, to deal with. Can't you just slow down a little bit," Mothers' voice is shaking like she is going to cry.

"I don't want to upset you Mother, all I want to do is move forward. If it means I get a job and my license and maybe my own apartment one day. This is where I am right now. I have finished my journal, and I have faced my fear of being not normal. I, I just don't know why you are fighting me on this mom, it's just a job. How are you going to feel when I ask you to look at apartments with me?"

"An APARTMENT? When did you start looking into moving out? Oh, Emmy, this is just too much, it's just too soon. I am sorry honey, but there are so many things you need to learn before you just go racing out into the world with nothing but ambition. I admire your tenacity, I always have sweetie, but how are you planning to manage cooking and bills and grocery shopping. Oh Emmy! You'll starve if left to your own devices," she says exasperated.

"Okay Mother, now you are just going off the deep end. Let's start with getting a job, then finishing my driving test and then we will see where I am at. And, by the way," I say with a crooked smile, "my brothers love my smashed potatoes!"

The conversation ends but I know very well it is not over. I complete four of the applications and gather my stuff into a pile and take it to my bedroom.

As we get into the car, I crawl into the backseat and Mother quickly corrects my action. "Please sit in the front seat Emmelia, there is no reason anymore you must sit in the back. I have treated you like a child far too long as it is," she says dryly, obviously still upset with me. "Besides," she says, "I'm tired of looking like a chauffeur when we go places." She smiles warmly to me.

I place the applications on my lap and click my seatbelt into place. We drive to the dress store first and I show Mother the dress that caught my eye.

"Emmelia, Darling, how have you been?"

"Johnathan," I say looking over at my Mother who looks completely perplexed. "Johnathan, this is my Mother, Edna Gage. Mother this is Johnathan, the man who has been helping Tory with the wedding dresses." They shake hands and Mother tells him it is nice to meet him. Tory has said such wonderful things about him and the store. He beams with the compliments.

"So, what are you ladies here for today? Oh, I hope it's not to try on your dress," he says looking my way. "It hasn't been altered just yet."

"No, my daughter and I are here so she may talk me into purchasing this dress for her," Mother says holding up the chocolate masterpiece.

"Oh, well then, let me see if I have your size in the back. That one is an eight, and would just simply drown your tiny figure," he says walking away briskly.

I shrug my shoulder and roll my eyes for effect as Mother and I continue to look through the racks of dresses. "I haven't found a dress for the wedding yet, maybe there is something here that will work," she says giving me a wink and starts looking around the boutique. By the time Johnathan returns from the stockroom, Mother has found a couple of dresses she would like to try on. He leads us to a different fitting room and closes the door.

"Oh, Emmy, that dress is just perfect," Mother says as she zips me up. "Turn around, let me look at you."

She admires me for a very long time before I notice she is crying. She moves closer and begins to pull my hair up.

"I think you should wear it up—like this," she says. "It will show off those beautiful shoulders and slender neck you have been so blessed to have inherited from your grandmother."

I stare into the mirror and admire the amazing woman looking at me. I think about everything she has had to sacrifice in her own life to care and provide for me. I see pride in her eyes as she holds my hair away from my face.

"Try on your dresses Mother. I want to see what they look like on you." Slowly, she releases my hair and it cascades past my elbows. She's right, it does look better pulled back.

Mother's first choice is a floor length, royal purple and white dress. It is short sleeved and fitted in all of the right areas to showcase Mothers' slender frame. Her second choice is pale lavender, mid-calf length, short sleeved as well. It is more airy than the other and the sleeves look like butterfly wings.

"Well, which one do you like best?"

"Oh, honey they are both so pretty," she says placing the second dress on the hanger. "I think I will ask Tory to make the final decision. After all, it is her special day."

She motions me toward the door. "Now then, grab that beautiful gown. It is my treat. You are going to be the most beautiful woman at the Gala this year.

"Thank you for the dress Mother." We are driving to the mall which is on the other side of town. Mother says she knows the perfect store to find items that will please me to wear. I tell her I just want something more grown up, nothing really fancy since I am the only one who will see them. She is opening up a lot today, about my past, and about my future. I feel like I can ask her just about anything.

"Mom?"

"Hmmm?"

"Do you think I will ever get married?"

Mother is very quiet and she keeps her eyes on the road. It takes her a few minutes to answer me.

"Emmy, there was a time when all I wanted was for you to wake up. Then all I wanted was for you to thrive in your schooling. I remember your piano teacher, Lisa, telling me how talented you were and all I wanted was to see you play. Every time I thought you were at your maximum, you were unable to achieve anymore," she clears her throat. "Well, you go on ahead and accomplish something no one expected from you. I believe now, more than I ever have before, you will accomplish everything you set out to do."

"How will I know when I am ready?"

"You mean, how will you know when you are ready to fall in love?"

I shake my head yes.

"Sweetie, when I met your father love, marriage, and children were the furthest thoughts from my mind. I remember him walking into class and choosing the seat right next to me. He hit me like a freight train. I ended up earning a "C" in the class because I spent more time staring at your father than listening to the teacher. At graduation, I told your father he was the sole reason I was not class valedictorian."

"So, you just knew he was the one?"

"There's really no other way to explain it. I wasn't looking for love when I met your father, but I knew what my life had been missing as soon as we started spending time together."

"Were you a virgin when you and Daddy got married?"

Mother stares at me for a split-second, and I realize I have caught her off guard with my question.

"Well," she says clearing her throat again. "Yes, I was a virgin when your father and I were married. But," she emphasizes the word, "I wasn't completely inexperienced." She glances over at me. My eyebrows are pinched together.

"So, you hadn't had sex with anyone… but you?"

"Yes, or um, no. I mean, no. I didn't have sex with anyone before marrying your father. But before we were married we did 'fool around a bit' if that makes sense."

Mother stops the car and I realize we have talked the entire drive to the mall. It is rare that we have this much to talk about. It feels good to ask her things and know I am going to get a straight answer.

"Are you ready to go shopping for some more, appropriate bras and panties?" She pats my knee and we are off.

Once we enter the store, I am taken aback by all of the choices. I'm not sure what the secret is about this store because everything you would possibly want or need in the likes of under garments is displayed quite beautifully. I walk over to a table with lace panties arranged in a circle. The sign reads 5 for $25, and I start looking for my size.

"Emmelia," Mother says from behind me. "Before we get too carried away, I want to have them measure you and find out which bras would fit best."

As if on command a young, full breasted woman appears with a measuring tape.

"Hello ladies, my name is Mandy. Is there something special I may help you find this afternoon?" She is cute, perky, and wearing way too much makeup. She looks like she just came from the cosmetic counter down the hall.

Mother explains I need to be measured and Mandy happily takes me into a fitting room and pulls a pink curtain. I remove my shirt and white front clasp bra and raise my arms out to my side. She's fast, which is appreciated. I just want to get some new bras and throw all of these ones away. She tells me she will write down my measurements and pull a few items from the store. She leaves and I proceed to put my shirt back on.

Mandy and Mother make quick work of finding choices for me. When I walk out of the fitting room, there is an array of strapless, lace, satin, multi-strapped. Some look padded while others do not, and they have chosen many different colors too.

I walk toward the counter as Mandy starts to explain the differences between the bras. Demi, semi, full-cup, push-up, padded, underwire, seamless—it's all overwhelming for someone has worn the same style of bra for the past decade. I end up choosing a demi in nude and a push-up in pale pink. Mother says I need a strapless bra for my dress and they have one in the same chocolate brown color. Mandy shows Mother a corset-style strapless contraption and Mother decides I need it as well. That one she chooses in black. I pick out some boy short style panties in colors matching my new bras as well as a couple of thongs because Mother says there are certain clothes you don't want to advertise a panty line.

Mother tells me to walk across the mall to the shoe store and she will meet me there. She says I need to pick out some shoes to go with my Gala dress. I do as I am told and walk across the mall to the shoe store. A young man greets me at the door and asks how my day is. "

Wonderful," I reply to him. I tell him I need a pair of shoes for a special event. He leads me over to an area where slickery shoes are on display. *Oh,* I think to myself, *thank goodness my kick ball days are behind me.*

He politely asks what size shoe I wear, and I tell him size six. He bustles around asking what color my dress is, how long it is, and so on. By the time Mother arrives, my sneakers and socks are sitting in a pile to my left and 'Brad' is lining up an assortment of fancy shoes.

Mother has four bright pink bags in her hands, each with white and pink tissue paper billowing out the top like cotton candy. She smiles and sets the bags next to me.

"Ooh, I really like these Em, try these on for me," she says as she picks up a pair of strappy brown heals. Brad sits at my feet and gently places the shoe over my heal and begins to lace the extravagant straps around my ankle.

"Now, we have these in a two, three, and four inch heal. Do you have a preference?" Brad asks looking first at me and then at Mother.

"I think a lower heal would be best, don't you?" I ask Mother.

"Mmm, yes, I think the two inch heals would be perfect. Can she try these as well?" Mother asks pointing to a pair of brown ballerina style slippers.

"I think I like the others better," I say to Mother, as I turn my foot to admire the slipper.

"I agree, and your dress is long enough to accommodate two more inches of height," she says and she purchases the shoes. Brad tries to sell her some gel insoles and waterproofing spray, but Mother declines while handing him her credit card.

We place the packages in the trunk and Mother asks where we need to go for the applications I filled out. I tell her all of the applications are for businesses on Main Street. She nods her head and we are on our way.

"How about we have dinner at Jackie's Place after we are finished?" I say as she parallel parks in front of Dan's Jewelry Store.

"Sure. In fact, I have a couple of stores I need to stop in, so how about we meet there in about 30 minutes," she says grabbing her purse. I tell her okay and tuck my applications under my arm.

I walk into Dan's Jewelry with my application ready. Dan is sitting behind the counter surrounded by sparkly diamonds.

"Well, good afternoon Emmelia Gage. You look well, how have you been?"

"I am doing well Mr. Wilkerson. It's nice to see you again," I reply walking toward him.

"I do hope you are not here to pick up Miss Tory's ring. I am afraid it is not sized yet," he says with a frown.

The funny thing about growing up in a small town is everyone knows who you are, who you are related to, and most of all everything has ever happened to you. Mr. Wilkerson's father was the man who helped my father pick out my Mother's wedding ring, and his son is the one Steve chose to trust with Tory's ring.

"No, no. I actually came by today to bring you an application. I am not sure if you are hiring," I stop and hand him the paper. He takes it and begins to read through it. I don't want to be rude and interrupt, so I begin looking at the cases filled with rings, necklaces, and bracelets. As I wander further to the back of the store, a baby grand piano catches my eye. It is white with a red velvet bench. I run my fingers softly over the ivory without making a sound, I pull the bench away and sit. The pedals are brass, gleaming and begging me to press them.

"You play?"

His voice startles me and I jump from the bench. "Yes, I-I am sorry, I just saw it sitting over here. It is a very special piano," I say trying to calm my nerves.

"You are correct. This is a very special piano. It was my daughter's and she played it every day here in the store. That is until she decided to get married and leave her old man," he smiles at me. "You may play it if you like. I was never talented enough or patient enough to learn. I crammed it back here because I was tired of all the little kids banging on the keys."

"Perhaps another time," I say. "I have a few more applications to drop off before I meet Mother for supper. Thank you though, it was very nice to see you again Mr. Wilkerson."

"Stop in anytime dear, and I will let you know if my summer help doesn't pan out." He gives me a hug and a quick peck on the cheek before returning to his stool behind the counter.

My next stop is two doors down. Readers Cove is a quaint little bookstore that serves pastries and tea. The owner, Jazz, doesn't believe coffee should be served with anything other than plain toast. Jazz and I would have graduated together if would have continued school. Walking through the door, I instantly smell lavender—so soothing and relaxing. The tables are empty and there are only a few people walking between the rows of books on display. I see Jazz standing near a large table. He's draping a bright yellow cloth over the round display table. I walk his way and notice he has box after box filled with the same books lying at his feet.

"Need some help?" I ask placing my applications on the nearby chair.

"Em! Holy moly! How have you been?" He asks as he wraps his arms around my waist. He grabs my hips and pushed me away looking at me the whole time. "Dang girl, you've grown up! You look fabulous."

I giggle, "Thanks. You look really good too! It has been too long! I mean, the last time I think I saw you was at the Gala last year. You and, um … Ben, right?"

"That was a while ago. Yeah, I was with Ben, wow! So he and I aren't a thing anymore. He decided to move to New York, and I decided he was an A-hole." We both laugh. Jazz is the only person I know who can bounce from one relationship to another without remorse or fear of rejection. "So what brings you in today, looking for the latest best seller?" He asks holding up a book from one of the boxes.

"No, I actually came into give you an application," I say, walking back over to the chair. "Here is it," I state, handing him the papers.

"Full-time or part-time? What are you looking for?"

I tell him I am looking for either, anything really, I just want to start saving up for a car and then move out of mom's house.

"Wow? Talk about waking from the dead," he says, and quickly frowns. "Sorry, I didn't mean it like it came out."

I laugh, "It's fine, glad to hear you're not one to hold back your real feelings."

Jazz offers me a job. It's four days-a-week to come in and help with the displays, clean the shelves, and a promise to teach me how to make his special lavender infused tea. I won't start for another three weeks. I am so excited by the time I get to Jackie's Place and find Mother in a booth drinking an iced tea. I tell her the news and she seems pleased as well.

"That poor boy has sure survived enough. I am glad he hired you. I think you both have a lot in common."

I am not sure what she means, and I am far too excited to ask any questions! I have checked off two items from the list. Dr. Weston is going to be proud of my progress.

Mother and I share a plate of nachos and finish our evening by carrying the purchases from the day into the laundry room. I hang my new gown on the back of the door and we start removing tags from my bras. Mother tells me to put them in the washer and instructs me on the correct wash cycle. She says I should never dry the bras as they will lose their shape. Hang and forget for a day she tells me. Panties get special treatment too. Air dry setting only and don't forget a dryer sheet. She says there's nothing worse than static cling on your bottom. I am exhausted from our day, so I tell Mother I will see her in the morning.

"Thank you for such a wonderful afternoon Mother. I had such a good time," I say kissing her cheek.

"Me too Emmelia, me too."

Katie's Drama

"So, why do you think he has had a change of heart?" I ask as I look through the clearance rack of summer tops.

"Your guess is as good as mine I suppose. He came home the other night and started talking about how empty the house is. How we don't have a legacy to leave when we're gone and then, oh geeze … who in their right mind would wear this?" She asked holding up a black lace top that probably wasn't meant to be worn alone. My first thought was Melanie of course, with her purple lace bra showing through.

"I don't know," I reply with a disgusted look on my face, and giggled under my breath.

"Anyway, so then he tells me we won't have anyone to take care of us when we are old and decrepit. Like that is the reason people decide to have kids these days!"

"I guess I don't understand what the big deal is. I mean, I think you would make a great Mother and you've always loved teaching."

"Teaching children and raising children are totally different Em. At school, I am only with them for a certain number of hours. I don't have to change diapers or clean up vomit, ghaw, just the thought of it makes my stomach sick. All that, and I get summers off. You don't get summers off when you're a parent. In fact, most kids these days don't even leave the nest until they are out of college," she says looking over at me.

"Or, something could happen and they don't leave home—ever," I say flashing her a dirty look.

"That's not what I mean. Your, um, situation is completely different. I am not talking about you when I refer to how long kids live with their parents. I'm sorry, it's just that we agreed when we got engaged kids were not part of our future and now he wants to reinvent the wheel. I am just really frustrated and I feel like he's doing this so he can have more control over me."

"How?" I ask completely perplexed.

"Well, if we have a kid or two, who do you think is going to have to stay home with them? You think he's going to quit his job? No, no, it will be me, stuck at home with screaming babies and stinky garbage cans just begging him to give me five minutes to take a shower."

"I think you might be overreacting a little, don't you? I might not know a lot about him, but from my viewpoint, it sounds like you are being really selfish."

"Selfish," she raises her voice and glares at me. "You have no idea what that word even means Emmelia. You have lived nearly your entire life in a precious little bubble protected from everything the rest of us have had to experience. Your Mother kept everything from you she thought would upset you. Why do you think we never played together or went anywhere together? You have no idea what 'real life' is even about. So don't ride your high horse and tell me that I am selfish!"

And that did it! The conversation ended and Katie asks if I can find another ride home. So this is what they mean when they say 'Drama Queen' I say to myself as I watch Katie stomp out of the store.

My What?

"MOTHER! MOM, PLEASE HURRY," I can hear my own screech in my head. Oh my gosh, I think I am dying and I don't know what to do. I hear the whoosh of the bathroom door opening and stand helplessly still as my Mother rips the shower curtain back. Her eyes are large and her color has faded in fear. She looks me over, up and down, and shakes her head quickly from side to side.

"What is the matter Emmelia? You nearly scared me to death. I thought you had hurt yourself," she stated still staring at me.

I couldn't move, I couldn't even breathe. I just started crying. Here I am standing, buck-naked, in the shower; sobbing hysterically trying to explain to my Mother without words I am dying right here in front of her. I feel weak, like my legs are going to give out at any minute so I lower myself into the bathtub, the shower still running. Mother isn't saying a word, she is just watching as I sit and continue to cry. I pull my knees to my chest and wrap my arms around them as if they would get away if I don't hold them in place. I drop my forehead until it hits my hands and close my eyes. I feel the convulsions running through my entire body. All this way and now I am going to die before I have really had a chance to live. I feel Mother place her hand on the top of my head in support. I can feel the steady stream of hot water trickle down my back but most of the spray is concentrated above my head.

I hear Mother take a deep, fast, inhale of breath. Like when you see a huge spider … or when a little kid on a bicycle almost collides with the curb … or when someone jumps out of the pantry to scare you … that kind of breath.

"Emmy, what happened? Where is it coming from? Emmelia, open your eyes. Look at me Emmelia," she says with pure panic in her voice.

Slowly, I open my eyes and raise my head toward my Mother's voice. She looks like she has seen a ghost.

"I think I am dying," I say to her and then I look down at my feet. There is a river of pink water running from between my legs into the drain. I am slowly bleeding to death.

"Emmy, where did you hurt yourself? Did you cut your leg shaving? Honey, please tell me what happened," she is frantic and prying at my legs. How do I tell her I was simply washing and the cloth came out red, blood stained from in between my legs? I hadn't even thought about shaving my legs this morning. I don't know what happened to me. I just started bleeding for no reason at all.

"I-I wasn't shaving, I-I," I stutter through the crying. "I was just washing and," I hold up the washcloth and show her the stripe of blood. I am crying even harder and I look at my Mother through my tears.

I am fighting against Mother's hands as she tries to pull my legs apart and I am thinking the very worst thoughts I have had since the days I lay in total darkness. I finally give into to her strength and allow her the opportunity to inspect my most private of areas. All of a sudden, Mother begins to cry and she is mumbling something about miracles.

You think it is a miracle that I am dying here in the shower with you staring at my nether region? "Mother! What are you doing?" I ask as she turns away from me and opens one of the bathroom cabinets. She's pulling out towels and setting them on the counter. "I have a towel Mother, what are you doing?"

"Emmelia Elizabeth Gage, you are not dying dear. You are having your period," she replies with a huge smile across her lips.

"My what?"

I remember hearing a conversation my Mother had with the brown light doctor. It was right around the time I got fitted for a bra, I think. Anyway, he was telling Mother that, most likely, I would not have a normal menstrual cycle and is likely may never have a period at all. I recall Mother saying it was probably best since it would unlikely I would have the mental capacity to raise children in my condition.

I remained seated in the tub while I watched Mother pull a clear tote from the cupboard. *So, does this mean I can have children?* I have never even thought about raising children or ... wait, it's all coming back. The sex education book my teacher had years ago. The anatomically correct (as she put it) drawings of the male and female reproductive organs.

"Okay Emmy," Mother interrupts. "Stand up now, let's get you dried off," she says holding a towel. I do as she asks and stand up just as a large amount of blood runs down my leg. I look up at her in shock.

"Really? I'm not dying?" I ask as I motion to the trail leading down my inner thigh.

"No, you're not dying, now rinse and hurry it up."

I step out of the shower and dry myself off.

"Alright, so we have options, but I am a little low on supplies so we will have to make due for now," Mother says as she hands me my underwear. "Now pull these on, just above your knees and then," she says as I am pulling them on. "Here, take this," she says handing me a small white pouch. "Open it up, it won't bite," she giggles.

I am still in shock standing in front of my Mother as she laughs at my terror. I've got my undies positioned just above my knees and I'm opening this weird, thick, long... pad. She tells me to remove the strip from the back which I do. There are three lines of what look like sticky tape on the bottom of the pad. She tells me to position the pad here, as she points to my panties. She says "That's all there is to it." I pull up my panties. It feels really awkward, I don't want to move. Mother retrieves a pair of sweatpants for me and tells me to take it easy today. *Yeah, what else would I be doing? I have a ginormous pad between my legs that make me walk like a duck! Lovely, just lovely!*
A few days later...

So, the blood bath/period/aunt flow thing is finally over. Mother decided we needed to go to the store and stock up on personal hygiene products so that is what we did. A little adventure to the grocery store with a list in hand. WHO IN THE WORLD prices this stuff? I swear, as Mother and I stood before a wall of maxi-mini-overnight, panty-liner, teeny, thong-style pads I began to wonder how normal women afford to have a period every month. Oh, and then there were shelves and shelves of junior, normal, super, super-plus tampons which come in every color under the sun! Some have applicators, some do not; some proclaim ultimate comfort, and other claim ultimate protection.

Mother tells me there are a lot more selections now compared to when she used to shop for these items. She's not really sure what to recommend. We read the labels and I look at the shape depicted on the front of the packaging trying to find the thinnest pads possible. It's like squeezing toilet paper to feel how soft it will be but instead, I just want to find something that feels less like a box of tissue.

After making our selections, we walk up to the checkout counter. The cashier gives us an odd look and begins ringing everything up. Since I only utilized nine pads during my first encounter, I can see why she's giving us the look. We could have been supplying a small village of menstruating women for a year or so. The total comes to $180 exactly and a whopping 16 bags! I wish I could say I was mortified by the experience. But, honestly, I can't wait to try some of them out. (Odd I know.)

The OBGYN

Mother leaves the exam room after explaining to me for the 'ump-teenth' time this is a normal appointment, "Don't feel embarrassed. You'll need to do this every year now to make sure you are healthy."

The female doctor walks into the exam room followed by a female nurse. The doctor positions herself at the foot of the examination table that I am laying on. She introduces herself and her assistant. She precedes to tell me what is going to happen during my examination. She must have already spoken to Mother, because she spends the first five minutes or so telling me I need to relax and breathe. This will be quick and there is nothing to worry about. She shows me a white, egg-shaped object and tells me it will feel cool. She tells me many times to relax my knees and at one point I lean up on my elbows to see what's going on.

Holy moly Martha May-who! The doctor's head in between my knees and the egg thingy is going in my … ouch! I lay back down as she is telling me I will feel a little pressure after I hear a couple of clicking sounds. Sure enough, click, click, and click … ugh. She reminds me again to relax. She wants me to relax my knees! *Seriously?* I already feel like they can't open any further, I look down at them. Okay, they are almost closed. I laugh at myself and start to relax them just a little bit more.

"Knock, knock," my Mother's voice sounds at the door. Instinctively, I slam my legs shut and smack the doctor on either side of her head with the inside of my knees.

"Ouch!" She says trying to remove her head from my panicked grip. I apologize and try to explain that the door scared me. She tells me it's fine. It has happened to other doctors although she said this was the first time it had happened to her. Mother made her way into the room and sat down near my head. I relax a little and after a poke, a swab, and three reverse clicks, I was free to get dressed. Mother spoke to the doctor about birth control pills and the two of them decided they were the way to go. After hearing the explanation and realizing it would keep my moods more even, lessen the amount of time I was having a period, and make sure everything was regulated, I was fine with the decision as well. Although, taking medication every day, was not something I was looking forward to doing again.

I Need to See Him

It has been so long since they buried him and I have yet to visit him. Other than the night he came to see me, to plead with me to tell someone about the accident. I think about him all of the time. I miss him, and I can't help but wonder if, in fact, he was able to get into Heaven. I want to go, and see for myself, where he has been laid to rest. I want to be alone, but I don't want to upset Mother. She has been easily angered these past few weeks. I grab the telephone and quickly dial the only number that comes to mind.

"Hey Emmy! What's up sis?"

"Tylar, I need a favor," I say into the receiver.

"Sure, anything," he replies.

"Can you come and get me? I want to go see dad."

There is a long pause in our conversation and I am worried I have upset Tylar. Of all of my brothers, Tylar is the one who never asks questions. He takes me at my word and never tries to read into what I am requesting, but the quietness is beginning to make me feel unsure of myself.

"Em, are you sure you want to do this? "

"I do, I really need you to take me there. Please Tylar," I plead.

"Okay Bug, give me a few minutes and I will come and get you."

"Thanks Ty. I love you," I say and hang up the phone.

A few minutes later, Tylar walks through the front door holding his sunglasses. He gives me a big hug and we leave mom's house.

"Where's mom?" he asks opening the passenger side door for me.

"She had an appointment this afternoon. She didn't say where, just that she would be home by supper time," I reply sliding into his car. He closes the door and makes his way around the front of the car.

"Does she know you called me?"

"Nope, and I don't really want her to know that you are taking me out there. It will only upset her and I really don't need any more drama at home if you know what I mean," I say in sarcastic tone. Tylar takes the parking break off and gently releases the clutch. We back out of the driveway, and I pay close attention to the symmetry of Tylar's movements as he changes gears. I will have to drive a stick shift for my DMV test in a few weeks and I have yet to try one.

"Do you think, now that I have my learner's permit and all, maybe I could drive with you?"

"You want to try and drive this beast?" He laughs and looks over at me. "Sure, we can go out and find a vacant parking lot or something."

We sit in silence as Tylar navigates the streets. He pulls up to the cemetery gate and looks over at me. "Are you sure you want to do this?" he asks in a whisper.

"Yes. But I don't want you to go over there with me. I know it sounds weird, but I have some things I need to talk to dad about."

"'s not weird at all Em, you never had the same opportunity to say goodbye that the rest of us had. I understand completely you want to be alone. I will show you where it is, and then I will wait for you in the car if that's what you want."

I nod my head yes and he pulls the parking brake then turns off the car. The gravel crunches under our feet as we walk down the pathway. He tells me it is the last grave on the right. I tell him I'm okay and I will try to be quick. I hear him walking away and I start to move forward again. I notice as I get closer, dad is buried by himself in a very large plot. There are several graves to the right of him but nothing but green grass to the left. His headstone is large and, as I kneel in front of it, I notice his badge is pressed into the cement. The grass is warm and dry, but plush and green. There are yellow roses in the flower container to my left. I rest back on my heals and gently touch the top of the headstone. I run my fingertips down one side and slowly graze over his police badge.

William Henry Gage
Respected Law Enforcement Officer
Beloved Husband and Father

I brush my hand across the inscription and read aloud as I go. It is warm to the touch but rough, uninviting. I fold my hands in my lap and whisper to him.

"Daddy, I don't know if you can hear me, but I want you to know that I am sorry. I am sorry it has taken me so very long to come and see you. I am trying so hard to be brave for you. I am trying to put all of the pieces together but it is hard and I get mad. I get so angry with Mother, and I know I shouldn't. I can't understand why I haven't seen you again. Why didn't you come back? Why didn't you let me know what happened after I told the white angel? I know it was her I was supposed to tell, but I never knew if you went to Heaven or not. It bothers me to think you are still out there, in between here and there."

"I miss you Daddy—I miss you every day. There are days which are so hard ... so aggravating I think I would have been better off if I hadn't survived the accident. I can't tell anyone though, they would worry and most likely put me on medication."

"Daddy, I don't know if I can move forward any further until I know you are okay. You're not rotting away underneath me. That you were able to get to where you needed to be. I need you to watch over me and help me overcome all of this drama everyone else deals with easily. I don't know what to do. I don't know who I am supposed to be. I don't know what I should do to make you proud of me. Please Daddy, please let me know you are okay.

The tears are running down my cheeks two at a time, and I cannot bring myself to open my eyes. I want to see him and I believe if I just wait, he will be there. In my mind ... in my soul. I wait and nothing happens. I know Tylar will be upset knowing I have been crying, but I cannot stop the tears. I miss him, I feel guilty for not coming here sooner. I need an answer, but no matter how long I keep my eyes closed, nothing appears to me. I unclasp my hands and wipe my eyes, then my cheeks, then my nose. I open my eyes and look straight ahead at his headstone.

There is a white butterfly facing me. It is slowly opening and closing its white wings but otherwise, it is not moving at all. My body relaxes and I feel my pupils dilate. I know I should sit still but I can't. I lean forward and whisper to the butterfly, "Thank you Daddy, I love you."

I walk back to Tylar who asks if I am okay. I assure him I am, and he drives me back to Mother's not asking anything else. I appreciate the silence as he drives.

Over My Dead Body

"Edna, if she finds out on her own, it will only make things more difficult to explain," Jenny says firmly.

"As much as I want to agree with you Dear, I just don't think now is the best time to tell her. She's only just beginning to discover her memories, and her potential. I don't think telling her is going to make forward progression impossible. I think there will be a more appropriate time to tell her. After she has had a chance to adjust to her newly found life."

"What has she told you? What does she remember from that day?" Jenny pressed.

"She remembers everything. She says she remembers everything," Edna looks down at the floor. "But, of course, there's no way to know for sure if her memory is correct," she looks up and glares, "because everyone else who was involved day is dead," she states coolly.

"Did she say anything about him?" Jenny asked her voice cracking.

Mother held up her hand. "Yes, she remembers his hand. She said it was rough and scratchy on her arm. She said she was trying to run away but he was holding her too tightly. She remembers him shooting her father and watching as he father fell to the pavement returning fire. She remembers her Daddy shooting her, Jenny! Is that what you want to know?"

"What else? What else does she remember, Edna?" her voice frantic.

"She said she remembered his hand behind her head. She said that he laid her down on the sidewalk. That is all, that was all," and she covers her face.

"Whose hands? Whose hands were behind her head? Edna," she yelled, pulling Mothers hands away from her face. "Who helped her lie down on the sidewalk?"

"Your Father!" Mother is sobbing. "She said she remembers his hand behind her head lowering her body. The hand belonging to the old man who shot her father. She said he swore and she heard him run from the scene," Mother cries.

"That explains all of the blood on his clothing when they found him," she said in a whisper. "I need to tell her! I need to tell her who I am before someone else does. She's no longer protected in this house, under your roof. Edna, she's out there, in the community and someone will say something."

Mother wipes her cheeks with the back of her hand and takes two deep breathes before placing both of her hands, palm side down, on the tops of her thighs.

"Over my dead body," she says leaning closer. "I will tell Emmelia—MY daughter—when I believe she is ready to deal with the truth. You, Jenny ... you will leave well-enough alone and keep your mouth shut. Do I make myself clear?"

Jenny lowers her head and her voice, "Yes ma'am. I understand."

Yettie

The written/book portion of the class is finished. I ended up with a B on the final exam which means I must receive a D on the driving portion in order to pass the class. Tylar is on his way to take me to a vacant parking lot. He says it will be a little easier to 'master the clutch' with no other vehicles pressuring me to make a move. I told him I needed to practice parallel parking as well. I am not too sure how this will work in a parking lot missing other cars and I assume we will do that portion somewhere else.

"Are you ready for this," he asks while holding open the door?

"Uh-huh," I giggle, "but are you?"

"Ha! You won't scare me; I am more worried about the car! Does mom know that we are doing this?"

"I told her yesterday about it, but when I got up this morning she was already gone. She left a note on the table though. It said she had a meeting and I was supposed to be careful. I'm not sure where her meeting was, but there's pork chops sitting out on the counter, so I assume she'll be home by supper."

We pull into the old Shop 'n Go parking lot and we switch seats. This is the first time I have driven a stick shift so Tylar gives me the run down. 'Give her gas and let out the clutch at the same time. You want to do it evenly, so more gas, less clutch.'

The car lurches then stalls. Tylar is laughing. Again, lurch, lurch, and stall. I am not laughing as I turn the key to start the car again. We go through this another dozen times before I finally get the hang of it.

"I think that's enough for today," Tylar says pulling on the parking break. "If you think you need more practice, I had better get a new clutch installed," he's laughing again.

As I walk around the car and hand Tylar his keys, I wrinkle my nose up. "What's that smell?" I ask him.

"Uh, that's my clutch Em, I think you done burned it up," he says, but he's laughing so hard I don't know if he's serious or not.

He drops me back of at mom's house and we see her car in the driveway. I thank Tylar for taking me out to practice and we make a plan for parallel parking next week. He says we will take mom's car because it would be easier.

I stall only once and it was right off the bat. The parallel parking went well and thankfully, I had to park between bright orange cones rather than real vehicles. I am nervous as I sit and wait for the instructor to add up my score. It is taking him forever! I woke up late this morning because I forgot to set my alarm. Thankfully, Steve and Tory came over to pick up some wedding stuff that was delivered to mom's house last week. Tory woke me up asking when my test was and when I told her it was at nine thirty, she totally freaked out. I was ready in 15 minutes and they drove me. I think Mother is picking me up, but I am not sure. Steve thought she had another appointment this afternoon, which seems odd she would have two appointments in the same day. She's been having a lot of appointments lately.

"Emmelia, your score is seventy-two," Mr. DMV instructor blurts out. "Congratulations, you've passed the course," he says with a smile.

He hands me a green sheet of paper and tells me to take it to the counter and they will process my Driver's License. I am so excited I run through the doors and forget to look for my Mother. There isn't anyone waiting at the counter and there is a really nice looking lady motioning me forward with a wave.

I hand her my green paper, and start digging in my purse for the envelope containing all of the other paperwork requested on the checklist. I place the envelope on the counter and watch as 'Lynn' according to her name badge, quickly types on the computer. She places all of the paper back into the envelope hands it back to me then staples some more papers to the green one and places it in a basket.

"Alright, that will be $59.12 please," as she hold out her hand, palm side up. I grab my wallet and hand her my debit card. She asks me to put in my pin number on the key pad. I enter 2580 and press the green button. While we are waiting for the machine, she asks me to sign my name here, as she points to a little black tablet and explains to me that it needs to be my legal signature. I do the whole loopty E's and finish with a wispy rendition of Gage. I hear the receipt printing and she hands me my copy and debit card and asks I go to the end of the counter for my picture.

Oh my gosh, I forgot all about the picture part! I look like I haven't showered or fixed my hair because I HAVEN'T! Oh no, oh great! I want to ask her if I can come back later for the picture part, but I don't think they do things like that. I stand in front a blue sheet and she tells me to smile but before I can even comprehend what I am being asked to do, the camera flashes and it's over.

She tells me it will take just a few minutes to print out a paper copy and the hard copy will come in the mail in a few days. I wait at the edge of the counter until finally she brings me a paper, the black and white version of my Driver's License. Oh dear, I am going to hate this picture in color. There's a huge cowlick on the left side of my head, causing my hair to stick up. And, because I didn't even brush my hair this morning, it is all matted down and I can almost see what looks like the making of a dreadlock. My eyes are scrunched together like I am trying to figure out an algorithm and my head is cocked to one side like I can't hear anything. My lips are wretched up and it looks like I am sneering, or growling. I shake my head and place the flimsy piece of paper in my wallet.

This will be a daily reminder to set my alarm for future appointments! I hope nobody wants to see the proof... I will just show them the receipt. I wrestle with my purse and push the front doors open. I scan the parking lot for Mother, but I don't see her car.

"Emmelia, over here," I hear Tory yell. I walk toward her as she is raises her arms out to her side. "Well, did you pass?"

I shake my head yes and feel lips part to reveal a huge smile. "I did! I got a seventy-two on the driving test. I stalled once, but did excellent on the parallel parking part." She wraps her arms around my neck and squeezes really hard.

"I knew you would! I am so proud of you! So, let me see it, let me see this brand new license!"

I hand her my wallet and she opens the clasp. She says nothing at first and then she starts laughing. "Oh my! Now that is a photo you don't want to post on-line! Don't worry though, once you get a new address, you can go have a new picture taken. I mean, unless this one is what you expected," she suddenly looked serious.

"Are you kidding? I look like a yettie!"

"A yettie?"

"Yeah, you know, the scary white snowman thingy children are taught to fear in the winter time in Norway, or somewhere like that."

"You don't look that bad, just disheveled. Almost like you didn't plan on passing the test!"

We walk toward Tory's car and I say, "Yeh, or I forgot to set my alarm," and we both start laughing.

An Idea

"Steve? Honey, are you home?"

"Tory, I'm in the kitchen. How did she do?"

"Good, she passed the test and has her license as we speak. You know, I was thinking it is about time I upgrade to a bit larger car. We've talked about a four door and well, what would you think about giving Em the Honda? I mean, she's going to need a car to get to work, and…" Tory trailed off waiting for a response from Steve.

"I think that's a really good idea sweetie," he said kissing the top of her head. "We should probably run it by Mother and make sure she doesn't already have something in mind for Emmy. I mean, I think what you want to do is perfect, but we need to ask Mother before presenting it to Em."

"Speaking of your Mother, and I don't want to overstep here, but have you noticed she has had a lot of appointments lately? Is everything okay with her?"

Steve places the newspaper on the counter and looks down at Tory seated on the barstool. "I haven't really thought about it. I know we, well you, have been running all over getting the wedding stuff figured out and all. Hmmm. I can ask her this Sunday during dinner."

No Fighting

"Mom, I have to go to the bookstore. Jazz is having a big book signing tomorrow and he needs help putting everything together. Mom?"

"Okay," I hear her holler from the laundry room. "If you get done early enough, bring him over for dinner."

"Thanks Mrs. Gage," Jazz says as we race out the front door. "Your mom is actually pretty cool ya know?"

"Yes, she is pretty cool," I reply while putting on my seatbelt. When we arrive at the bookstore the lights are on and there are boxes all over the place. I look over at Jazz and he explains he was trying to get it all done himself and then realized it was just too much stuff to do for one person. He thanks me a hundred times while we are carrying boxes and table clothes.

He has set up a leather recliner behind a large round table in the corner and we are filling the table with a paperback version and hardback version of the same book. I read the inside cover and realize this is a local author. Jazz says the book is a Sci-Fi story and has been flying off the shelves, partly because the author is local. Well, pretty local, he lives only thirty minutes from here which is why he agreed to do the book signing.

There are five more boxes. We remove hardback copies and stack neatly on a rectangular table near the front door. Jazz tells me to grab the boxes of markers on the counter and find a basket to place them in. Of course, what he means is, find a basket and fill it with tissue paper which matches the book cover and doesn't clash with the table clothes. Then, place all of the markers so they are facing the same direction. It's funny, after only two weeks of working for Jazz, I understand what he is implying but never says. I had made the mistake of serving a cup of tea without a saucer. You would have thought the entire world was going to come to a complete stop and explode.

Three hours later and Reader's Cove is ready for its first book signing. It looks amazing and very retro-chic with just enough chrome to give the feel of Sci-Fi. I think I will ask Jazz to help me decorate when I get an apartment. He definitely has an eye for style.

"Should we head over to my brothers' house and see what there is for supper," I ask walking toward the door?

"Sounds good to me. You're sure I'm invited?"

I give him the look I usually reserve for Katie or my brothers. The one that says, 'seriously?' and then I slug him on the arm. *Katie, I haven't spoken to her for over three weeks. I wonder if I should call, or just let her cool off. Although, I am still not sure what I did that could have irritated her so badly.*

Sunday Supper

"Mom! Hey, come in. Tory and I are in the kitchen just finishing up," Steve yells toward the front door.

"Oh, wow! Look at all of this. What's the occasion?" Mother asks looking at the large number of plates on the counter.

"Well, Tory wanted to get everyone's opinion on the food for the wedding. She had a heck of a time getting the caterer to deliver all of this stuff to the house. Especially on Sunday, I swear," he winks at Tory, "this woman has the power of suggestion."

"Edna, where's Emmelia?" Tory asks looking outside.

"Oh, she had to go in and help Jazz. I guess he's having a book signing tomorrow and he's in panic mode. I told them to come over after they were finished."

Tory looked over at Steve who shook his head giving her his silent approval.

"Edna, Steve and I have been considering well, discussing our transportation needs. We are looking at upgrading to a four door. Now, I know it's an older car and everything, but I can assure I have maintained it well. It runs great and we were thinking of giving it to Emmelia. But," she added quickly, "we wanted to run it by you first and see what you thought."

"Yeh, so what do you think mom? Win-win right?"

"I think it is a very generous offer Tory. And yes, it is a win-win Steven. But..."

Tory and Steve look over at one another questionably.

"But," she continues, "Your sister may not accept a car as a gift."

"What do you mean?"

"Steve, she's trying to find her independence. She is desperate to prove to herself she is capable of providing for her own needs. I am not suggesting you cannot give her a car. But maybe consider selling it to her for a manageable amount.

"'s actually a really good idea mom," he says while looking at Tory. "That will give her instant ownership and if we have her pay every month, she would really get a quick life lesson on payments."

"Okay, well I will go along. I just want it known I do not like the idea I am taking money from your sister for something I wanted to give her for free," Tory states. Steve kisses the top of her head and promises they will do something for Emmy with the money.

"Mom, Tory and I have been noticing," Steve looks over to Tory then continues, "you have had a lot of appointments lately. We just wanted to make sure everything okay with you."

Edna turned toward her son and the tears began to swell in her eyes. "I was really hoping to keep this to myself until it came time to go."

"Go where," Tory asks with a look of pure horror on her face?

"To go and finally see William again sweetheart. I have been attending chemotherapy treatments for a few months now. I didn't want you children to worry."

"You have cancer? Mother, what kind?"

"Stage four lymphoma." The treatments are small doses of radiation. I could have gone for a more aggressive form of treatment, but the hair loss and fatigue would have been too much for me to handle. Please don't be upset darling." Edna reaches over the island and takes Steve's hand. "I have lived a long life, fulfilling life, raised four wonderful children, and I am ready. I cannot, rather, I choose not to fight my way through this." The tears fall as the front door opens.

"Anyone home," Tylar yelled from the front door. "Corbin called me and said he was going to be a few minutes late. Something about Julie needing him to drop something off at her office," he said walking into the kitchen. "I never pretend to understand that relationship. I mean, Tory I have seen you more at Sunday dinners in the last year than I have seen Julie in the past eight!"

"Tylar, don't start, and don't judge your brother or his wife. Their relationship works for them therefore, it works with us," Mother says in her this is the way it's going to be voice.

"Where's Em?"

"She will be late as well. She is at the bookstore with Jazz," Tory answers.

"Jazz? Who's Jazz? Male or female?"

"Sorry, sorry. Jazz is a boy. Actually he is Emmelia's boss. And I have no idea… nor will you ask should he show up."

"Ask which question? Whether he is gay or if he's dating my little sister? What kind of name is Jazz anyway?"

"Tylar."

"Sorry Mother, I promise to be on my best behavior," Tylar says opening the fridge and pulling out a soda. Turning toward the counter Tylar realizes he had interrupted something. His Mother's eyes are red and Tory is looking down at the platters of food on the counter.

"Mom has cancer," Steve blurts out staring at Tylar.

The questions continue to be asked and answered throughout the evening while the food on the counter remains untouched. Corbin and Julie sit together at the table while Tylar, Steve and Tory remain in the kitchen listening intently for Emmelia to arrive.

The Funeral

It's Saturday afternoon and the house is eerily quiet. The funeral was exactly one week ago and although I know she's gone, I still expect to see her when I walk into the kitchen. Instead, all I see are the dirty dishes I left in the sink last night after making myself some macaroni and cheese.

I unload the dishwasher and place the dirty dishes on the racks. I fill the tea kettle with water and turn on the stove. While I am waiting for the water to boil, I wipe down the counters and pull down her tea cup. I rest against the counter and wait.

After five minutes of silence, the tea kettle whistles. I place a bag of lavender tea in the cup and watch the clear water begin to turn a light purple. I am restless today—the tea is too hot to drink and I don't have the patience to wait for it to cool naturally. I walk to the freezer to retrieve an ice cube. I drop it into the hot water and watch as it slowly dissolves. Smaller and smaller, it melts away until it disappears completely. It reminds me of Mother's last week of life.

Hospice had delivered a special bed for her and set it up in her room. The last six days of her life were spent lying in a partially inclined position staring blankly at the ceiling.

On Friday, she called each of us, one-by-one, to her bedside. I am not sure what she told my brothers or Tory but she told me I needed to continue to grow. She told me that I am fully capable of doing anything that I set my mind to.

She handed me an envelope with my name written on the front in her handwriting. She told me to remember to forgive. Not to hold grudges, and always be kind to others.

I look over at the dining room table. The envelope sits alone still unopened.

Her funeral was small. Consisting of a graveside memorial. Corbin wanted to do more for her, but he said he would abide by her wishes. Jenny was the only one present who spoke on behalf of our family. She shared stories of my father and the love he had not only for all of us, but for our Mother. How they were once again united in Heaven and watching over us.

Corbin, Steve, Tylar and I all placed white roses on the top of Mothers' casket. Tory placed a pink rose and Jenny laid a yellow rose in the center of ours. We all held hands and watched as four men lowered her body into the ground.

The emptiness I felt that day was only overshadowed by the grief and despair shared by my brothers. Now, alone in her home, I am feeling anxious and unsettled. Corbin told us Mother left the house to the four of us to split should we all decide to sell it. My brothers decided it wasn't a good time to sell and it was ultimately up to me whether I wanted to keep the house or move out. I told them I would actively look for an apartment. But today, I am not actively doing anything other than watching the ice cubes melt in a small tea cup.

I know I have to move soon. If I stay here much longer I am afraid I won't have the energy to move forward.

The Final Gala

  I told my brothers I would meet them there. I just want to take my time getting ready. I take the dress Mother purchased for me and remove the plastic bag.

  Further back in my closet, I pull out the shoe box. I haven't even looked at them since that day. I open my dresser drawer and remove the black corset and lace thong panties. I think back to my Mother saying, "There are just some occasions a girl doesn't want to advertise panty lines'. I think this is just one of those occasions Mother was referring to.

  The hot rollers have been plugged in for a few minute now and I am pretty sure they are hot. I push in the plunger and turn the hot water on. I sprinkle some rose scented bath salts into the stream of water and return to the mirror.

  Sectioning my hair, I carefully roll each segment around a large roller and pin it in place. After securing the last one, I unplug the contraption and turn off the water. Steam is rolling out of the tub as I drop my robe to the floor.

  I slowly lower myself into the hot, rose scented water. I close my eyes and rest my head back until the curlers make contact with the ledge. I remember sitting on the bathroom floor coloring while my Mother would lie back as I am now. The bathroom smelled of roses, just as it does now.

  Sometimes we would talk, but most of the time she would just quietly lay back and breathe. I miss her dearly.

  The water turns tepid so I drain the water, dry myself off and apply lotion. I shaved this morning, hoping any little red bumps would be gone by the time I needed to get ready. Thankfully, I didn't nick myself once with the razor, which for me is a miracle. I swear, the skin behind my knees must be as thin as a piece of tracing paper. I purchase a new lotion just for tonight. It has a bronze shimmer to it and the girl at the counter selling it said it would make me look like I was just kissed by the sun. *'s the only thing I've been kissed by* I wanted to tell her, but I didn't. I pull my robe back on and grab my laptop. This was the first thing I purchased with my paycheck. Corbin sold it to me for fifty dollars because he said he just didn't need it any longer.

I connect to the internet and type in 'smokey eyes' and press enter. A ton of pictures come to life on the screen. I scroll until I find eyes similar to mine in both color and shape. I line up my brushes and eye shadow. I apply a layer of foundation and then some brightener on my eyelids. I put a little concealer under my eyes and on the bridge of my nose. Powder to set the foundation and then I apply a layer of light cream colored eye shadow from lid to brow. The picture shows a deep copper from the lid to crease so I follow suit. Not too bad if I do say so myself as I look at myself in the mirror. Next is a dark brown from the outer corners to the crease. This one's a little trickier but I manage to get both sides pretty equal. I take the brown eyeliner pencil and draw a broad line over the top lid. Then, I sharpen the pencil and make a fine line across the bottom lid. The photo says smudge under it and it shows a photo of a cotton swab. I smudge a little then a lot. It's starting to look like the picture and I am really excited!

Next is the blush. A light peach tone is what is recommended so I dig though my supply of make-up. Cheek bones done, now for mascara. Layer, layer, blink, blink and my eyes are nearly finished. I lean in closer to the mirror and brush my eyebrows upward and then smooth them into a neat line. I apply a neutral tone of lip line and a pale peach gloss. The face is finished and I am very proud of the way the make-up on my face looks pretty close to the face on my computer.

Now I type in 'updo' and press enter. Awe the things I can accomplish with the internet. While I am waiting for the page to load, I take out the cooled off curlers and place them back where they belong.

Photos are up and I start scrolling through them with renewed energy. Mother said my hair needs to be worn up to show off my shoulders and my neck. Okay, mom, help me out here… which one, which one?

As I scroll, I come across a photo of a girl who has her hair pulled up into a loose, messy bun. The hair is really cute, but what gets my attention is the tattoo in the middle of her neck. It is a butterfly! Alright, there's my sign. Thanks mom!

It takes 18 bobby pins and two crystal covered clips to achieve the end result. I hold the hand mirror over my shoulder and check it out. *Dang, for a newbie, this isn't too bad at all!* Maybe I have a future in hair design. (No, not really, but it really doesn't look too bad at all.)

"Good evening Miss Gage, you look lovely tonight," Gregory says holding the large door for me.

I lean in close to him and whisper, "Thank you Gregory." There are two men at the elevator dressed the same as Gregory. White tuxedos with white roses in the lapel.

"Good evening Miss Gage. Please enjoy your evening," they both look at one another and the taller one smiles. "I'm sorry dear, I didn't mean to sound insensitive. We are all saddened by the sudden loss of your Mother. Please accept our condolences sweetheart," he says and squeezes my hand.

"Forgiven, and thank you. I know she loved this event more every year that we came. I know she and my father are both with is this evening," and I step into the elevator.

"Emmelia! Wow, you look amazing."

I turn to see who is speaking and recognize Jazz. "What are you doing here tonight? Are you operating the elevator?"

"Yeh, Jenny was short-handed and I offered. Sheesh girl, if I knew you cleaned up this well, I would have expected more out of you at work! Hmmm," he says with an odd look on his face.

"Good-bye Jazz, I will see you in a few hours." I exit the elevator and take a deep breath.

The first thing I notice when I step through the threshold is the color Jenny has chosen to decorate with. Yellow, the color of my Mother's light. My breath is taken away as I look at each table. The linens are pale yellow and each table has a large center piece filled with white and yellow roses. Each rose is in its own vase and I assume Jenny did this so each guest could take one home after the evening is over.

I think of the flowers we laid on Mothers' casket.

The chairs are covered in shear white fabric, each tied in the back with a satin yellow bow.

The twinkle lights are bright white and yellow. It's perfect and I know my Mother would be pleased. On the back wall, where the photos of my father are usually hung; there are pictures of my Mother. Some are with her and my father together, while some are with her and the four of her children. There is one in particular that must have been taken the year my father died. It is a family portrait I have never seen before. We all look so young and healthy and I stare at the perfect family as though I hardly recognize the people standing and smiling for the camera.

I am suddenly aware the room is silent and everyone has stopped whatever they were doing and they are staring at me.

I look in the direction of my family's table and see Corbin and Julie holding hands. Tory is smiling at me and Steve has his hand on her leg. I look for Tylar but he's not at the table.

As I continue to scan the room I notice a familiar face staring back at me. He's wearing a police uniform. It is the same person I saw at the diner with Katie. She told me I would remember him, but I don't. I can't figure out why he is someone I recognize, I don't even know his name. He smiles and I smile shyly back.

"Emmelia Elizabeth Gage," a man whispers in my ear.

Startled from my thoughts, I turn around and see my brother Tylar. His elbow is popped out giving the impression he is my escort tonight. I tuck my arm the crook and he begins leading me to our table.

"You look all grown up Emmy, I hardly recognized you. In fact, I think most of the room was trying to figure out who you are. By the looks on the faces, I am thinking I should have brought a gun," Tylar says as he winks and we make out way across the large room. When we reach our table, he pulls my chair out.

"No guns tonight, and thank you Ty," I reply as I adjust my dress and take a seat.

Our center piece is like the others except there are four white roses, one yellow and one pink. Ours though, is in a single vase. Jenny thought of everything.

I lean toward Corbin, "Has anyone seen Jenny tonight?"

"No, as a matter of fact, I haven't," he replies.

's odd, she usually waits by the front door for us to arrive. I look over toward the door once more and then again around the room, but I still don't see her.

Tory leans across the table to ask me where I found my dress. She says it is very elegant. I tell her I saw it at Janessa's when we were looking for bride's maid dresses.

Her face drops a fraction, no one else would have noticed, but I did. She tells me I look like a goddess. She tells me my hair and makeup is flawless.

After Mothers' death, Tory cancelled the wedding. Not postponed or rescheduled, no she cancelled the wedding. She said a celebration was not an appropriate reaction to the events that transpired within the family. Steve was upset, but he said he would support her.

I think Mother would be disappointed. I think she would want Steve and Tory to get married and celebrate their love for one another. I was told by Steve that this is something that was Tory's decision and we were not to argue or try to persuade her otherwise. Still, I think it is a mistake.

I tap on Tory's shoulder and ask her if she recognizes the Officer in the corner by the photo wall. I watch as she nonchalantly scans the room. She catches his eye and he begins to walk toward our table. Tory places her hand on my knee under the table.

He stops at the head of our table and says hello to Miss Garrison and Mr. Gage and proceeds to apologize to Tory for the miscommunications during their previous meeting. I have no idea what he is apologizing for, or how he knows my brother and Tory. I assume it is from them working together at Steve's company.

Tory smiles graciously and tells him it was a night filled with them. Steve shakes his hand and thanks him for his service to our family and the community. I watch as he glances in my direction and I feel the sudden urge to run out of the room. Instead, I stand and feel my dress straighten itself. I extend my hand and say, "I am sorry, but you look unusually familiar to me. I'm Emm…"

"Emmy Gage, yes I remember," he says reaching for my hand. "I'm Thomas."

"EMMELIA!" A stern voice yells from across the room. The tone causes an instant panic to occur within me.

It feels like someone is warning me not to place me hand on the burner of the stove because it is hot. I pull back my hand before Thomas has a chance to shake it. I turn around, toward the voice and see Corbin crossing the large span between us and he was walking very fast. His face is flushed and he looks very angry.

"Jenny wants to see you in the hall," he quips.

"Okay," I reply not wishing to argue with my brother in a room filled with people. I take one last look at Thomas and walk toward the door. I step into the hallway and look to my left and then to my right. Jenny is nowhere to be seen. Jazz is standing outside the elevator watching me.

"Lose something?"

"Have you seen Jenny?" I walk toward him.

"Nope, haven't seen her most of the night," he says. "Man, Em, if I wasn't interested," he says wiggling his eyebrows up and down, "I would definitely be interested."

"Enough Jazz! Corbin said Jenny was out here looking for me. 's just weird," I say with a sigh. He shrugs his shoulders and promises to keep an eye out for her. I turn just in time to see Thomas walking toward the stairwell. His face is red and he's saying something under his breath but I can't make out what it is. He looks angry. His hands are in fists and he's swinging them like a mall walker, or a kid that is throwing a tantrum. He pushes the door open with vengeance and disappears from my view. I hear a female voice from his radio and then the door slams loudly.

I question whether or not I should follow him but remember my shoes. For most women, two inches is nothing. But, for me, two inches would make the difference of whether I ended up at the bottom of the stairs on my bottom or on my feet. *Oh, would be a lovely sight, 'Thomas, Thomas wait…" then I lose my balance and end up at his feet with my dress wrapped around my neck advertising the flimsy panties don't even cover up my bottom.* No, not tonight I decide. I walk back into to Gala. Corbin is standing behind Julie and I tell him I couldn't find Jenny.

"Well then, she must have figured it out on her own," he says rudely. He grabs Julie by the elbow, "We have to go." And they both leave rather abruptly.

I look around our table, dumbfounded. "What was that all about?" I look at Tylar for an answer.

"Nothing. Don't worry about it. Hey," he says rubbing my arm, "Thomas said to tell you it was nice to see you again and he was sorry he had to go. He said something about an alarm call he got called out to."

Tylar, my youngest older brother, was the very worst liar in our family. I know there is more to this story, but I choose not to delve further.

Hey Thomas

"Dude, isn't that your girlfriend?"

"Nah, that's his wanna be girlfriend huh Hayden," they tease.

Thomas turned his head to see what his fellow Officers were jarring about. It only took him a second to recognize the woman standing in the doorway. "Emmelia," he whispered. Her blond hair was pulled back with only a few curls gracing her shoulders. Her eyes were darkly lined and seemed to be taking in the entire room. Her dress was a rich mocha brown, strapless with ornate, bead-like crystals that sparkled each time she took a breath. He watched as the very tops of her breasts press against the dress when she inhaled. Her waist was tiny, perfect and the dress was not one to hide any imperfections. She didn't have any to hide. He watched her look around the room, searching for someone. He held his breath hoping she wasn't there with anyone in particular and then, she caught his stare. He smiled, she smiled in return and when he saw her brother escort her to their table, only then did he take another breathe. He knew he shouldn't stare, but it was simply too much to make his eyes advert. She was beyond beautiful, beyond perfect. He secretly watched her all night. The way her face lit up when she laughed, and how she folded her napkin in her lap. How she flexed her claves under the table. He stared at her shoulder blades and imagined kissing the back of her neck. Suddenly, he caught the attention of Miss Garrison. She was looking right at him. This was it! This was the invitation he was waiting for. He walked over to the table and greeted them. He watched as Emmelia stood and placed her napkin to the right of her plate. She said he looks familiar, tried to introduce herself and then… He watched as she walked into the hallway.

"Listen. You keep your eyes off of my sister. In fact, keep completely away from her. Do you understand me kid?"

Her eldest brother Corbin to the rescue.

"I didn't do anything, I just came over and, she recognized me!"

"I mean it Hayden. Stay. Away. From. My. Sister."

After watching Thomas run through the stairwell doors, I decided I needed a walk. Tylar said he would be happy to accompany me, but I requested to be alone. Tory seemed to see what I needed and persuaded Tylar to let me be for a few minutes. As I crossed the parquet floor, I saw Jenny at a far table. She was clearing plates and silverware.

"May I help with this?"

Jenny looked up at me with a horrified face. "I can't believe you are actually speaking to me," she says while balancing three empty wine glasses in one hand.

I scrunch my eyebrows together and reach for a dirtied plate. "Why in the world would I not?"

Jenny's face fell. "She didn't tell you," she nearly whispered. Jenny set the plates and glasses back down on the soiled tablecloth and proceeded to take the plate from my hand, spilling the fork in the process. It clanged on the floor but no one noticed. She sat in the nearest chair and motioned for me to sit across from her. She took both of my hands in hers and I watch her lip begin to quiver.

"Jenny, what is it? What is wrong?"

"I don't know where to start," she said shaking her head back and forth. "I was truly hoping your Mother would have told you before she passed. Oh, it would have been so much easier than trying to tell you myself. She promised me she would tell you and I told her I would keep quiet until she felt you were ready to know." Jenny desperately grabbed at a pale yellow napkin and blew her nose. "I'm so sorry Emmy, I just can't do this tonight." Jenny stood quickly and exited through the hallway.

Dumbfounded, I sat in the chair for what seemed like ages. Tylar finally appeared and asked if I was alright. I shook my head yes, and told him I was just getting ready to call it a night. After saying goodnight to Tory, Steve and Tyler, I walked out into the hallway looking to see if Jenny was there. She wasn't but Jazz was standing outside the elevator.

"Leaving so soon?"

"Yeah, these shoes are killing my feet," I lied while stepping into the elevator.

"Did I tell you that you really look beautiful tonight Emmelia?"

I smile warmly and give him a hug. "Yes, Jazz. You might have mentioned that a few times so far. Thank you."

He pressed the button and the elevator door closed. "Is it still okay that I have Mother's piano delivered to the bookstore tomorrow?"

"Of course, I can't believe you were going to put it in storage. At least it will be enjoyed in the store rather than collect dust in a dark unit somewhere," he replied holding the elevator door open.

"Jazz," I sigh, "Thank you for everything. I mean it, everything." I give him a quick friendly kiss on the cheek and quickly walk to my car. I made the final payment to Tory last week. Five hundred dollars was a bargain. I really have so many blessings to be thankful for, I think as I fastened the seatbelt.

As I pull into the driveway of Mothers' house, I notice a white, newer pickup sitting in front, near the curb. A uniformed Officer is leaning against the tailgate, watching as I pull in. I press the garage door opener and wait as the metal door comes to life. The Officer remains, no movement at all. I pull forward and pull the parking break and turn the ignition off. I grab my purse and open the door. A strange hand extends and offers assistance. I look up and realize it is Thomas!

As my fingers slip across the open palm of his hand, an electric bolt races up my arm. Every instinct is telling me to pull my hand away, but I can't. Not because he won't let me, but because I don't want to. He gently captures my fingers in his lightly bound fist and assists me in getting out of the car. My entire body feels like it has fallen asleep. Tingling sensations everywhere, my hands, arms, legs, I feel light-headed and I am suddenly very glad he is there.

"I just wanted to make sure you made it home okay," he said.

I watch his lips as he speaks. Full, pouty and then, suddenly I watch as he licks them. His tongue darts out and sweeps across the top and bottom at the same time leaving a glaze as it retreats back into his mouth. I can feel the constraints of the corset as I try to catch my breath but no matter what I do, my breathing is labored and loud. Embarrassed and confused, I look away from his mouth to his shirt. *HAYDEN* is embroidered above his left breast pocket. *Oh my, oh no way. Thomas Hayden! TH! I heart TH.* A sudden rush of air hit my hungry lungs as I feel his fingers under my chin. Softly pushing my face, my eyes, back to his. His lips slowly part revealing the most amazing, most possessing smile I have ever seen and I feel my knees stutter to hold my weight.

"Are you okay?"

"No, I-I don't know what's happening. I feel, I just feel really light-headed, dizzy," as I ramble on he wraps his arm around my waist and walks with me toward the back door. I turn the knob and take two steps into the kitchen before I turn around. He is standing, still in the garage, smiling at me. I watch as he moves inside the door and closes it behind him. The tingling feeling rushes back as well as a dose of adrenaline. He walks toward me, long strides, his eyes are piercing. I take a step back and lean against the kitchen counter for support just as he leans toward my ear. No part of his body is touching mine but his mouth is so close to my ear I can feel his breath. He is breathing hard, short, shallow breaths into my neck. His breath is hot and moist and I place my hands on the counters edge to keep from falling toward him.

"Your brother would kill me if he knew I was here with you," he whispered. The words send a shockwave through my body only to fade quickly into a tiny tingles up my spine. He turns and walks out the back door but before closing it she says, "Make sure you close the garage door after I leave." And then he was gone. I walked to the door and pressed the button, watching the garage door noisily close. From the front window, I watch as he drives away. It wasn't until he was out of my view I realize I am trembling.

After the Gala

Jenny went home after cleaning up from the final Gala with a heavy heart. She was not prepared to speak to Emmelia about either of their father's. Especially knowing Edna hadn't told Emmy before she passed away, it only left Jenny with two options.

She could keep the secret and pray no one ever mentioned it to Emmy. But that would mean Jenny may never get the answers she had been in search of for the past 20-two years.

Her other option was to tell Emmy about her father. Tell Emmy that Jenny's father was the old man at her bus stop. The old man whom killed her father and the reason William Gage returned fire. Jenny's father was the reason Emmy had suffered and her family had suffered.

Jenny sat quietly on her couch debating internally. After careful consideration of Emmy's initial shock, the potential of her finding out from someone else, and her own selfish need for an answer, Jenny made up her mind.

Walking to her bedroom, Jenny grabbed a photo of her father. Then, pulling open a drawer in the kitchen, she retrieved a pen and some stationary. The letter would be her last resort. She hoped Emmy would allow her the opportunity to talk. She knew it may be too much, too soon which was what Edna had feared.

Jenny had waited so many years for these answers and she couldn't wait, would not wait any longer regardless of the consequences. Jenny began writing,

Dear Emmelia,

I can only assume our discussion did not go as well as I had hoped. This letter you are holding was to be my last resort in trying to help you understand why your memories of my father are imperative to so many questions have never been answered for me.

My Mother left my father and me when I was almost eight years old. My father spent the following two years trying to convince me her leaving had nothing to do with me. Although, looking back, when my Mother was around she had spent most of her time entertaining men other than my father and doing drugs. When I was six, one of my Mother's many 'johns' sexually abused me. After he had finished with me, he made me watch as he had sex with my Mother. He told me while he was slamming into himself into my mom, he would kill me if I told anyone what we were doing. He told me it was our dirty little secret.

After my Mother left, all of the men and drugs left with her. I had nightmares of that man on top of me, underneath me, touching me, and sticking things inside of me. I never told anyone though. I was so afraid if I did, he would come back and make good on his promise.

The nightmares eventually decreased. I would have one every couple of nights, then once a week rather than every time I fell asleep. I had boyfriends off and on throughout high school, but I never allowed myself, or them, to get too close. I was afraid that they would figure out what had happened to me. It wasn't until my junior year of college I finally let my guard down. His name was Blake and he was Co-captain of the basketball team. I was absolutely, without question head over heels in love with him. We dated for about eight months before I decided to offer myself to him in the physical sense.

I won't go into detail as I know it would cause you distress, but the encounter was rough, unemotional on his part. He immediately reminded me of the man who stole my virginity so violently as a child. Blake and I broke up. He told me I had serious issues and told me I needed to see a shrink. I dropped out of school over Christmas break and moved back home with my dad. I locked myself away in my room for nearly three months. I thought about taking my own life every day. The nightmares had returned and I did my best not to sleep.

It was an afternoon in late May. My father had come home from work early and hollered for me to come to the kitchen. Reluctantly, I made my way out of the fog that had become my new reality.

He was sitting at the kitchen table, his back to me and I stood and watched his shoulders tremble. I sat down directly across from him and watched, horrified as tears raced down his face. He asked me if it was true. He asked me when it had happened.

I told him everything. I told him everything Emmelia.

My father left the house that evening and I didn't see him again for two weeks. I saw him on the news, accused of killing your father and attempting to murder you.

Emmelia, the person whom shot and killed your father was not the man you think he was. He was a kind man who loved me. I don't know what happened to him after he left the house. I don't know where he went or what he was planning on doing. But I do believe he was trying to track down the man who raped me when I was little.

The toxicology report came back and it confirmed my father had methamphetamines in his system. He had never done drugs while I was growing up and he was adamant I never try them. In fact, I can count on one hand the number of times I witnessed my father drink alcohol.

The only thing I can think happened is he found my Mother and the man who raped me then lost it. Or maybe he met up with my Mother and she drugged him.

I don't know how he ended up on the corner. I don't know why he shot your father.

These are these questions that I think you can help me answer.

Although, knowing you are reading this letter, you may choose to never speak to me again. But, perhaps Emmelia, there are some questions I may be able to answer for you.

I won't bother you and if you decide to allow me back into your life, I will be waiting.

Jenny signed the letter with love and placed it into a matching envelope. Sealing it, she turned it over and 'Emmy' on the front. As she laid the envelope on the table near the photo of her father, she silently prayed Emmy would listen to her plea.

Sealed Envelopes

The envelope is still sitting on the dining room table. I haven't had the courage to open it yet. Every morning, I walk by, pretending it doesn't exist. It has been nearly seven weeks, almost two months since her death. Other than going to work, I have spent all of my time at the house.

Tory has been a recluse as well. She and Steve were to be getting married in a couple of weeks and I think she is thinking about that. The thing I have learned about Tory is, she would rather suffer in silence than cause anyone else to suffer with her.

I feel badly for her. I can't imagine finding my soul mate and then feeling as though I cannot marry him for fear of upsetting an already fragile family network. I pick up the phone and dial her number.

"Hi, this is Tory, please leave me a message and I will return your call as soon as I am able."

"Tory, it's Emmelia. Give me call. Love you."

Just as I hang up the phone, there's a knock at the front door. I look through the peep-hole and yank the door open wide.

"Hi, I just left you a message!"

"I say you were calling just as I pulled into the driveway," she laughs. "I guess great minds think alike huh?"

"Come in, come in," I say gesturing her into the house. I follow her to the dining room table. She looks tired and stressed, although she is all put together. It's her eyes that give her away. I ask her how everything is going and she tells me she had gone to Janessa's to return all of our dresses.

I tell her I think Mother would be very disappointed knowing she has created such havoc that Tory no longer feels comfortable enough to have a wedding.

"It's not just that," Tory says to me and then buries her head in her hands.

"What? What is it then?"

It takes me more than a minute to persuade her to tell me what is going on, what she is so upset about.

"It all just started so fast. It happened so quickly and now I am afraid ..." she trails off and starts crying again. "Can we talk about something else please?"

I don't know what to say to her. I can't think of anything to talk about so I just sit there, at the table and fumble with the white envelope.

"Emmelia. Is that the envelope from your Mother?"

"It is," I shake my head. "I haven't worked up the courage to open it yet. I am not sure I want to know what it says," I say feeling the blood rush to my cheeks.

Tory smiles and wipes her eyes. "I tell you what, I will make you a deal okay? I will tell you what is really going on in my head if you promise to open that letter sooner than later."

I agree and it is easy to do so since Tory didn't tell me when I have to open the envelope. Of course I plan on opening it, I just haven't felt the right moment to do so.

"Alright," she says with a deep breath. "I met Carter when we were still in High school. It was one of 'love at first sight' relationships. We dated for three years before Carter proposed. It was magical Em. He took me to Louis, my favorite Italian restaurant. I had the lasagna and he had the manicotti with red sauce. We shared some gelato and then he surprised me! He came to my side of the table, bent on one knee and opened a black velvet box."

"He asked me to spend the rest of my life with him, by his side and it hardly takes me a second to answer yes."

"The ring, oh the ring! Emmelia, it was the most beautiful ring I have ever seen in my entire life. There was a bright princess cut diamond in the center and 13 sapphires surrounding the center diamond. And not just any sapphires mind you," she smiled. "Carter special ordered them from Montana. They were the purest, deepest, most beautiful shades of blue. Each one different, but similar enough so without really examining, one might think they were cloned. Even the depth of the Pacific Ocean didn't come close to intimidating the luster and color of that ring. Carter had told me later it took three months to get the ring after he had ordered it."

"Our wedding was from a fairytale book. My dress was so amazing. My parents had been divorced for a long time and at the time and my mom had no symptoms of dementia. I called my father to tell him and I only got his voicemail. Mother sent him an invitation which he mailed back saying he was unable to attend. He enclosed a one hundred dollar bill and wished me well. My Mother was infuriated, but I wasn't really surprised. He did the same thing for my high school graduation but enclosed fifty dollars for that accomplishment."

"Anyway, my dress was white," she looks over at me, "yes, I was still a virgin. It buttoned up the back. It had a really different neck line. It was high in the back and cut low in the front like a reverse geisha dress. It opened into a heart shape, so much I had to wear a corset to compensate the heart shape. The sleeves we long and full of intricate beading and near the shoulder and wrists, the fabric was cut in kind of a fleur delis pattern and lined with lace. There was also a lot of beadwork on the bodice. The dress was really form fitted and the slit up the back went above my knees. It was kind of inappropriate, but the nine foot train detracted the eyes from the back of my legs."

"The train was detachable and it was scalloped around the edges like a fancy dinner plate. It also had beadwork and similar cut outs as the dress. My shoes were the old fashioned lace up boots. They only came to my ankles, and only had a two inch heal, but they were simply elegant."

"My favorite part though, had to be my veil. It was made with little twigs painted white and it came to a 'v' on my forehead. It had beads and sparkles and a shear train that fell all the way down my back. I remember my Mother telling me the veil cost almost as much as my dress. It was so delicate and pretty, I didn't ever want to take it off."

"Our colors were royal purple and white. Melanie was my maid of honor and her dress was just as breathtaking and complex as mine. Hers had the same neck line but her dress was layered and fuller. Imagine a petty coat. That is what the bodice looked like. That part was the deep royal purple and just below the sternum, the coat portion of the dress opened up and was cut at a reverse angle. The reveal of the coat was a white petticoat dress that went to the floor."

"I really wanted hydrangeas for our wedding flower but it was the wrong time of year. My Mother, bless her heart, decided to make my flowers. She not only made my bouquet, but another I could throw, all of the boutonnieres, and enough for all of our respected family members too."

"She looked everywhere for ribbon that would match Melanie's dress. She was frantic and purchased spool after spool of purple ribbon. After about the third trip to the fabric store to return all of the items, she called the seamstress and requested the scrap material. As tall as Mel is, they still had to hem the dress three inches."

"I watched as my Mother cut the scraps into ribbon-like strips. Then she sandwiched the between two pieces of lace then she stitched around the edges. The hydrangeas had extremely long stems, so Mother arranges baby white roses in my main bouquet then wrapped white silk ribbon around the stems. She used the ribbon she made from Mel's dress to weave between the flowers and then cascade out of the bouquet."

"Em, they were so pretty," she says and I notice her eyes are moist but she hasn't started to cry. "She deconstructed some of the flowers to make smaller versions for the guys and for family."

"Carter was adamant he picked out the Tux's. He was so persistent my Mother finally caved as long as he promised no jeans, and no hats. I had to laugh because I knew this day was just as important to Carter as it was to me. He chose well, black tuxedos with white pin stripes. He also decided bow ties and cumber buns were out dated and chose royal purple ties instead."

"The invitations had a photo of Carter and me standing on the beach. We had the photo created in black and white and the invitations were black as well. The R.S.V.P. cards were purple."

"The day of our wedding arrived and mom spent the day bossing everyone around. She was polite about it, but everyone knew she meant business. I was oblivious, upstairs in the bridal suite having my hair and make-up applied. When it came time for me to get dressed, mom pushed everyone else out of the room except Melanie and me. They helped me into my dress and my mom tediously buttoned the back of my dress as Melanie held my hand in support of my big day. Melanie attached the train and Mother handed me my veil. I stood in front of the mirror and watched as

Melanie and Mother fluffed and doted some more with my dress."

"I remember hearing the music begin and hugging Melanie as she walked out of the room. It would be only moments until Mother led me down the aisle. Mom turned to me and asked me if I was sure I wanted to spend the rest of my life with Carter. I told her I was willing to promise two lifetimes if it were possible."

Tory stands and walks into the kitchen. She returns with a stack of napkins and places them between us on the table.

"I truly believed that Emmelia, I believed Carter and I would be together for as long as we both had breath to breathe," she says and then begins to sob.

"So, what happened? I knew you were married before, but all of this is, well crazy." I say completely confused.

"We were married for 16 years. I decided almost seven years ago to go back to school and that was when everything in our relationship changed. He started working more and staying home less and less. I was so busy with homework and study groups I really didn't even notice. Then, he tells me he wants a divorce and he's seeing another woman. He told me about her and said her name was Erin. But then there was the accident, and your brother was so kind. And Carter admitted there never was an Erin and he had made her up. He was insecure about our future. He thought I would want someone better after I graduated. But that wasn't true! I wanted Carter, I had always wanted Carter. He died in the hospital that night just minutes before our divorce was supposed to be final. I thought so badly of myself because of what happened on the stairs with Steve. I had no idea until a few days after Carters' death that the divorce had been finalized the afternoon of the accident."

"What happened with Steve?" I ask and watch as her face turns red from embarrassment.

"Oh Em," she sighs, "I kissed him! In the heat of all that was happening, I kissed him!"

"I'm lost," I say. "First you tell me you have this magical wedding and then happily ever after is interrupted because you want to get an education? Then he makes up a woman to have an affair with? Then dies just after he tells you she wasn't real?"

"Yep," Tory replies. "I guess that sums it up," she blows her nose into one of the napkins. "I just don't think I can recreate such a perfect day, and I don't want to try. I went to Janessa's and saw the dresses your Mother set aside and I knew I couldn't marry Steve in the traditional way. I can't do the fairytale again."

"Have you talked to my brother about it?"

"Yes, and he said he doesn't even need a piece of paper to tell me how much he is committed to me. He said he will love me forever regardless of whether we get married or not."

"Wow, so now what?"

"So," she says, adjusting herself in the chair. "That actually brings me to why I stopped by. I am moving in with Steve! I know, I know, all of these magical stories about marriage and fears of trying to duplicate something I know I never will; now I have decided to throw caution to the wind and try a different approach." She pauses and folds her hands on top of the table. Her face is serious, "I don't know how you feel about living here, and I haven't had the conversation with Steve yet. But, I have five months left on my lease and I was wondering if you would like to take it over?"

"What do you mean take it over? Like, move into your apartment?"

"Exactly. You don't have to though, I can sub-lease it out to someone else. I just wanted to give you the first opportunity."

I sit there quietly thinking about her offer. A place of my own! Somewhere I can try to decorate, try to discover myself. Now that Mother is dead, this house feels so lonely, so desolate and sad. I know my brothers said the market for home sales was soft and I am sure they are not going to be too thrilled about having an empty house for sale. But, this is something I have wanted to do.

"We should probably have a family meeting and see how my brothers feel about the offer. And, I will need to know how much everything is because I don't want to be short on money. I don't really know what to say Tory, I mean I am really excited and at the same time, I am really scared."

She gives me a big hug and tells me she will get my bothers together for dinner and we can all discuss it then. She turns to leave and thanks me for listening and apologizes for 'dumping her drama' onto my lap. She says no matter what I decide to do with the apartment or Mothers' house it needs to be my decision.

Who is that?

I carry the last of the boxes filled with my clothes from Mothers' house up to my new apartment. I walk in and feel the positive energy immediately. Tory and Katie helped me paint the walls a light mocha and we kept the crown molding white. Tory purchased an area rug that transformed the bedroom area almost immediately. We shopped for hours and found so many fun accessories including a lamp made completely of seashells. It seemed fitting to decorate in beachy colors since the apartment rested just above the ocean and shore line. The pops of aqua bounce to life when I turn on the light in the kitchen. I place the boxes on the counter and marvel at my new little sanctuary.

My bedding is teal with sand colored sheets and the bed skirt has polka dots. Not quite grown up yet, but not so childish either. Tory and Katie were adamant I pick things that spoke to me, made me smile and feel happy. The whole room has made me feel all of those things. I have only one photo on my walls and it came from Jenny. It was the one she had made for the Gala of our entire family. She had it mounted on canvas and turned the photo into a black and white version of the original. I cried so hard when she brought it over, I told her it was so what I needed. Hung above my bed, it is a reminder of everything I have to be thankful for in my life. No matter what happens, I know I am loved and protected by my family.

"Coming," I yell toward the knock at my front door. I peer through the peep-hole and discover it is Jenny standing on the stoop. I have wanted to speak to her about what happened at the Gala, but haven't found the right time. Hoping this was that time; I opened the door and invited her in. After accepting my offer for tea, she sat down at my dining room table set for three.

She began fidgeting with the table cloth telling me there was something we needed to talk about. I was quiet, not wanting to interrupt her thoughts as it seemed she was having a difficult time telling me what she needed me to know. I turned my back to grab two cups a saucers as well as the Lavender tea Jazz insisted I offer everyone who's a guest in my new home.

As I turned back toward Jenny, I notice she was looking down at my table. Her eyes are moist and she was slowly shaking her head. I looked in the direction of her gaze and I am staring into the same eyes I did so many years ago. The tea cups and saucers shatter on the tile floor as I grab the back of the chair to steady myself as all of the blood rushes to my feet.

"Where did you get that?" My voice is harsh, loud and shaking. "Answer me Jenny," I demand. "Where did you get that?"

"It's mine," she sobbed.   "This is my father."

Breathe Em, just breath. It's a nightmare, just breathe.

"Emmelia, this is a picture of my father, and this is what I need to talk to you about. This is what I told your Mother I wouldn't tell you. But there are some questions I need answered and you are the only person who can answer them for me."

"Get out," I shriek racing to the front door. "Get out NOW!" Jenny stands and walks toward me, pleading with me to 'just listen' to her for a minute. Her eyes are already red, she is crying, begging me to close the door. I extended my pointer finger and in a low growl tell her to leave before I call the police.

Slamming the door behind her, I race to the bathroom and begin to vomit, violently. The tea kettle begins to whistle but I cannot move. My stomach is retching every three seconds and I can't catch my breath.

It was at least five minutes before I could stand and walk to the stove. I removed the kettle and turned the burner off. I stared over at the broken china lying hap-hazardly on my clean kitchen floor. The image in my mind though was of those eyes. Jenny's father was the old man who killed my father and nearly killed me.

As I scan the table, I notice a white envelope occupying the space where his picture was presented to me just a few minutes ago. 'Emmy' is written across the front. *I haven't even read my Mother's letter yet. Jenny, what makes you think I am going to read yours?* But the truth is I would read Jenny's letter before I would read the one from my Mother.

I tossed and turned before drifting off to sleep.

A Recital of Sorts

I arrived shortly before the moving van pulled up in front of the bookstore. The two men slowly, carefully unloaded the piano and slid it into place in the back near the counter. Jazz smiled as they left and turned his attention to me.

"Want to try it out? Make sure they didn't mess anything up?"

I returned his smile and quickly made my way over, pulling out the bench and lifting the lid. I made a couple of adjustments and began to play.

Jazz opened the front door and patrons started filing in, drawn by the quiet melody emanating from the store. Emmelia's eyes were closed and she was entranced in her motions. Jazz placed a large bowl on the piano and placed a five dollar bill in it then walked behind the counter.

It was the beginning of summer vacation and he was in awe at the faces that began to fill every table in his little shop. One by one, they ordered tea and some even wandered the store looking and reading the covers of books he has for sale. Jazz couldn't remember the last time there were so many people in such a small space. People were mingling, talking to one another, commenting on the beautiful woman playing the magical music. Many made their way to the piano and deposited money into the bowl. Emmelia was oblivious to the furry happening around her.

She had spent the night before, barely sleeping, haunted by the image of the old man. She was disturbed by the thought that such an awful human being could actually be the father of one of her favorite people. She knew that she needed to read the letter Jenny had left on the table after she was so rudely asked—no demanded—Jenny to leave but even this morning, Emmelia's stomach ached. Another reminder last night was not a nightmare, it had actually happened.

Emmelia played from her heart and not from the memory of sheet music. No, this was her composition, her life in the notes. The music began to build as she thought of the old man and of her father. But as soon as she thought of her Mother the tone changed to a more soothing, softer melody. She thought of Thomas and his whispers, his touch, his hot, moist breath. Her eyes shot open as she felt her cheeks warm. She looked around the bookstore for a moment and then saw the multitude of people clapping for her. She stood by the piano and made an effort to bow.

"Jazz, where did all of these people come from?" she asked as she rounded the corner and stepped by him behind the counter.

"Um, you brought them in," he said staring at her with his mouth wide open.

"As soon as you started playing, I opened the door and they just came in, one after another until…" he gestured around the room. He left her side just long enough to retrieve the bowl he had placed on the piano. "Take it into the back room and count it, Em."

"What is all of this?"

"I put the bowl on the piano for people to give you a tip. Now go, see how you did," he smiled brightly pointing her to the backroom.

Ten minutes later, Emmelia emerged from the back.

"$45.00," she whispered into his ear.

"Sweetie, you will never make another cup of tea again," Jazz said turning his head toward the piano.

She played for about 20 minutes every hour. Each time, new faces walked through the door. Jazz told her it was the best day in sales and tips he has ever had. He said there were people that came in he had never seen before. Many purchased a book to read while they waited for her to play. Emmelia ended the day $105.00 richer. She offered to split the tips with Jazz, but he insisted she was good for his store and she had earned every penny.

She unlocked her front door and walked over to the table. The infamous letters lay flat where she had left them. The one from her Mother and the one from Jenny, both silently demanding her attention. She deposited her purse and keys on the table beside the door and kicked off her shoes.

Well, it's either now or never. I need to find out what Jenny needs and if I am able to help her. But to go back and relive this again? I just don't know if I am ready to deal with it.

I grab the envelope and open the French doors to the balcony. The wind is warm and the tide is full. The waves are crashing noisily on the sand. I decide I need a cup of tea and fill the kettle. After placing it in the stove, I begin fiddling with the envelope. I inspect the front, then the back and begin picking at the small piece in the corner not adhered to the other piece. I wait for the water to boil.

A Serious Blunder

Emmelia walked over to the table, still fidgeting with the envelope Jenny had secretly left behind. Her telephone buzzes and interrupts her thoughts as well as progress of opening the envelope. Reaching over, she grabs the phone and reads a new text message from Katie.

'Is it ok to give your number to Thomas?'

She quickly types a response: 'Thomas Hayden?'

Almost instantly, Katie replies, 'Yes'

"Oh geeze," she thought, "He wants my number!" Excited, she once again responded to her best friend.

'Sure, that would be fine.' Trying to calm her heart rate, she stood and took a tea cup out of the cupboard. She was down to only two since the mishap with Jenny.

Her phone buzzed again. She looked at the screen and did not recognize the number. It had to be him! She read the simple message.

'Hi'

She replied back, 'hi?'

'It's Thomas'

'Hello' she responded feeling her body tingle.

She started to reply just as the tea kettle began to whistle. She placed her phone on the counter, turned off the stove, and poured the scalding hot water over the lavender tea bag. She returned to the table, setting her cup on the saucer and continued her message to Katie.

'I can't believe I had a crush on him when we were kids'

Buzz. 'You had a crush on me?' She stared at the screen for a moment giggling to herself and replied.

'No you goof! Thomas' and pressed send,

She stirred her tea feeling giddy at the thought that Thomas wanted her phone number, 'buzz'. She read the text on the screen three times before she realized what she had done.

'This is Thomas. I can't believe you had a crush on me!'

In her rush to turn off the stove and quiet the tea kettle, she had forgotten she had hit the reply button to Thomas instead of Katie. "Oh no, no, no," she said aloud to herself. "How could I have been so stupid?" Another text arrived.

'Hi' it read. It was Thomas. She didn't respond right away and another message popped up.

'Do you want to start over?' She smiled and replied.

'Yes. Please.' She waited for another message, but nothing happened. Instead, her phone began to ring.

"Hello?"

"Emmelia, it's Thomas. Uh, I thought it may be easier if I just called you," he said and she could he him stifling a laugh.

"I am so sorry about that. I-I, uh thought I was texting Katie."

"Absolutely the dumbest thing I have ever done," I tell Katie. She is laughing so hard I find myself laughing with her.

"Hold on, oh, I can't breathe Em," she tells me holding her palm toward my face. I am shaking my head from side to side.

"So, what did he say when he called?"

"He asked me out on a date!" My excitement is more than I can contain.

"When?"

"Saturday night," I reply giggling once again.

"Okay, so that's what, uh, four days away. You need to figure out what you are going to wear," Katie says pulling me away from the table toward my closet. We open the closet and start flipping through my wardrobe, both of us squealing like little girls. For a moment, I feel so blessed to have Katie back in my life.

We had gone for weeks without speaking to one another after our argument at the mall. Then, one afternoon, she walked into the bookstore and we started talking like nothing had ever happened. She said she was trying to get pregnant and start a family. Surprising me with her revelation and asking me about my recovery. She had heard Mother had passed away and apologized she wasn't able to attend the funeral. She said they had gone on vacation and hadn't found out until they returned. It was a quick conversation filled with 'I'm sorry, no I am sorry' that ended in a hug and a promise we would never go that long again without talking. Now, she and I were pulling outfit after outfit having a wonderful time together.

Music to My Ears

Jazz is standing behind the counter as I walk through the door.

"Ready to play?" He has a huge smile plastered across his face.

"Is that where you want me today?"

"After what happened last week Em, behind that piano is the only place I want you during your shift," he replies with a chuckle.

While Emmelia readied the instrument, Jazz propped open the front door and placed a large tip bowl on the piano. Again, he seeded it with a five dollar bill. Within ten minutes of her playing, the patrons began filling the tables.

Thomas and his partner, Pete, parked the patrol car near the bookstore. Their sergeant had assigned them to the downtown area for patrol today, so they would walk Main Street for the next ten hours. Not a difficult task, although the tourist traffic does increase the potential for encountering drunken patrons. But on day shift, most likely the most excitement he and Pete would encounter could be a violation of the "No Shirt, No Shoes, No Service" policy of the small shops.

"Hey Thomas, let's hit up Jackie's before we get going," Pete says as he shuts the door.

"Sounds good," Thomas replies feeling a growl in his belly. They both walk across the quiet street taking notice all of the shops are still closed. Most wouldn't open until ten. A few welcomed customers around eight. They wouldn't be missing anything for about an hour.

After taking a seat nearest the front windows, they both ordered the breakfast special which consisted of two pancakes, two eggs, two sausage links and two slices of bacon.

"So, did you get ahold of her yet or did you heed her brother's warning at the Gala?"

"Funny," Thomas replied with a smirk. "After seeing her at the Gala, I decided even her brother, as intimidating as he is, couldn't squelch my pursuit."

Pete stirred his coffee, mixing the cream and sugar. "What now? You plan on marrying her?"

Thomas thought of her in a wedding dress. She would look amazing on his arm as his wife. But what did he really know about her? She had accidentally admitted she had a crush on him when they were both younger. He knew she had suffered from a horrible incident and her father was killed in the line of duty. He had read the report but very few details about Emmelia were included. Most of her medical records were sealed after the District Attorney's Office closed the case.

The few photos of Emmelia were of her wound prior to surgery, 30 in all. They were taken from every angle imaginable. Her eyes were closed in each one of them, her purple iridescent lids softly shielding her from the horror that was happening around her. He stared at her, remembering her in class. She had always tried to join the boys in a game of kickball at recess. She was good, but very clumsy. Always tripping or falling down. When he was chosen as team captain, he always picked her first for his team. He remembered the feeling of anger and sadness when the other team captains would pick her last.

Images of the crime scene popped into his mind. The photos showed two distinct areas where blood had pooled. The investigation revealed Sergeant Gage had died quickly. The red stain was substantial, considering the fact his heart had stopped pumping minutes before the medic unit arrived.

The other pool was larger. Once Thomas had realized it was Emmy's blood, he was shocked she had survived the ambulance ride to the hospital. The crime scene was re-created with public servants portraying the victims and the suspect. The chief of police at the time had his daughter portray Emmy and lie on the sidewalk with her eyes closed for the forensic analysts who were processing and taking photos. It was a haunting image for even the most seasoned officers.

He hadn't thought of her for quite some time. Then, after seeing her out to lunch with Katie, he was infatuated by her. The way she smiled across the room and the way she walked so gracefully with her slender arm tucked into her brother's arm. She had grown up, turning into the most beautiful woman he had ever seen, while no one was watching.

"Well, I am watching now," Thomas said to himself.

"Dude!"

Thomas jerked his head toward the voice.

"Seriously? I have been having a one-sided conversation for the last five minutes," Pete said shaking his head back and forth.

"Sorry," Thomas replied as the waitress delivered their breakfast.

"Thanks Tracey," Pete said and both Officers began to eat quietly.

Emmelia finished her first "set" and walked from the piano to the counter where Jazz was busy making his famous tea.

"You are such a blessing Em," he said giving her a quick peck on the cheek.

"I am glad you feel that way," she smiled and blushed slightly.

"Um, do you think it would be okay if I took Friday and Saturday off this week?"

"Sure, why? Got big plans this weekend?"

"Well, sort of," she blushed.

"Hmmm," he replied, eyebrows wiggling. "With whom?"

She giggled to cover her nervous embarrassment, "Thomas Hayden," she quipped looking down at the floor.

Jazz smiled and nudged her arm. "He's a very, well-respected young man, Em. I think he is a good choice for your first."

Her eyes shot up and the look of utter shock was obvious. "First," she whispered to herself. "Jazz, what is it like?"

"What is 'what' like?"

"Um … you know," she said moving closer to his ear. "Sex." She said it so quietly he barely heard her.

He laughed! He laughed so loudly three patrons stopped mid-conversation to stare at him from the seats nearest the counter. Slowly, trying hard to subdue his outburst, he turned to her. His pupils enlarged.

"I am probably not the right person to ask, Em. My experiences with sex are going to be very different from yours," he replied between chuckles.

"But …" she tried to interject but he interrupted.

"I would be able to explain what he will experience. But honestly Em, I have no idea what you should expect as a woman." His voice was full of sincerity, all joking and laughter aside.

Jazz walked around the counter with a tray filled with cups and saucers. Emmelia watched as he delivered each one to an awaiting guest. When his tray was empty, he vanished behind a row of books.

Curiously, she waited for him to reappear. When he finally did, his serving tray was brimming with paperbacks.

"Okay," he said briskly walking toward her. He piled the books on a nearby table and sorted them into three stacks. Then he motioned for Emmelia to come closer.

"So," he said pointing to the first stack of books. "These are pretty tame, mostly educational books about sex. This pile ..." he said shifting to the right, "these are less education and a little more graphic. And these," he said pointing to three similar looking books, "these are three of the bestselling books in the store. I have read them and they are very graphic." He emphasized the word *very* and waited for her to respond. Nothing. She looked at him like a deer caught in the headlights.

"Let me know if you have any questions. And use the internet. But keep in mind, not everything you read on line is correct." He handed her the stack of books and silently hoped the trilogy wouldn't totally freak her out.

"So," she smiled while balancing the stack, "am I good to take Friday and Saturday off?"

"Emmelia, you have a lot of homework to do before your date. Finish today and take tomorrow too. That should give you a little time to 'research' your topic," he grinned.

"Really?" He nodded in response. "Okay, I will finish out today. Oh Jazz, thank you," she squealed while packing her books to the back room.

"Can you hear that?" Thomas asked as he and Pete made their way down Main Street. It was the sound of a piano. A soft melody drifting through the air.

"Yeh, wonder where it's coming from," he said sarcastically. Pete pointed to the line of people staring through the windows and walking through the open door of a shop on the next block.

The two officers continued to walk in the direction of the music.

"It's a bookstore," Pete said stopping near the entrance.

"Have you ever been in there?" Thomas took a step closer.

Pete shook his head indicating he had not. He walked through the threshold first, followed closely by Thomas.

Jazz looked up just in time to see two uniformed officers walk through the door. He quickly scanned the crowd, counting heads. Thirty-two, thirty-three, ending at thirty-nine, well under the maximum occupancy.

The Officers made their way to a clean table and sat down while adjusting their duty belts filled with an arsenal of weapons.

Jazz made his way through the crowd, "May I get you gentleman anything?"

"Who's playing the piano?" Pete asked as Thomas tried to peer over the many heads obviously enjoying the music.

"That's Emmelia Gage," Jazz replied watching Thomas's face light up. His eyes opened wide, his pupils contracted as he raised himself from the table and looked in the direction of the piano.

Thomas stood to watch the stunning woman sitting properly at the black piano. Her hair cascading over her shoulders, eyes closed and her head was slightly inclined back. He watched her fingers move gracefully, without effort, over the ivory keys. Her foot was pressing the brass pedal in a slow beat. Not recognizing the song, Thomas could only imagine it was music from her soul. The lower notes were sad and dominated the melody. She was expressing her emotions through her instrument. The melody suddenly changed and the little bookstore was filled with the sound of happiness. A smile formed on her lips as she continued to play the light, quick pulses of sweet music. The smile was infectious as he continued to watch her.

"Hayden …. Hayden! HAYDEN! You want some tea?"

He turned and looked down at Pete, grinning from ear-to-ear.

"Nah, we best be getting back to the sidewalk. It wouldn't look right if we only patrolled one shop on Main Street."

Pete stood and Jazz turned to walk away. Thomas grabbed Pete's elbow, shoving a single bill into his hand motioning for Pete to place it in the bowl on the piano. Pete gave him an odd look, placed the money on the pile already accumulated in the bowl and met up with his partner on the sidewalk.

The afternoon passed by quickly as Emmelia took the tip bowl to the counter. She heard the familiar click of the deadbolt and watched as Jazz ran the daily report on the register.

She started sorting through the money by denominations. Fives, tens, a hundred dollar bill!

"Holy crap, Jazz!" She yelled holding a single bill in the air for him to inspect. She glared as a huge smile consumed his face and lit up his eyes. She shook her head, "You can't do this."

"Em, it wasn't me, I promise." He winked, "Em, if it works out, I truly believe you will be one very happy woman."

She placed the money on the countertop and stared through Jazz. "He was here," she said—more a statement than question.

Jazz smiled again, "So, Moneybags, how did you do today?"

"Two-hundred and thirty-five dollars," she replied with a surprised expression. *He came and listened to me play*, she thought to herself.

"Let's see here," Jazz said, ripping the daily report from the cash register. "Huh, looks like you made me another small fortune today, Em."

"How much do I owe you for the books silly?"

She walked out of the bookstore with a bag of books, her wallet full of cash and her paycheck. She has a lot to do over the next few days, for sure.

Final Walk-Through

Making a quick trip to the bank to deposit her earning, she drove through the local coffee stand then headed back to her apartment. Corbin had called this morning letting her know there were two offers on Mother's house. He seemed optimistic, one way or another, the house would close before the Holidays.

Steve had already packed up the boxes from Heaven and Tylar had removed a few things from his old bedroom. There was to be an estate sale soon, to try and clear out the remaining items in the old house.

Emmelia suddenly turned her car around and headed toward the familiar street. Pulling into the driveway, she killed the engine and sat for a moment admiring the house which held so many memories for her. So many of them good, and that is what she focused on as she stepped out of the car. She walked up to the front door and entered the living room. Walking through and to the hallway, she turned into Steve's old bedroom and opened the closet. One by one, she carried the three banker's boxes to her car. Making her way into her old bedroom, she made quick work of gathering the few items she wished to keep rather than having a stranger purchase them at the estate sale.

Two pieces of paper caught her eye as she turned to leave. The infamous "I heart TH" and "The List" she had presented to Dr. Weston. Tucking them into her pocket she returned to the living room. After another glance around the room she left, locking the front door behind her. She was nearly to her car when she looked to her right. It looked as though the corner had disappeared, but she knew better. It was still there. She hadn't walked around the blind spot since the accident.

"I can do this," I say out-loud to only myself. My feet feel like they weigh 200 pounds each. One foot in front of the other I take small, cautious steps toward my goal. I glance over my shoulder, and I can still see the house. My breaths are short now. I hear my heart thumping in my ears and my head is beginning to feel dazed—like I am in a dream rather than reality. The corner is closer. I look over my shoulder again and the house is no longer in my view.

I stop. I see him.

He is talking, yelling at someone named Justin but there is nobody there. His light is pale, a light blue color. I see the yellow school bus and hear the brakes squeal as it comes to a complete stop. The stop sign on the corner flashes amber colored spots and the door opens.

A moment passes and I see a little blond-haired girl rush down the stairs, jumping from the last one landing on the street just below the sidewalk. Her light is a deep purple, almost black.

She tosses her purple backpack over one shoulder and waves at another little girl seated by the window. The bus pulls away and the waving continues until the yellow bus rounds the corner and is no longer in sight. Her purple ribbon is waving in the breeze as she turns to look at the old man. She smiles nervously and steps toward him. She and I hear the sirens at the same time; both of us turn and look in the direction.

She smiles—I shudder. I know what's coming. I try to scream but my voice is gone. I try to run to her, but I am frozen in place.

"Daddy!" the little girl yells!

I watch as the old man grabs her arm.

"Jenny, is that the man," the old man asks the little girl?

"Emmy, run," the officer yells.

I look at him, the officer—my father. There is pure terror in his eyes, etched across his face.

"Jenny, don't move Honey. Daddy is going to take care of him. That sonofabitch won't hurt another little girl again," he says, and then I watch as he pulls a gun out and points it at the officer.

The little girl is watching too. She is yelling her arm hurts, she is trying to runaway but she can't. The little girl looks determined, not scared as she and I watch the officer pull his gun out too.

The little girl and I both cover our ears from the sound of a loud bang. She looks confused as we see the officer falling to the ground. Still falling, he points his gun at the old man who is pulling the little girl closer to his chest. It looks like he is hugging her. I hear the second gunshot and I jump.

The officers' body makes a "thud" sound when it hits the sidewalk. I turn back to the little girl. The old man is gently holding her head as he lowers her to the sidewalk.

"Jenny," he says staring at her with tears in his eyes. "Jenny Honey, open your eyes baby girl," he pleads with his hand still behind her head.

The little girl opens her eyes and looks up the old man. I can see the blood starting to drip, then flow quickly onto the gray concrete. He is pulling her to his chest, sobbing.

In a tiny voice, the little girl says to him, "I am not Jenny. My name is Emmy. Emmy Gage," and closes her eyes once more.

The old man and I watch the blonde hair turn deep crimson as he lowers her down on the sidewalk. He is staring at me now. Blinking his eyes and shaking his head quickly as though he is trying to clear his mind.

He stands and stares for a moment at the officer lying lifeless on the concrete. The officer is dead! I know this because I can no longer see his light. The old man looks back at the little girl.

"Fuck!" He exclaims.

We both look up the street and see a woman running toward us. He turns the opposite direction and runs away. I hear Every time his feet hit the ground. He is running fast, and I can no longer see him.

The woman is wailing, she is getting closer and closer, but everything is happening in slow-motion. My vision is beginning to cloud. The woman vanishes before reaching me. Then the little girl and the officer slowly fade away. I stare at the police car, waiting for it to go away as well, but it doesn't. Instead, two Policemen step out. One of them is calling my name and I recognize his orange light. He is running toward me, and I can feel it getting dark. I feel strong arms around my waist and I crumble, I close my eyes and allow the darkness in.

A Proposal

"Steve, Steve where are you?"

"In the basement Tory, you need me to come up?"

"Um, yes, if you can please." Tory had spent the majority of the morning rummaging through her old wedding magazines. She felt Steve arms before realizing he was there.

"I think I am ready," Tory stated. There was a long silence as Steve looked at the wedding magazines cluttering the dining room table. He turned her around by her waist.

"Really? You want to go ahead and finally make an honest man out of me?" There was hesitation is his voice. Since Tory told him her fears, concerns really, about getting married again, he had backed off. He was happy she had decided to move in with him. He had convinced himself he didn't need a little piece of paper to know she loved him.

Tory nodded and wrapped her arms around his neck, nuzzling her mouth into his neck. "I do," she breathed into his sweaty skin. Just then, his cell phone rang in the kitchen. "Let it go to voicemail, I think you need to take a shower and I would love to assist," she said arching one brow.

Halfway up the staircase, Tory's phone began to ring. They both looked at each other. If it were a client, they would have left a message for Steve and waited for a return call. Family would be the only ones who would try her phone after he didn't answer.

They raced to the kitchen and Tory picked up the phone and pressed speaker, "Hello?"

"Tory? It's Corbin. Where is Steve?" His voice was elevated, excited and he was talking fast.

"I'm here," Steve yelled at the phone. "What's going on?"

"Em, its Em. I just got a call and she's been taken to the hospital. Julie and I are on the way, but we won't be there for another 30 or 40 minutes."

"We can go right now," Steve yelled from across the room. He had his keys, wallet and cell phone already in his hands. Tory grabbed the phone, her purse, and her keys out of habit.

"Thanks, and I will give Tylar a call and meet you all there."

"Do you know what happened?" Tory could feel the tears stinging her eyes as she asked the question.

"No, Thomas called from Emmy's phone. All he said was she was being transported by medics and her car was parked at Moms."

"Okay, we are just leaving. I will call you from the hospital if we hear anything else before you get there. Hey and Corbin, drive safely."

"Will do, I have Jules behind the wheel so I can call everyone. She's a cool cookie under pressure … you on the other hand …" he paused long enough to for Tory to pipe up.

"Got it. I will be driving, don't worry Corbin." With that, she clicked the key faub in her hand and Steve crawled into the passenger seat. They ended the conversation with Corbin and quickly drove to the hospital.

The Unknown

All I can hear are muffled voices and machines beeping. I know these sounds. I remember the darkness, the beeps, and my Mother begging me to open my eyes.

Please don't let this happen again. I am too strong. I have come so far, and I don't want to start all over again. Wake up, wake up Emmelia! Be stubborn, fight the darkness. Fight it!

Tory parked the car near the Emergency Room door. Steve jumped out of the car and raced to her door even before she had turned the ignition off. She slid out of the seat and they both walked quickly, hand-in-hand across the vast parking lot. The last time they were here, the parking lot was filled with police cars and flashing lights. This morning, there was only one patrol car but no flashing lights. The automatic doors opened with a whoosh of sterile air. Looking left then right, Steve pulled Tory in the direction of the reception desk located to the left.

"May I help you?"

"Yes, I … we, are looking for Emmelia Gage."

The red-head looked down at her computer monitor and typed away for a moment. She picked up the white phone on her desk and pressed three numbers.

"Yes, this is Jan at reception. I have," she paused and looked up at Steve and Tory. She covered the receiver and asked, "Who are you again?"

"This is her brother, Steve. And I am her sister-in-law, Tory."

"Sorry, I have some family members of Ms. Gage in the lobby area. Is she accepting visitors yet?" There was a pause. "Very well, I will send them your way then, thank you." She returned the receiver and looked up at the pair standing in front of her.

"You will find your sister on the second floor. Check with Cathy and she will show you to her room."

"Thank you," they said in unison and ran toward the stairs.

Steve pushed the large steel door open and they approached the desk. Cathy, as her name tag indicated, was busy typing, staring at her fingers when they arrived, slightly out of breath. She looked up and smiled.

"Hello, may I help you?"

"Yes, Jan said you would show us to Emmelia Gage?"

"Of course." She slid her chair away from her desk and straightened her jacket. "I don't know what you have been told, but please don't be alarmed when you see her." She stopped in front of room 202 and knocked lightly. Both Tory and Steve shot one another a strange look. After a moment, a uniformed officer opened the door slightly. When he realized it was Gage, he pulled the door quickly, revealing another officer crouched at the side of his sister's bed.

Pete quickly cleared his throat hoping to arouse his partner. It worked … it worked well. Thomas lifted his head, realized how inappropriate he must look and immediately jumped to his feet placing his hands at his sides.

"Mr. Gage, Ms. Garrison, I am so sorry. I, I didn't hear the door. I didn't realize anyone other than Pete was here," he said looking over at the other officer.

Steve took a few steps forward and placed his hand on Thomas' shoulder. He felt the kid's muscles tense. "Thomas," he said calmly. "Corbin said you called him. What happened to her?"

"I don't know, I mean, we were patrolling and we saw her on the corner. She was as white as a ghost. Pete stopped the car and I yelled her name. She was looking through me. Like she didn't really see me and then she closed her eyes. I started running toward her and as soon as I had her in my arms, she collapsed."

Thomas shook his head. "Pete got on the radio and requested medics. I rode in the ambulance with her and she just kept asking for Jenny."

Steve and Tory exchanged glances and Tory stepped back into the hallway, closing the door behind her.

"Once we arrived here," Thomas continued, "Doctor McInnes took her straight to radiology."

Steve removed his hand from Thomas's shoulder, leaned over and brushed the hair from his sister's forehead.

"Corbin's was the first name I recognized in her phone, so I called him while Pete and I waited for her to come out of radiology. I would have called you, but his was the first number I pressed," he said lowering his gaze to the floor.

"You did fine," Steve said, not taking his eyes off Emmy.

"Her vitals were strong the whole way here. The medics said they couldn't find anything wrong but knowing her history ... her previous injury ... they brought her here."

Steve gently grabbed her hand. *Such a fragile little white butterfly,* he thought to himself. Just then, Dr. McInnes walked through the door. Steve quickly stood and shook his hand.

"John, what happened?"

The doctor stood in the threshold and smiled. "As far as I can tell, Gage, nothing out of the ordinary. Her scans are clean although very active, and vitals are normal. Blood sugar levels are a little low, but that's it." He walked over to Emmy and held her wrist between his large fingers.

"Why isn't she responding to anything?" Both Steve and Thomas take a step toward her bed. Their eyes meet and Thomas stops, allowing Steve to progress toward his little sister.

"She is, just not how you would want her to." He turned toward Thomas and Pete. "Medics reported you two picked her up, she was standing at the place where she was shot, had watched her father die." He turned back to Steve. "That alone is a lot of information to go on. She's processing Steve, she trying to compartmentalize the accident. She never should have gone back there alone," his glare pierced Steve like a red-hot poker in his gut.

"I had no idea she was going back there," he replied in disgust.

Tory quietly while stepping into the hallway to make a call.

"Hello?" the familiar voice answered.

"Jenny, it's Victoria. I need you to come to the hospital."

"Oh my God, Tory what's going on? Is it Emmy?" *Oh please, let this not be about Emmelia.*

"Yes, it's Em, she's unconscious and she is asking for you. I don't have any more information, can you please come?"

"Yes." Jenny's voice trembled as she hung up the phone.

Edna, oh Edna please. Don't let anything happen to her. I know, I know this is my fault. I never should have left the letter, I should have tried harder to speak to her face-to-face.

Jenny raced to the hospital and waited for Tory in the waiting room. She watched as Katie and Jason walked in the waiting area, followed by Jazz. A few minutes later Corbin and Julie walked in and head straight to door 202. After a moment, she watched as Tylar walked quickly and also disappeared behind the door. She heard Tory's voice behind her and turned to see her. She was speaking with an older lady wearing a floral skirt and button-up blouse. She was asking Tory questions to which Tory was answering and shaking her head. Tory led the woman to the door, opened it and after a few minutes Jenny watched as the room emptied. It resembled a clown car at the circus, first came Corbin and Julie, then Tylar, then Steve and Doctor McInnes followed by Officer Wiseman, Officer Hayden and then Tory. She closed the door behind her. The only person in the room with Emmy was the lady in the floral skirt. Jenny stood up to get Tory's attention.

"Emmelia, Emmy, it is Dr. Weston, Dear. You are safe, you are not hurt and you need to open your eyes."

"Jenny?"

"Not yet. Emmelia open your eyes and then you can see Jenny."

I don't hear the beeps any longer. I stretch my legs, my arms, my back and I feel no pain. She's not lying, I don't hurt anywhere. I open my eyes, blink a few times to focus and look at Lesley. She is standing over me, her pink light bright and pretty. She is smiling.

"What happened," I ask completely perplexed.

"Why don't you tell me young lady," she says to me while pulling over a chair.

"Can I sit up?"

"Of course, there's nothing wrong with you."

I look around the room for a moment and smile, "Really? Then why am I in the hospital?"

"Again, you tell me."

I prop myself up and look at my arms. No IV's, no machines, nothing. In fact, I am wearing my clothes rather than a hospital gown. I gasp and turn toward Leslie.

"I went back to Mother's house to get the boxes. And I was ready to leave and then," I cover my mouth and I can feel the tears beginning to build up. "I walked to the corner. I wanted to see. I wanted to see if the … if the blood was still there. I wanted to be sure it had happened. But when I got close, I froze. I was watching it happen all over again. Only this time it was like I was outside myself watching it all unfold. I couldn't stop her—me! I couldn't change anything!

I saw myself getting off the bus. I saw Katie waving and the old man. I tried to stop it all from happening but my voice was silent and my feet rooted. I heard and saw things for the first time, through new eyes and ears." I turn to Dr. Weston, "I really need to talk to Jenny. Is she here?"

"I can check for you. I think it would be a good idea if I were here as well. Emmelia, the encounter you had today, it was so much information. I was truly afraid I wouldn't be able to bring you back."

"Where would I have gone?" But I know the answer. I would have reverted back to the way I was for so many years.

Dr. Weston raised an eyebrow and walked out of the room, closing the door behind her. I can hear the ruckus, everyone talking outside asking about me. Only a moment passes and the door opens again. Dr. Weston is accompanied by Jenny. The tears I only felt before now tumble feely over my eyelids in rapid succession. She sits on the corner of my bed apologizing over and over about the letter. Dr. Weston moves the chair back and stares at the notepad on her lap.

"I didn't read the letter," I admit to Jenny.

"Wh … what do you mean? Tory said you were saying my name. I thought … I thought you read the letter and …" now she is sobbing as well.

"He thought I was you, he called me his baby girl." I watch as Jenny's eyes glaze over.

"That is what my father used to call me. I was always his baby girl. When did you see him Emmy?" Her voice was shaking.

I look over at Dr. Weston and she smiles. "I went back to the house today…" I watch Jenny's face contort into so many emotions throughout the events. I tell her everything that happened like I was replaying a movie. As soon as I mention her father was talking to someone named Justin, she becomes extremely upset. So much I stop and ask her if she wanted me to continue. She tells me between sobs the man named Justin was the person who raped her and then made her watch as he had sex with her Mother.

My head is swimming, trying to comprehend what type of person would do such a horrible act against a helpless child. *Not that I think it's any less wrong to do to it an adult. But a kid, come on. This Justin guy needed some justice.* Dr. Weston waits for me to finish and then she escorts Jenny into the hallway. There is another loud commotion outside the door. People asking questions and talking over one another, it sounds like utter chaos. I open the door and everyone stops. That old saying, "You could hear a pin drop" well, trust me, at that moment I could have tested the theory.

A second passes and then another before the room erupts in questions.

"Shouldn't you be in bed?" "How are you feeling?" "What happened to Jenny?" "Emmy have you been crying?" "Why did you go back by yourself?" I listen to each of them yelling their question louder than the last person. I see Pete, he is standing in the back of the room and he has hand on his partner's back. "Emmy where are you going?" "Wait Em, what happened?" The questions continue as I make my way past them, all of them. I turn around and everyone is silent.

"I am okay. I didn't know I was going to walk around the corner this morning. I just stopped to pick up some last-minute things from the house. It was scary. I was terrified and I don't know what happened after Thomas arrived. All I know is he was there; he was there when I needed him. I am so sorry I made all of you worry, I feel fine. I feel weird, like I was stuck in a horrible nightmare, trying to change the events from so long ago but there was nothing I could do. I am thankful for all of you. I cannot imagine how scary this was for all of you." Steve is the first to step toward me; wraps me in a hug, followed by Tory. It doesn't take long for everyone to hug, touch, and assure themselves I am okay. Everyone, except Thomas, approaches me. I turn to see him sitting in the far reaches of the waiting area. Tory nods her head and I understand there is a recognizable attraction between Thomas and me. Not in an inappropriate or immature way. I don't know how he was able to sense I was in need. All I know is, I have to let him know I want to move forward with him. I make my way to where he is and stand in front of him. He doesn't move, he doesn't raise his head.

I drop to my knees in front of Thomas and lean close to his ear. I whisper loud enough he can hear over the crowd quickly approaching us.

"I knew it was you because I instantly felt safe," and a lump forms in my throat. He doesn't raise his head, and I don't move mine.

"I was so scared. I was so scared I was going to lose you before …" and his eyes shoot up. I am trying desperately to control my emotions. I don't want to cry in front of him but my brain and I aren't on the same page yet. Tears fall like raindrops, hard and fast.

"Before what?" A deep baritone voice explodes through the crowd. I look up and see Pete move in front of us. My shoulders slump, I close my eyes and stand. Facing the back side of Pete, I tap his shoulder. He shuffles to the left and I make my way around him. My hands are clinched into fists and I feel the adrenaline rush through my veins. I shake my head toward Steve and Tylar, they stand and walk toward us. Corbin's face is bright red, I know he is angry but I am not backing down. He stops, staring around me, through Peter, at Thomas.

"I warned you Hayden, do you not remember?"

"That's enough Corbin! You can't keep me in a glass house! You can't keep me from living like Mother did! Quit warning. Quit commanding. Quit being so over protective of me!" My voice is shaking I am so upset. Corbin lowers his eyes and looks at me. "I am not six anymore, you have to see me for who I am now." I am sobbing again.

Corbin takes both of my fists into his hands. "He's not right for you Emmy, he's going to end up breaking your heart Em. I am just saving you from the pain."

I know he is speaking the truth. I know he is trying to protect me the best way he knows how. Even though I know this, I explode in a tirade, a tantrum of sorts in front of everyone I know—and Pete—a person I just met.

"You," I say pulling my hands from his and pressing my index finger into his chest. "You cannot protect me from pain Corbin. I hurt because I miss Father. I hurt because I miss Mother. I hurt for Tory and Steve, for you and Julie, and for Tylar because we all lost her. I hurt for Jenny. I have never hurt so much in my life! I remember when I didn't hurt. I remember when the only pain I felt was when Katie had to leave my birthday party or Mother said we couldn't go sledding, or when you guys got to go and watch the fireworks and I had to watch them on television. Corbin, I don't want to go back to that kind of hurt." I look back and see Thomas standing next to Pete. "If Thomas hurts me, it will be because I allow him to. If I choose to let him get close to me, it will be my choice. It will not be yours Corbin." I see his shoulders relax. I know from experience this is over—that this conversation will never happen again. One thing I have learned about having brothers is once a topic has been argued, it is not argued again. Ever.

We each step forward at the same time. I lean forward and he kisses the top of my head. "I'm sorry," he whispers. I wrap my arms around his waist and hug him. I feel exhausted, I just want to go home and go to bed. After promising I will be at Sunday dinner, everyone filters out of the waiting room except for Jazz, Pete, and Thomas. We all walk out together not saying a word. Thomas smiles as he slides into the patrol car, Pete waves, and Jazz plops down in the driver seat of his car. I open the passenger door and settle in. He's taking me to get my car. I look at his dashboard and it says 7:30. *Nothing like spending another day of my life in a hospital room.*

So Long

It has been two years since that afternoon in the hospital. Thomas and I are sitting on the couch watching a movie, eating microwave popcorn. He's running his hands up and down my legs. He knows I love to feel his touch. He makes me feel safe, powerful, and appreciated.

Over the past 18 months, things … feelings have progressed slowly. He is so careful not to push too fast when we are alone together. I, on the other hand, loose control as soon as he wraps me into his arms.

Dr. Weston has been teaching Thomas how to bring me back to center, just as she did in the hospital after my flash back. She is also seeing Jenny as a patient, helping her to come to terms with her childhood. I never read Jenny's letter. Instead, I returned it to her in the original envelope. It just seemed to be the right thing to do.

Katie lost her baby during the first trimester. Last week, she called me and said they were going to start trying again.

I finally read Mother's letter. It took a few tries before I was able to make it all of the way through. She wrote she would not have changed anything about her life. She had four, healthy, happy children and the love of a man she would see again soon. She told me to focus, to always look forward, and she reminded me to forgive others and myself. I tucked her letter into the third photo album along with the letters she had written to my father after he died.

I look over at Thomas and twirl the ring on my finger. It won't be long before the next chapter of my life begins. It has been a whirlwind. Sometimes easy, sometime difficult to adjust to a *normal* life.

Helping Tory transform the bedrooms at their home into nurseries was a lot of fun although we all laugh about it now. The twins slept with them the first year, because Steve was worried something might happen and they wouldn't be able to hear it.

Strangely enough, throughout my life I learned if you want something, take the steps to get it. If you owe someone, repay them. Smile in the face of adversity, and never try to fit into a box someone else created. While I am the same as everyone I meet, I am still unique.

The Wedding

The guests are seated quickly so as not to delay the ceremony. Jenny has planned everything down to the final seconds and she is determined to keep everyone on schedule.

The room above City Hall had once again been transformed. But this time, it was a wedding rather than a memorial Gala. Steve had delivered the boxes two days prior and the girls helped place each ornament on the trees that lined the back wall. The red runner was the last piece to arrive, just this afternoon.

Tory took a deep breath and Emmelia squeezed her hand, "I will see you in just a few minutes."

She skipped down the stairs and was escorted to her seat, next to her husband. He held out his hand and leaned over. "Do you wish we would have had a ceremony like this instead of going to the Court House?"

She turned to face him, shaking her head, "No, ours was perfect just the way it was."

The music began and her heart stammered. *This is it, the moment I have waited for.* She watched from a hidden staircase as the bridesmaids met up with the groomsmen and walked down the aisle. The girls were dressed in red, floor length, satin dresses. They each carried a bouquet of white poinsettias. The boys were dressed in white with green ties and they had holly for their boutonnieres. Next she watches the ring bearer and the flower girl, which were her niece and nephew. They are twins who look nothing alike, but they are the spitting images of their parents, Steve and Tory. On their best behaviors, Aaron held tightly to the rings while Anya dropped glittery snow. They look like a miniature version of the wedding party and the spitting image of her brother and Tory. She watched as they both smiled up at their parents on the way down the aisle. Emmy could only hope she and Thomas would make such beautiful babies together.

The music changes, I take a deep breath as I hold my bouquet of red poinsettias and holly tightly in my hand. I tuck my arm in Corbin's and we stop at the closed doors. Jenny is on one side, Jazz on the other. In unison, they pull the doors wide open and I can't help but cry. The trees are decorated with our gifts from Heaven, and hundreds of white butterflies are suspended from the ceiling. Iridescent glitter is scattered on the red carpet leading to the alter. The chairs are covered in red satin complimented with white bows. Garland and white lights flank both sides of the aisle.

Corbin leans down and asks, "Are you ready, Em?"

I look to the front of the room and I see Thomas smiling. His perfect teeth showing. He is so masculine and strong. I look up at Corbin. "I have been ready for this for three years." We begin walking and I lose track of everything but Thomas. I can't stop looking at him, tears streaming down my face. I feel Jenny adjust my train and smile, I know this day is important to her as well. It's like walking on a red cloud, a dream I never want to wake up from. Corbin stops, wraps his arms around me and, when asked, says, "My brothers and I." He kisses my cheek, gives my hand to Thomas, and sits down next to Julie.

"You may all be seated," the loud voice booms into the microphone.

"We are gathered as friends and family to witness the marriage … the union of two extraordinary individuals. I have been told each of them has prepared their own vows," he says smiling at Thomas who is patting his pockets. My eyebrows shoot up and I hear a few giggles from the crowd. I see Pete pull a sheet of paper from his lapel and hand it to Thomas with a smile. I turn to Katie and she hands me mine.

Thomas is first. He holds onto my left hand as he reads from the paper.

"Emmelia. Over the past three years, I have been given the honor of loving you and in return I have been truly blessed by you."

"You are my fire when I feel defeated, you are my salve when I am wounded, you are my constant voice of reassurance, you are my support when I waiver, and you are my loudest cheerleader when I accomplish even the smallest of things."

"You take my breath away with your smile and break my heart with your tears. I promise to love, honor, cherish, and protect you even after death do us part."

"Thomas. Of all the dreams I have had, I never imagined I would ever find someone who sees me for whom I am, and would accept the vision of whom I want to be. Not only have you accepted my past, but you have patiently let me find my way, find myself, and you have encouraged me to grow. The woman I am today has grown to be a better person because of you."

"You are kind and patient when I am a blubbering mess of memories. You are as hard as steel when I need strength and you are flexible when I need space."

"You understand I am a challenge and you are patient. When I am wrapped in your arms, the world disappears and I feel safe, sacred, and loved."

"Thomas, I promise to love, honor, cherish, and protect you long after my light fades."

I feel my knees buckle. I lose my grip on his hand. The room becomes darker. I feel a strong energy, like a lightning bolt, enter through the top of my head.

A Choice

"Emmy... Emmy sweetheart, over here Honey."

I look around, everything is bright. There are white lights everywhere! I look toward the voice and all I can see are two bright objects walking toward me.

"Dad?" I rush to hug him. He looks better than he did the day he visited me in my bedroom. "Where's Mom?"

"Right here darling," she says. She is flawless, beautiful and glowing white.

"Daddy, where is Thomas?"

He takes one hand and my Mother takes the other. We start walking toward a white gate. My father gently squeezes my hand, "He will be here soon dear."

The End? I received many comments regarding the ending of Emmy's Story. Many readers wanted to read a happy ending. Emmy survived once. Can she do it again? "The Darkness" will be book four—the final book in the Ocean Series and is will be completed in 2013.

ABOUT THE AUTHOR

A. L. Elder is a wife and a step-Mother, a career girl and a student. When she's not at work or studying, she is spending time with her wonderful family. For as long as she can remember, she has written stories long and short. Finally gathering the courage to self-publish in the summer of 2012, she has written three books and is working on her fourth.